OLGA ROMANOV

RUSSIA'S LAST GRAND DUCHESS

OLGA ROMANOV

RUSSIA'S LAST GRAND DUCHESS

by PATRICIA PHENIX

PENGUIN BOOKS

PENGUIN BOOKS
Published by the Penguin Group
Penguin Books Canada Ltd, 10 Alcorn Avenue, Toronto, Ontario, Canada M4V 3B2
Penguin Books Ltd, 27 Wrights Lane, London W8 5TZ, England
Penguin Putnam Inc., 375 Hudson Street, New York, New York 10014, U.S.A.
Penguin Books Australia Ltd, Ringwood, Victoria, Australia
Penguin Books (NZ) Ltd, cnr Rosedale and Airborne Roads, Albany,
Auckland 1310, New Zealand

Penguin Books Ltd, Registered Offices: Harmondsworth, Middlesex, England

First published in Viking by Penguin Books Canada Limited, 1999

Published in Penguin Books, 2000

1   3   5   7   9   10   8   6   4   2

Manufactured in Canada.

CANADIAN CATALOGUING IN PUBLICATION DATA

Phenix, Patricia
Olga Romanov: Russia's last Grand Duchess

ISBN 0-14-028086-3

1. Olga Aleksandrovna, Grand Duchess of Russia, 1882-1960.
2. Russia – Kings and rulers – Sisters – Biography.
3. Russia – History – Nicholas II, 1894-1917.   I. Title.

DK254.04P43 2000   947.08'3'092   C00-930403-7

Visit Penguin Canada's web site at www.penguin.ca

THIS BOOK IS FOR
MY FAMILY,
LEONARD, VERNA AND JOHN

Contents

Descendants of Emperor Alexander III

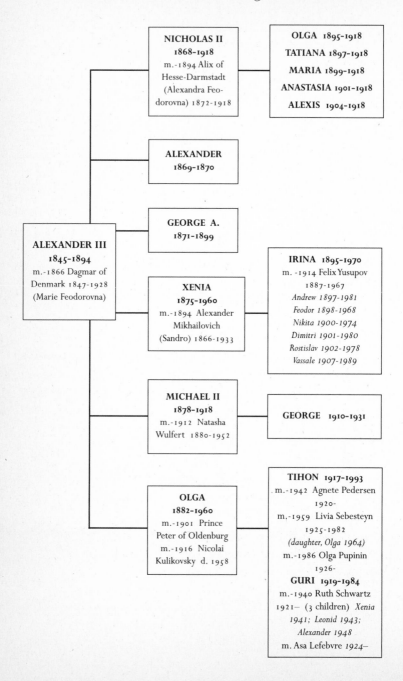

ALEXANDER III
1845-1894
m.-1866 Dagmar of
Denmark 1847-1928
(Marie Feodorovna)

NICHOLAS II
1868-1918
m.-1894 Alix of
Hesse-Darmstadt
(Alexandra Feo-
dorovna) 1872-1918

OLGA 1895-1918
TATIANA 1897-1918
MARIA 1899-1918
ANASTASIA 1901-1918
ALEXIS 1904-1918

ALEXANDER
1869-1870

GEORGE A.
1871-1899

XENIA
1875-1960
m.-1894 Alexander
Mikhailovich
(Sandro) 1866-1933

IRINA 1895-1970
m. -1914 Felix Yusupov
1887-1967
Andrew 1897-1981
Feodor 1898-1968
Nikita 1900-1974
Dimitri 1901-1980
Rostislav 1902-1978
Vassale 1907-1989

MICHAEL II
1878-1918
m.-1912 Natasha
Wulfert 1880-1952

GEORGE 1910-1931

OLGA
1882-1960
m.-1901 Prince
Peter of Oldenburg
m.-1916 Nicolai
Kulikovsky d. 1958

TIHON 1917-1993
m.-1942 Agnete Pedersen
1920-
m.-1959 Livia Sebesteyn
1925-1982
(daughter, Olga 1964)
m.-1986 Olga Pupinin
1926-
GURI 1919-1984
m.-1940 Ruth Schwartz
1921- (3 children) *Xenia*
1941; Leonid 1943;
Alexander 1948
m. Asa Lefebvre 1924-

$\mathcal{F}$OREWORD

I WAS FIFTEEN YEARS OLD WHEN my parents separated. Soon after, I moved permanently into a small house on Camilla Road in Mississauga, Canada, with my grandparents, Grand Duchess Olga Alexandrovna and her husband of forty years, Nicolai Kulikovsky. I felt more at home with them than I ever felt even with my own parents. Despite their advanced ages, my grandparents were open, artistic, sentimental and utterly and completely devoted to each other. Their love was a tangible thing, even magical, and the small house we lived in was suffused with great warmth and security.

Grandmother and I spent many hours sitting beside the fireplace in our cozy living room reading books we borrowed from the local library. As I grew older, I also grew wilder and harder to handle. I was always dashing in and out of the house. Once I juggled three steady boyfriends at the same time. Even so, my grandparents showed endless patience with me. There was no topic I couldn't discuss with them, even sex. My grandfather and I were especially close. We shared an interest in the history of many countries, such as Egypt and Greece. He never disparaged me, even when I became convinced that I was a reincarnation of an Egyptian cat. Instead, he remained always curious, open to new experiences, and eager to learn.

My grandmother Olga had been forced to leave Russia in 1919, so all of her life she dreamed of the forests, lakes and rivers she had left behind. In Canada, we couldn't pass a birch tree without her saying how much it reminded her of Russia. Yet as sad as her memories of her turbulent past made her, they also uplifted her. She was not the type to waste time being bitter about the fate life had dealt her. If she had one regret, it was her first marriage to Prince Peter of Oldenburg, whom she had naively married at nineteen so she could remain in Russia. She often lamented that the many years she spent with Oldenburg were years she could have devoted to the greatest love of her life, my grandfather Nicolai. Fortunately, once she freed herself from Oldenburg, she and Nicolai were able to make up for lost time and remained devoted to each other until his death in 1958.

I shall never forget the morning Nicolai died. I was asleep in one of the upstairs bedrooms of the house. My grandmother gently shook me awake and asked me to come downstairs with her into the living room. We descended the short staircase and entered the living room. Nicolai lay face-up on the couch, looking as if he was in a deep sleep. "He's dead," Olga said tenderly. I remember feeling sad but not frightened. Olga did not cry. Instead, she reached over and gently crossed my grandfather's hands across his chest and kissed him goodbye on the forehead.

My grandmother wore white to the funeral and remained brave throughout the service. Nevertheless, in the weeks and months after Nicolai's death, she began to fade. It was as if the light in her soul had been extinguished. After two years of emptiness, she too lost the will to live.

If there was anything my grandmother would like to be remembered for, it was her love of country, flowers and her kindness toward other people. She was a selfless and generous person, who always put others' concerns above her own. She was a Grand Duchess, yes. But, that was something she was, not something she ever chose to be remembered by.

Xenia (Kulikovsky) Nielsen
Karlslunde, Denmark
March 1999

OLGA ROMANOV

RUSSIA'S
LAST GRAND
DUCHESS

CHAPTER ONE

CHILDHOOD

A SLIGHT BREEZE RUSTLED THE cellophane-covered flowers scattered across the graves in the Orthodox section of York Cemetery in Toronto. On August 25, 1996, more than two hundred friends and family members, as well as network news teams, gathered to witness the unveiling of a bronze plaque dedicated to Grand Duchess Olga Alexandrovna Romanov, the younger sister of Tsar Nicholas II of Russia. The ceremony was one part piety, two parts public relations.

As a black-robed Orthodox priest murmured prayers, a Zsa Zsa Gabor look-alike, better known as Olga Kulikovsky-Romanov, the third wife of Grand Duchess Olga's late son Tihon, distributed pamphlets advertising the Russian Relief Program from a canopy-covered table set up nearby. The Russian Relief Program, a charity created by Tihon and Olga Kulikovsky-Romanov in memory of the Grand Duchess who died in 1960, currently sends food, clothing and medical supplies to the poor in Russia and survives thanks to the steely-eyed determination of Olga Kulikovsky-Romanov, its chief executive, who uses her adopted Romanov surname to secure donations from White Russian émigrés passionately loyal to the Romanov name in general and to Grand Duchess Olga in particular. In 1998, thanks to Olga Kulikovsky-Romanov, the late Grand Duchess even acquired her own Website.

The legacy of the Grand Duchess is not limited to her family. From Bangkok to Banff a sophisticated cottage industry has grown around the possessions she once owned. A simple paintbrush she used might fetch more than a thousand dollars; a hand-knitted sweater, five figures. The hand-embroidered lace nightgown she wore on the night of her wedding to her first husband, Prince Peter of Oldenburg, lies folded in a trunk in the living room of an antique dealer in Smiths Falls, Ontario. Priceless Fabergé picture frames, multicoloured malachite eggs and hamburger-sized diamond brooches belonging to the Grand Duchess remain locked in her daughters-in-law's curio cabinets as family descendants battle over which items should be bequeathed to whom. Mystery still surrounds the whereabouts of a pearl necklace rumoured to be missing from the dead woman's neck.

Virtually lost in all the machinations over her material possessions is the essence of Olga herself. Born to supreme privilege, waited on by countless servants, inhabitant of seven palaces, poised to co-inherit a fortune worth more than $30 billion, object of murder attempts by Bolshevik revolutionaries, Olga—feisty, slightly eccentric and fiercely proud—died in relative poverty cared for, not by her two sons, but by loyal members of the Russian émigré community with whom she had always shared an affinity.

CHURCH BELLS CHIMED IN every Russian capital to celebrate the June 1, 1882 birth at Peterhof of Grand Duchess Olga Alexandrovna Romanov, daughter of the Emperor Alexander III and the Empress Marie Feodorovna.

Her arrival was the one bright spot in an otherwise blood-soaked year and a half. The previous winter, Olga's grandfather, Alexander II, known throughout Russia as the tsar liberator because of his attempts to invoke constitutional reforms to benefit the working classes, was murdered. His carriage had just left the Winter Palace in St. Petersburg when a blinding explosion enveloped his horseback-riding Cossack in a cloud of smoke and whirling snow. As Alexander rushed from his carriage to inspect his Cossack's injuries, another blast erupted. This time the cloud of smoke cleared to reveal a horrific sight. Both the Emperor's legs had been eviscerated beneath the knees; one of his arms hung by a thread; and a great portion of one side of his face was shredded beyond recognition. His left eye stared out lifelessly as the right was sealed shut by coagulated blood. Shards of his wedding ring were embedded in the flesh of the third finger of his right hand.

"Quick home, carry to Palace, there die,"[1] he moaned, as his mangled form was carried into the palace, where his wife, clad in a nightgown, threw herself on the floor by the settee where what remained of her husband was laid. After more than sixty excruciating minutes, Alexander II finally died. Little did the murderers know that they had thwarted their own ambitions. The first constitution to create parliamentary reform lay forever unsigned on the dead Emperor's desk.

Mere yards above where his father bled to death, a tight-jawed Alexander III, now the new Emperor, stared out the window. Beside him his wife, Marie, tremblingly clutched a pair of skates she had worn during an outing with their first son, Nicholas. On the street below, the murderers were rounded up and arrested, while the curious plunged their hands into snowdrifts searching for bits of clothing and other gruesome talismans of the disaster.

Suddenly turning around, all vestiges of youth erased from his face, the new Emperor announced, "The army will take charge of the situation. I shall confer with my ministers at once in the Anichkov Palace."[2] With that, he motioned to Marie, and together with little Nicholas and a team of Cossacks, they quickly departed the palace.

Alexander III would not make the same concessions as his father. With the explosion of the bomb that had killed his father still reverberating in his ears, he had the murderers brought to trial, then hanged in public. It was a bloody display of force. With his accession to the throne, the age of liberalism came to an end.

Not long after the assassination of his father, Alexander III whisked Marie and the rest of their family away to what became their permanent main dwelling, Gatchina Palace, forty miles west of the politically unstable city of St. Petersburg. Commissioned by Catherine the Great, the nine-hundred-room limestone palace, complete with a draw-bridged moat, was outwardly austere in design, resembling a barracks more than an emperor's home. Inside, the family lived like tenants, confining their living quarters to the Arsenal, a portion of the palace that had formerly been reserved for servants.

In his teens, Olga's father had no particular interest in politics; his grasp of foreign languages was spotty and his patience for protocol nil. If he felt any sense of duty, he hid it well behind his passions for hunting and courting the young ladies of St. Petersburg. Unlike his wife, he remained a poor horseman, never overcoming his perception of the animals as conveyances of destruction.

He was big, lumbering and clumsy, and tilted his head down between his shoulders like a bull aiming for a red cloak. His father's nickname for him was Bullock.[3] Nevertheless, beneath his less than aesthetic exterior beat the heart of a true patriot and born administrator. He distrusted his father's liberal advisers and decided to chart a more conservative course for the country based on a model of religious purity and self-discipline. Most significantly, as a man who preferred borscht over crème brûlée and civvies to ceremonial garb, he was seen by the populace as one of their own— a ruler by fate, a peasant by mentality.

Alexander III and his wife, Marie Feodorovna, the daughter of King Christian IX of Denmark, enjoyed one of the most successful and faithful marriages in Europe. Marie had given up her home country of Denmark, her family and her Lutheran religion to marry Alexander, a man she barely knew. But although their union had been motivated by Russia's desire to ensure shipping passage out of Russia through the Baltic, Marie and Alexander soon fell madly in love, so much so that Alexander claimed the marriage would "mean my happiness for the rest of my life."[4] The couple's empire, the largest in Europe, covered an area of eight and a half million square miles, one-sixth of the earth's land mass. It was so vast that as the sun set at one end of the empire, it rose in another.

Most comfortable when bedecked in priceless jewels and French designer gowns, Marie enchanted the Russian upper classes whenever she swept into the sumptuous fancy imperial balls thrown by the couple. While her husband ambled grumpily around the edges of the dance floors, the multilingual Marie shook hands and chatted gaily with guests. She instinctively understood that to the Russian people the appearance of greatness was as important as greatness itself.

Before her husband became Emperor, Marie had five children: the shy Nicholas (1868); Alexander (1869-1870), who died shortly after his birth; the frail, tubercular Georgy (1871); the pixieish and party-loving Xenia (1875); and the tall and athletic Michael, "Misha" (1878). Tomboyish Olga, three and a half years younger than Michael, was the only child born "in the purple," that is, during her father's reign.

Olga began life as an underweight, somewhat sickly baby. Despite her physical frailty, or perhaps because of it, she quickly became her father's pet. As she grew older, he nicknamed her Badger, for her propensity to burrow herself in mounds of earth and snow. Propping Olga on his massive shoulder, he would jog her across the rolling hills of the private park surrounding Gatchina Palace.

For all her outward strengths as the partner of the most powerful man on earth, Marie was a diffident mother, especially toward Olga, whom she dismissed as "plain-faced." As the newly crowned Empress, Marie soon became utterly immersed in organizing official functions and, accompanied by her older children, joining her husband on State trips abroad. It was therefore no sacrifice for her to hand over the care of Olga to a small, plump English governess named Elizabeth Franklin, a surrogate mother who from Olga's infancy became her constant emotional salvation.

As a sunny and cheerful infant, Olga was happy just crawling across the sweetly scented grass. Predictably, her first faltering steps were witnessed by Franklin, who bragged by letter to Empress Marie that Olga "insists upon walking everywhere 'all alone.'"[5] Already determined to achieve the kind of independence she would be renowned for in her adulthood, Olga exclaimed to Franklin, "I no can ride in my little carriage any more, I quite big now, just like Misha."[6]

By the age of two, she was an agile walker, in addition to already being a precocious talker. Franklin wrote, "[Olga] delights me. Yesterday as she was running in the garden she said, 'I so happy Nana.' I said why are you so happy my darling and she answered, 'You are so stupid, Nana, you must know the sun shines, and I do good and I love all these things and everybody: Papa, Mama, Nicky, Georgie, Xenny, Misha, all the flowers.'"[7]

Still, Olga's dependence on imaginary games and playmates increased Franklin's exasperation with the absentee Empress Marie. In an extraordinarily critical letter written in 1884, Franklin barely conceals her impatience, "I wish so much that Your Majesty could hear all her [Olga's] pretty talk and see her sweet engaging ways. She misses Your Majesty very much and says she cries every time you go out. Poor Olga! No Papa. No Mama go to see her." Franklin signed it, "I beg to remain Your Majesty's obedient servant, Elizabeth Franklin."[8]

In another letter from the same year she wrote, "[Olga] is very pleased to write these telegrams every morning to send to Your Majesty and never forgets that it must be done before going out. Many times during the day she says, 'I like best for Papa and Mama to be at home—I like to see them.'" [9]

As they grew older, Olga and her brothers chased each other down the endless parquet-floored corridors of Gatchina Palace and played hide-and-seek behind adult-sized Chinese vases. [10] During breaks in play, it was not unusual to find Olga sprawled on her back on the floor, counting the number of crystals on the magnificent chandeliers that hung from gilded ceilings. While her father and mother entertained thousands of dignitaries in the palace's great ballrooms, Olga dangled her small frame over balcony railings and scattered flower petals on the guests' heads before being sternly escorted back to her room by Franklin.

By contrast, at night, conforming to a militaristic ritual initiated by her great-grandfather Nicholas I, Olga and her sister, Xenia, slept in a dorm-like room on thin-mattressed camp cots and one flat pillow and, when they rose at dawn, rinsed their faces in cold water. [11]

The emotional distance between Olga and her mother only widened over time. "I never felt at my ease [with my mother]," Olga recalled years later to biographer Ian Vorres in his book *The Last Grand Duchess*. "I tried to be on my best behaviour. She had a horror of anything beyond the frontiers of etiquette and propriety." [12] As a result, when Olga coughed, it was Franklin who spoon-fed her medicine; when she fell down, it was Franklin who bandaged her wounds; and it was Franklin who brushed her hair one hundred strokes every night.

Some of the letters written by Olga as a young girl are

heartbreaking in their plaintively expressed desire for her to be closer to her mother. Written on delicate stationery, each is illustrated with a miniature sketch drawn by either Olga or her English tutor, Mr. Heath, who seemed to specialize in waterwheels and landscapes.

Most letters are punctuated throughout by the words "I miss you." "I miss you all very much and especially in the morning when I want to run down and take Mr. Foxy [her dog] for a run,"[13] she writes in one. "Goodbye, mother dearest, from your loving daughter, baby Olga,"[14] she writes in another, as if trying to remind her mother of who she is. One particularly poignant letter includes a moist P.S. in which Olga writes, "Everyone sends their best compliments, and the dogs lick your hands."[15]

In the midst of this strained emotional climate, Franklin's task consisted of finding ways to amuse Olga. In the winters, there were forays into snowdrifts as "high as a horse's belly," and often "higher than a man's head."[16] As the second youngest, Olga's brother Michael, nicknamed Floppy for his propensity to sprawl lazily in chairs, was also frequently left behind when his parents went on trips, so he often joined Olga and Franklin sledding down steep hills.

Supervised by Franklin, the two children wrestled, made snow angels, and skated across mile-wide ice rinks formed on the natural lakes nearby. Snowshoe racing was a particularly fierce contest, as Olga describes in one of her letters. "Misha and I fly down the hills . . . [and] I fall on my face and my poor shoes stick out of the snow, and when I try to get up, I fall further in, up to my waist . . . [Misha] gets down better, he is more used to it, but I can walk along the snow better than he as I am lighter."[17]

As she grew older and more conscious of her mother's abandonment, Olga became obsessed with protecting the defenceless. One day, walking upon one of the estate's frozen lakes, she and Michael spotted a goose's egg unprotected on a small island in the centre of the ice. "The greatest care must be taken of it,"[18] she wrote in her diary. For nights on end she lay awake fretting excessively about the safety of the small gosling inside. Risking frostbite, she took daily walks to the site until the mother goose returned to protect her young.

Another incident involving a helpless, old, blind dog sickened her. While being taken for a walk by a family friend, the dog had fallen into a pond, pulling the friend in with him. Though the friend was saved from drowning, the dog was poisoned to death by the family doctor to prevent it from committing similar misadventures. Soon after this tragedy, Olga began collecting stray dogs in addition to the dogs she had as pets. For the rest of her life, she would never be without an animal by her side.

Whenever the entire family was home at Gatchina, the morning ritual remained the same. Shortly after Olga awoke and dressed, Franklin escorted her to the breakfast table where all the children ate porridge and when the servants' backs were turned, pelted each other with bread rolls. Like their parents, the children ate bland, but hearty, meals.

After breakfast Olga cherished the half-hour visit she was allowed to her father's study, where he made her laugh by tearing decks of cards in half, bending cutlery, or pulling out of the top drawer of his desk his menagerie of miniature china and glass animals which he had kept since childhood. Lifting his daughter onto his lap, he would then clasp her fingers around the handle of the Imperial seal and help her press down on envelopes addressed to ministers and other government officials.[19]

Now and then Olga and her father flipped through the pages of an album of pen-and-ink sketches of an imaginary city called Mopsopolis, inhabited by Mopses (pug dogs), which Alexander had whimsically drawn when he was eleven.[20] Although her mother was an accomplished and enthusiastic watercolourist, it could be argued that Olga acquired her later love of art sitting on her father's lap.

THE FAMILY SHUTTLED AMONG several dwellings. In the spring they travelled to the stone-coloured Anichkov Palace situated on the Nevsky Prospekt in St. Petersburg. It boasted a white marble staircase, bordered on each side by green marble columns. Encircling the banquet halls were silk damask curtains of sea-green, aquamarine and gold. Blue and white sparkling chandeliers appeared to set the bejewelled heads of the female guests aflame. One of Olga's favourite rooms, the huge main-floor conservatory, was remarkable because its entrance was guarded by two enormous turquoise-coloured stone frogs, each with jewelled eyes as big as one of Olga's fists.

For six weeks in summer the family moved to Peterhof Palace, nicknamed the Russian Versailles, located northwest of St. Petersburg on the gulf of Finland. It was here that the children had their only chance to see their father's subjects in relaxed settings. On carriage rides they often passed parents and children bathing naked in various small lakes.

"Our arrival would not upset them in the least. The [children's] screaming and laughing would be silent only momentarily; their mothers would bow slightly and smile in acknowledgement to their Tsar, and then they would continue enjoying their bath,"[21] said Olga. Only Nana disapproved of the vacationers' flagrant lack of modesty.[22]

Peterhof, built by Peter the Great, was an architectural novelty and included a staircase leading from the palace to an ornamental lake. From the lake flowed a tree-bordered canal that emptied out to the sea. Close by, a yellow and white neo-Gothic villa named Alexandria stood in the middle of a park. On balmy evenings, Marie and the rest of the family savoured orchestral music at the open-air theatre nearby.

One evening, Olga and Michael's conspiratorial bursts of laughter discombobulated fellow concert-goers. The source of the siblings' amusement was an eccentric old gentleman who liked to pose as a member of the orchestra. "He loves music, but cannot play at all, so he sits with an instrument while a man plays music for him and is especially paid for that," wrote Olga to Nicholas, adding, "Don't you think it's funny?"[23]

Because they were the youngest, Olga and Michael shared lessons from nine to three o'clock in Gatchina Palace's dining room, which had been converted into a gymnasium. Between lessons the grinning twosome relaxed by photographing each other with the new Brownie cameras that had just come on the market. "Michael and I had so much in common. We had the same tastes, liked the same people, shared many interests and we never quarrelled,"[24] recalled Olga in later years.

Horseback riding lessons were mandatory. Even in youth,

Michael was an adroit horseman, galloping far ahead of his younger sister, who struggled with the reins of an elderly horse named Kopchaka. Every morning, Nana Franklin ran in circles trying to feed Kopchaka sugar from a basket, while Olga "nearly fell out of the saddle with laughter." [25]

Although they were surrounded by some of the most magnificent artworks of the Russian Empire and wealth beyond imagining, Olga and Michael grew up isolated from the company of other children. Because of this, their social skills remained underdeveloped and each sought emotional sustenance within the womb-like gymnasium, where several tutors instructed them in languages, Russian history, drawing and dance. Olga was a gifted student, whose reading skills were well in advance of most children her own age. By six she was already reading at the level of a child twice her age.

Olga's favourite tutor was Mr. Heath. Heath had a thatch of curly white hair, a genial smile and a gentle manner. He loved the classics, Shakespeare in particular, and advised Olga that one of a girl's greatest attributes was to possess clear and legible penmanship, which Olga studiously practised by the hour. Heath was also an accomplished swimmer, horseman and all-round athlete and used to accompany Olga on biking and boating trips on the palace grounds. Olga fondly referred to him as "Old Man."

On one occasion Olga was invited to attend an amateur performance of *Hamlet* at an uncle's house. Despite her distaste for the classics, Olga agreed to go along with her mother. Shortly after Olga and her mother entered the room where the play was to be performed, the hostess for the evening, Olga's aunt, took Empress Marie aside and whispered something in her ear. Marie, stricken by what she heard, looked at Olga and said, "Olga, I think you should turn around and go home again. *Hamlet* is not a piece for young girls." An embarrassed Olga insisted that she had read the play several times with "Old Man," but Marie would not be dissuaded. Olga returned home alone and began to reread the play, finally theorizing that Empress Marie was trying to protect her from being exposed to an enactment of the Danish Prince's tortured relationship with Ophelia.[26] Apart from visiting relatives' homes, Olga was allowed few outings and was allowed even fewer friends. There were, however, exceptions.

Every Sunday, a group of aristocrats' children was permitted by Alexander to journey by train from St. Petersburg to Gatchina to play with Olga and Michael. Far from being allowed to lose themselves in games, the imperial children remained intensely conscious of possible attacks from outsiders and got used to the sight of hired protectors "darting in and out from behind trees and shrubs."[27]

The gigantic park that adjoined the palace was encircled by a high wall. Neither servants nor employees were allowed in or out of what Olga called a "beautiful prison" without showing a special piece of paper, whose colour was changed every week for security reasons. Sentries, placed twenty-seven yards apart outside the palace gates, were changed every hour.

A special expert was hired to inspect the palace's interior for any wires or electric batteries rigged to bombs that might be lying in its corridors or apartments. In spite of his best efforts, there were often security leaks. Once, the Emperor noticed a beautifully painted Easter egg sitting on his desk. When he opened it, he found inside a small silver dagger, two carved ivory death's heads, and a slip of paper on which was ominously written, "Christ is risen. We also shall rise again."[28] The perpetrators inside the palace were never found.

Gossip was enthusiastically exchanged among Gatchina's servants, their favourite stories usually involving Olga's older brother Georgy, who despite suffering chronic coughing fits and muscle weakness from as yet undiagnosed tuberculosis, engaged in endless pranks.[29] Tall and blond, with almost translucent skin, Georgy was the most well read of the family. As a child and later a teenager he delighted his fellow siblings by mimicking his tutors, his favourite victim being the kind-hearted Mr. Heath. So memorable were some of his rejoinders that Nicholas, whose schoolroom was next to Georgy's, scribbled them down on scraps of paper and for the rest of his life, including his joyless days as Emperor, kept them in a small box, from which he removed them whenever he needed a laugh.[30]

Nicholas, by contrast, was a quiet child. When Olga was born, he was already fourteen years old and terrified at the prospect of one day becoming Emperor. Early on, he developed a love for military service and eventually commanded a squadron of the Hussar guards, but out of modesty never accepted a post higher than colonel. He was a man who liked to be ordered rather than to order. Shy and dependent, drawn more to the quiet joys of nature, or discussions about horses, ballerinas or the latest French songs than the rigours of court life, he regularly turned to his mother for reassurances about the most minute family matters.

As she matured, Olga grew to resemble her father in her even temperament and heavy features. Her sister, Xenia, with her velvety brown eyes, was a china-doll-like replica of her mother. She loved fine clothes, jewellery and parties.

Deeply religious and quiet by nature, Xenia became her mother's confidante and companion. Certainly, of the two daughters, she was the most obedient and subservient and a far cry from her grass-stained and tree-climbing sister.

CHRISTMAS WAS THE OCCASION when all petty grievances and resentments were laid, if temporarily, aside. Before the family celebrated the day privately, gifts were bestowed on all the imperial servants, who numbered five thousand. Incredibly, each gift was accompanied by a handwritten note from the Emperor himself.[31]

In the weeks preceding Christmas Day, representatives from some of the finest jewellers in Europe, including Cartier, descended on the palace with boxes overflowing with priceless trinkets.[32] Sapphire-encrusted perfume bottles, 18-karat gold watches embedded with more diamonds than the eye could count, walnut-sized cabochon emeralds and gem-studded icons were quickly purchased and gift-wrapped for delivery to the wives of foreign dignitaries.

The imperial children, spoiled enough by the gems given to them by relatives such as Queen Victoria and Grand Duke Ernst of Hesse, received only plain wooden toys, books and clothes from their parents.[33] Unlike her sister, Xenia, who preferred to snuggle up in fox-fur wraps, Olga knitted and crocheted her own homemade presents. Each year she gave her father a pair of flaming red slippers, cross-stitched in white. For the rest of her life, red remained Olga's favourite colour.

On Christmas Day all the children flooded into the

banquet hall, which contained seven or eight ornately decorated trees. The children's gifts were stacked under two trees, while the adults attended trees of their own. The gay ripping and tearing of paper continued late into the evening when, with their eyes drooping from fatigue, the children were finally escorted back to their rooms by the servants.

After Christmas the children were expected to write thank-you notes to each gift-giver. Georgie, the future King George V of England, one year unwittingly caused some post-Christmas sibling rivalry between the practical no-nonsense Olga and her glamorous older sister when he wrote a personal letter to one and not the other. Olga, in her teasing way, made him aware of this gaffe:

> Darling Georgie,
> Thank you tremendously to have sent me
> that pretty present, and thank May [Queen
> Mary] too *very* much; it was awfully kind of
> you both. I was delighted to get a letter from
> you and I gave Xenia your message. She was
> furious that you did not write to *her* and
> called you any amount of bad names! [34]

Dismantling the trees was a family affair that occurred three days after Christmas. Branches were clipped off the mammoth trees and the handmade ornaments distributed to servants.[35] If possible, Olga tried to include a string of popcorn and cherries she had made weeks before the event.

OLGA'S GOLDEN LIFE WAS tarnished almost overnight by a traumatic event that remains unsolved to this day. On a wet and overcast autumn day in 1888, Olga and her entire family boarded a train from Gatchina to travel to the Caucasus. It was six-year-old Olga's first train trip and, propped atop a stack of pillows, she excitedly pointed out the lakes, rivers and forests of her father's empire as they whizzed past her window like an elaborate slide show.

At approximately noon, just as the train approached the small town of Borki, family members, as well as twenty-two members of the entourage, gathered in the train's dining car for lunch, which consisted of hearty servings of beet soup, hot rolls and fresh strawberries with cream. The servants had just begun removing the used dishes from the table when an ear-piercing scream like that "which one could imagine on the last Day of Judgment,"[36] recalled Empress Marie, filled the passengers with terror.

Olga, playing with Franklin in the children's coach behind the main dining car, clamped both hands over her ears. A second, higher-pitched scream tore through the taut autumn air. The Emperor grabbed his wife. Nicholas and Georgy reached for Xenia, as the car lurched forward. In the brief, eerie silence that followed, two pink vases slid off the table where Olga sat and smashed to the floor. "I was frightened and Nana took me on her knees and put her arms around me,"[37] she remembered later.

Yet another lurch backwards converted the interior of Olga's car into a tornado of broken glass and flying metal. The other wagons passed under the floor of her carriage, shearing off the wheels. Before she could catch her breath,

Olga watched the earth and sky somersaulting until she thudded, face first and shivering with shock, into a muddy puddle at the foot of a steep hill.

Clambering to her feet and blinded by tears, Olga ran in circles. Some of the train's cars, propelled by momentum, slammed into each other, teetered, then also began thundering down the hill toward Olga. A footman snatched Olga into his arms. Hysterical, she began tearing the skin from his face with her nails and crying out for her family and Nana. Moans from injured and dying passengers wafted through the smoke and fog that surrounded the wreckage. The footman, limping and bloodied himself, gently carried her to her father, who subsequently took her to one of the undamaged cars where Nana lay groaning and half-delirious. Her chin and cheeks were deeply bruised and two broken ribs had punctured her liver.

Shortly after Olga was carried into the car, she was joined by other members of her family, cut, bloodied and bruised, but miraculously all safe. Olga's father's injuries appeared initially to consist only of a bruise on his leg from the thigh to the knee, while her mother and the rest of her siblings nursed blackly bruised and cut hands, legs and feet.

Months after the accident, theorists speculated that the family had survived because when the iron walls of the main dining car pressed inward, the roof, instead of caving in, warped upwards, sparing the family severe head injuries. Others, including Olga, insisted that the Emperor held the heavy iron roof above his family while they crawled to safety. No matter what the true story, the family's survival, said Empress Marie, was like "the resurrection from the dead."[38] In the end, the crash killed twenty-two passengers, with twenty-five more injured.

At first the derailment was deemed to have been caused by a band of revolutionaries, one of whom was executed, but no concrete evidence of a plot or bomb was reported to be found, although as Charles Lowe, Alexander III's biographer, wrote, "In Russia it is next to impossible to get to the truth of such things."[39] A commission appointed by the Emperor concluded that the train had been travelling too fast across rotted railway lines, an explanation that Alexander was reluctantly forced to accept.

Despite the innocent explanation for the crash, Alexander was never certain that it hadn't been a thwarted murder attempt. His health, once robust, noticeably deteriorated. On good nights, he suffered insomnia; on bad nights he awoke drenched in sweat. His dislike of horses intensified and he avoided riding because of severe back pains. The London *Daily Telegraph* of October 16, 1894 reported that after the crash "the Emperor grew more moody and reserved than ever before. He lost his confidence in the ability of the most trusted and the devotion of the most intelligent of his Ministers. He avoided even more systematically than before all public ceremonies and amusements."[40]

For Olga, the true cause of the Borki crash remained shrouded in sinister mystery. Years later she admitted, "I was only six but I became conscious of a danger lurking somewhere."[41] Back at Gatchina Palace, she quickly became used to the increased security measures implemented by her father. At night, members of the élite Blue Cuirassiers army unit rode horses bearing lanterns strapped to their heads by her window, searching for intruders. Other soldiers stood outside her private apartments. "Hearing them tiptoe outside my door in their soft leather socks gave me a wonderful sense of security," she said. "They had been especially selected for this duty because of their physiques and they soared above me like creatures from 'Gulliver's Travels.'"[42]

It is not impossible to imagine that even at her tender age, Olga must have succumbed to the fear of enemies seeking to take her and her family's lives. Guarded round the clock, her movements restricted to the confines of her own palaces, encouraged to be suspicious of all others on the "outside," and perhaps overhearing her parents discussing the assassination of her grandfather, Olga understandably felt that her innocence had been shattered and that the seemingly carefree days of her youth were consigned to the past.

Witnesses to the crash recall the prescient words of Olga to her father as she clung to his shoulders shortly after the crash. "Oh Papa dear! Now they'll come and murder us all!"[43]

CHAPTER TWO

TURNING THE PAGE

IN THE YEARS THAT FOLLOWED the Borki crash, Olga clung even more closely to her father and brothers. Prompted by "the mournful calls of the hunting horn,"[1] she accompanied them on fox and rabbit hunts from the family's lodge at Spala, near Warsaw. The days were made into family outings, with gifts bestowed on the hunter who bagged the biggest bounty. Some observers found it odd that Olga, so weepy over the fate of a small bird or dog, didn't flinch at seeing the carcass of a giant moose lying mere feet away from her.

Nana recovered slowly. Olga pushed her wheelchair-bound patient across the palace grounds to take some sunshine. She pampered her with lemonade and bowls of succulent fruit. When the sun disappeared behind clouds, Olga draped shawls over her lap. Within a few months, Nana was back to her regular chores, a profound relief to Marie, who had watched Olga's fussy ministrations with a jaundiced eye.

After the Borki incident, Alexander and Marie's emotional stability teetered as precariously as the railroad cars that had ultimately crashed down the Caucasian mountainsides. Although he attempted to hide it from his children, Alexander could not shake off his continued exhaustion and the acute pain that afflicted his lower back. He began to drink heavily. Instead of striding ahead of his family as he had once done, he now often lagged behind, using work as an excuse.

The keenly observant Olga sensed a change in her father before any of her fellow siblings. "We are always with dear Papa, except when he is busy and now he has so much to do we often have to start for the walk without him and wait at the shore until he comes,"[2] she noted.

Between 1889 and 1893, the family shuttled among their Russian palaces, and every summer boarded a yacht which steamed across the Baltic toward Fredensborg Palace in Denmark. There the family would entertain in lavish fashion the great families of Europe, including the Prince and Princess of Wales, the Duke of York and Queen Olga of Greece. Michael and Olga learned to distinguish the members of royalty by their smell: the English smelling of "fog and smoke," the Danes of "damp, newly washed linen," and the Russians of "well-polished leather."[3]

Denmark meant freedom to Olga. It was the only place she could walk the streets without tripping over a bodyguard's sword. When she was fully recovered, Nana drove Olga into Copenhagen's finest shopping areas. "I shall never forget the thrill of walking down a street for the first time, of seeing something I liked in a shop window and knowing that I could go in and buy anything I pleased,"[4] Olga confessed.

Olga's favourite destination, however, remained the villa of Alexandria in Russia, located just off Peterhof Palace. Olga and Michael loved to race bicycles along the seashore, struggling to see how long they could pedal through the wet sand before their wheels stuck and one or the other was catapulted into the surf.

Distractions such as these did little, however, to relieve the two children's anxiety over their parents' health. Even their seemingly indomitable mother had aged noticeably since the Borki crash. She had turned grey-haired almost overnight.

Indeed, Marie had become less a wife than a truant officer, preoccupied with trying but failing to stop her husband from consuming alcohol. In the evenings, while playing card games with his favourite partner, General Peter Alexandrovich Cherevin, the head of his own Life Guards, Alexander and his partner secreted flat field flasks in specially made boots, and they took swigs every time Marie moved away from the table. General Cherevin recalls, "[Alexander] liked this game . . . And we called it 'necessity is the mother of invention' . . . One, two, three! . . . and we drink." [5]

Marie's heartaches increased with the news of Xenia's engagement to her first cousin once removed. Grand Duke Alexander Mikhailovich, nicknamed Sandro, was a temperamental lothario, possessed of charm as creamy as his wit was sharp. Marie's despair at losing her daughter to an impetuous flirt, coupled as it was with the decline in her husband's health, nearly capsized her.

Marie tried to have the engagement broken, first by arguing that her daughter was too young, then by explaining that in order to marry, the cousins would have to receive a special dispensation from the Holy Synod. Olga saw through her mother's excuses and provided a far more practical explanation for her objections: "My mother just did not want to lose all control over Xenia. She meant her to stay on as a companion to herself."[6]

Shortly after the engagement was announced, during a trip to the Caucasus, Sandro and Xenia's brother Georgy discussed Sandro's growing feelings for Xenia and, in light of the Emperor's poor health, the prospects for a Russia ruled by the weak and vacillating Nicholas. "We both hoped that Alexander would reign for many more years and feared that Nicky's total unpreparedness would handicap him stupendously should he ascend the throne in the near future,"[7] recalled Sandro in his 1932 memoirs, *Once a Grand Duke*.

Even as his father's health failed, instead of attempting to prepare himself for assuming the throne, Nicholas distracted himself by concentrating on his blossoming courtship and eventual proposal to the shy and sombre-faced Princess Alix of Hesse-Darmstadt, Queen Victoria's favourite grand-daughter. (Princess Alix, as she was then known, only became Empress Alexandra Feodorovna upon her marriage to Nicholas.) In the summer of 1894, Nicholas visited England to ingratiate himself with the English royal family, who always disapproved of what they considered their slightly mad Russian relations.

Nicholas and Alix's courtship enraged Sandro and Xenia, as they saw their union, scheduled for July of 1894, might be upstaged by the nuptials of Nicholas and Alix. In response, Nicholas and Alix agreed to postpone their wedding until the fall.

Unfortunately, once again due to poor health, Georgy was unable to attend a family event and sent Xenia his apologies, promising to visit them when his health improved. In a June 7 letter to her mother, Olga expressed her sorrow to discover that "dear Georgy can't come to Xenia's wedding," adding that "it [is] nice to know he will come later."[8]

For several months preceding the wedding, Olga and her sister unwrapped hundreds of boxes of incredible wedding gifts from china to gold plates for sixty-nine persons, coats and wraps of every kind of fur including mink and chinchilla, as well as five-string pearl necklaces "each holding more than a hundred pearls." There were also "diamonds, rubies, emeralds and sapphires, with tiaras and earrings to match."[9]

Sandro was not overlooked in the gift-giving department. His future father-in-law bestowed upon him dozens of shirts and a sixteen-pound silver dressing gown, which Sandro claimed made him look on his wedding night like "an operatic Sultan."[10]

On July 25, 1894, the wedding ceremony commenced at Peterhof Chapel, located on the grounds of the palace of the same name. It was stiflingly hot inside the church and several spectators nearly fainted. The assembled held their collective breaths as Xenia and her father, pale but otherwise steady on his feet, slowly walked down the aisle. Xenia was perspiring heavily under the weight of a diadem with a huge pink diamond, a crown of large diamonds and her robe.

Observers did not fail to notice that Empress Marie, escorted down the aisle behind the bride by Sandro, could barely see out of eyes that were swollen nearly shut from tears. Olga and Michael, next in line down the aisle, winked at Sandro, causing him to "strain every muscle of his face not to laugh."[11]

The couple's escape from the wedding reception to their honeymoon suite turned into an inauspicious comedy of errors. Shortly after they left, the horses drawing the coach in which they sat were startled by lanterns strung along a bridge and bolted, tipping the coach and its passengers into a muddy brook.

*U*NTIL THE LATE SUMMER OF 1894, the public had not been informed about the desperate state of the Emperor's health. By early fall, as if sensing the end was near, Alexander summoned Georgy to Peterhof Palace, whose corridors were renowned for their draftiness. After a day spent shooting ducks, the two men retired to their beds. Sometime in the middle of the night, with the help of his manservant, Alexander arose and, slipping on a robe and slippers, walked to his son's room and sat by his bed to watch him sleep. It is generally believed that while walking down this cold corridor he developed the severe chill that hastened his death a few weeks later.

Palace doctors officially diagnosed the Emperor as suffering from nephritis, or a shutting-down of the function of the kidneys, as well as what today would be termed as congestive heart failure. Both conditions were deemed incurable, and death was predicted within four to six weeks.

Alexander received the news of his impending death with outward peace, but suddenly, even guiltily, fretted about the fitness of his eldest son, Nicholas, for the role that awaited him. An announcement was released to the public stating only that the Emperor was suffering from nephritis and that on the advice of his doctors he was trying to recuperate at Livadia in the Crimea.

Toward October his condition grew grave. The former leviathan could no longer eat or sit without falling into a semi-comatose stupor. Olga sat on a stool by his chair and spoon-fed him ice cream, which Marie had forbidden him to eat, but which slid down his throat with such cooling ease that he could not resist it.

Near the end, the dying Emperor summoned Nicholas's fiancée, Alix, to Livadia, where the two "officially" met. Though the contents of the meeting were never revealed, his doctor concluded that it "strongly excited the patient, in spite of the joy it caused him."[12]

Alexander began to say goodbye to the members of his family. During the last days he kissed all of them one by one and summoned a priest to hear his final confession. During the confession, the priest asked Alexander if he had prepared Nicholas for the throne. "No, he himself knows everything,"[13] Alexander replied almost inaudibly.

The priest placed his hands on the Emperor's head, which seemed to momentarily relieve his distress. Soon after, his breathing became laboured. No family member was more distraught than Nicholas, who was overnight transforming from a carefree young man to Emperor of all the Russias. The thought terrified him. "Poor sweet Nicky, who is to begin this life at such an early age,"[14] his mother lamented. Complicating emotions even more was the fact that Nicholas's marriage to Alix was slated to take place in mere weeks.

On October 29, the anniversary of the Borki train wreck, the half-dead Emperor defiantly roused himself enough to take the Sacrament and reply to a telegram of congratulation sent by the troops of the Moscow district. It was the last telegram he would ever send.

His final hours were excruciating. An oxygen mask was intermittently placed over his face to help him breathe. On the morning of November 1, after a sleepless night, he told the Empress that he felt the end was near. *"Tu vois comme je suis calme, tout à fait calme,"*[15] he sighed. Placed in a chair by an open window, with his wife in a chair beside him, her head slumped against his cheek, he finally, almost imperceptibly, slipped away, bearing "a smile of bliss"[16] on his face.

The entire family, including twelve-year-old Olga, filed quietly into the room and knelt in prayer. The Empress slumped against her husband for almost an hour before an attendant became aware she had fainted. Weeping, she was led away as each child approached Alexander and kissed him on his head. Then each kissed Nicholas's hand, which was ice-cold with fright. Olga declared herself beyond tears.

Moments after his father's death, a panicked Nicholas urgently steered Sandro into another room and exclaimed, "What am I going to do, what is going to happen to me, to you, to Xenia, to Alix, to mother, to all of Russia? I am not prepared to be a tsar. I never wanted to become one. I know nothing of the business of ruling."[17]

"Who could have predicted that the Emperor Alexander III would die at the age of forty-nine, leaving his work as a monarch unfinished, and leaving the fate of one sixth of the world in the hands of a trembling and unhappy youth," [18] Sandro later mused.

JUST TWO DAYS AFTER the death of Alexander, Princess Alix was anointed with the holy oils, completing her conversion to the Orthodox faith in preparation for her marriage to Nicholas. In grotesque juxtaposition, the couple then recited the prayers for the dead. Their marriage was still scheduled to take place a few days after the funeral, so the family struggled under a burden of sorrow so profound that in his memoirs, Sandro was moved to remark, "I doubt the greatest of theatrical producers could have staged a more appropriate prologue for the tragedy of the last Tsar of Russia." [19]

Olga, who felt strained to the point of screaming, was now without a steady male hand to comfort or guide her. As a recent bride, her sister was no longer even a remote confidante. And since her mother was preoccupied by the physical and metaphorical loss of the two greatest loves of her life, her husband and son, Olga found herself roaming the corridors of Anichkov Palace alone, forbidden even to play her violin or piano. There was no one left to show her affection but Nana Franklin.

By some miracle, the death of her father and the desperately sad 1,400-mile funeral journey past throngs of sobbing subjects toward St. Petersburg, along the same train track that had carried the family to Borki, did not permanently dampen Olga's essentially optimistic nature. The funeral, or near "canonization," as the press called it, took place over several torturous days. The Prince of Wales attended the funeral to provide support to Marie. Kings, queens and foreign dignitaries from myriad other countries paid homage. Five thousand wreaths were sent from France alone.

Thousands of subjects braved the cold, slush and mud to arrive at the Cathedral in St. Petersburg where the ornate coffin was placed, although cynics claimed their presence was ensured by the free dinners Nicholas, as the new Emperor, ordered that they should receive during the Romanovs' period of mourning. The officiating priest laid a band of silk upon the forehead of the dead Emperor, which each member of the family kissed. Amid cannon bursts and artillery blasts, the coffin was finally lowered into the ground.

Less than two weeks after the death of the Emperor, on November 14, 1894, Nicholas and Alix recited their vows in front of eight thousand guests in the chapel of the Winter Palace. The wedding procession started at the Arabian room, where Olga, Xenia and Marie helped Alix fix her hair into two long curls and to fasten several magnificent necklaces and brooches to the bodice of her dress.

Enormous corridors throughout the palace were filled with spectators as the procession began its walk toward the chapel. Leading the procession was Empress Marie, accompanied by her father, King Christian IX of Denmark. She wore white, a few shades lighter than her own face. This was to be her last walk as Empress. Though Nicholas would not be formally crowned Tsar for another year and a half, he was already recognized politically as Alexander's successor.

Next came Nicholas and his bride, who wore a simple circlet of diamonds on her head. An unsmiling Alix stared grimly at the floor during the ceremony and seemed to be melting under the heavy gold mantle lined with ermine that she wore around her chest. Nicholas, jumpy and flushed with excitement, anxiously fiddled with the handle of the sabre attached to the uniform of the Hussars of the Life Guard that he had donned for the ceremony.

Once the ceremony commenced, he too gazed floorward, as courtiers held crowns above his and his wife's heads. Once or twice spectators thought Nicholas might break down sobbing. Later he admitted that throughout the ceremony all he could think of was the cavernous space created by the absence of his beloved Papa. At five minutes past one, as the gold wedding band was slipped onto her finger, Princess Alix became Alexandra, the new Empress of all the Russias.

Within the space of two weeks, Marie had lost her husband, her son in marriage and her title. Adhering to a centuries-old custom, on this occasion alone, she was compelled to walk behind her new daughter-in-law as members of the procession grimly filed out of the palace toward their carriages. Thousands of citizens lined the streets loudly cheering their new Empress. Regrettably, far from possessing her mother-in-law's gracious and winning charm, Alexandra barely managed to nod in the direction of her subjects. Instead, the carriage bearing the bride and groom sped like an ambulance toward the Anich-kov Palace, where the couple had set up apartments at Marie's request. There would be no honeymoon. Arriving by carriage at the palace ahead of the newly married couple, the now Dowager Empress Marie greeted Nicholas and Alexandra with a plate of bread and salt, a Russian custom of greeting.

In letters afterwards, Nicholas described the day of the wedding as "absolute torture,"[20] for him and Alexandra.

Alexandra both pitied and admired her mother-in-law. "She is an angel of kindness," she wrote to Queen Victoria, ". . . and is more touching and brave than I can say." [21] Her tender benevolence toward Marie was, however, short-lived. As Nicholas's passion for his new wife increased, and Marie's role in his life began to decrease, relations between the two women cooled.

Olga returned home to Anichkov Palace deeply depressed after a day of high emotions. At thirteen she was too old for toys, yet after donning the nightclothes Nana Franklin had laid on her bed, she knelt beside her oak treasure chest and withdrew her favourite doll, a blonde curly-haired girl dressed in full Cossack regalia, complete with sterling silver sabre and lambswool hat. Climbing between the crisp sheets, she clutched the doll to her chest and finally, understandably overcome by all the stresses of the previous weeks, began to cry.

*E*IGHTEEN-NINETY-FIVE PASSED quietly, with Xenia and Alexandra bearing children—both girls. Xenia and Sandro's child was named Irina. The first daughter of Nicholas was named Olga. She was an enormous child, ten pounds, with a full head of hair, a wide smile and intelligent blue eyes. Nicholas ecstatically savoured his role as husband and now father and did not share his sister Xenia's disappointment that her brother's first child was not a boy.

Both Olga and Michael were blossoming into charismatic teenagers. Michael had no trouble attracting the attention of members of the opposite sex. He was tall, slim and boyishly

handsome, with a sense of courtliness that made him particularly sweet. He even charmed Queen Victoria, who had
thought his father Alexander III "a boor." [22] Like his sister
Olga, he retained a weakness for children and dogs.

Olga was as homely as her brother was handsome, but
she had a glorious smile that captivated whomever it was
directed toward. Her grey-blue eyes, so similar to those of
her brother Nicholas, conveyed both deep sadness and
immeasurable warmth.

As 1895 drew to a close, palace staff members speculated that a feud had erupted between the Dowager Empress
Marie and Alexandra over who should have Nicholas's ear in
affairs of state. Marie, already disgusted that Alexandra possessed a tin ear when it came to statecraft, increasingly gave
advice to her son, so much so that Alexandra came to refer
to her mother-in-law as the "Angry One," who manipulated
Nicholas according to her whims. As the day approached for
his coronation, Nicholas was without doubt a man torn
between two women.

Preparations for the coronation, which was to take place
on May 14, 1896, in the Kremlin in Moscow, were placed in
the hands of a special commission headed by Grand Duke
Sergei Alexandrovich—an uncle of Nicholas and the Governor General of Moscow—whom Sandro accused of being
a "complete ignoramus in administrative affairs." [23]

During rehearsals, Nicholas grew increasingly irritable,
declaring the occasion "a great trial sent to us by God." [24] He
smoked so compulsively that Alexandra feared he would
have no voice left for the ceremony. Making matters worse,
the sky opened and it rained for three days. Had it been
possible for Nicholas to snatch the crowns and place them on

his and his wife's heads in the privacy of their apartments, afterwards making a brief appearance on the balcony to wave to the crowd, he would have done so.

Olga was experiencing anxieties of her own. On May 12, the Sunday before the ceremony, she awoke in her room in the Petrovsky Palace in Moscow still suffering the lingering effects of a cold she had caught in the rain. After breakfasting with her mother and Michael, she, her mother, Michael, and Nicholas and Alexandra attended church. To her dismay, the service was exceedingly long. "I felt giddy from the beginning," she recalled in her diary, "but at last I could not stand and kneel any longer so off I went to my room and laid down on Nana's bed, while she sat beside me until the others came from church and we all went down to lunch." [25]

Shortly after lunch, Nicholas and Alexandra returned to the Kremlin for more rehearsals. A scheduled parade was cancelled because of the rain. For most of the afternoon, Olga stayed in her room and painted. Her external calm was deceptive. That night she confided to her diary that she was dreading the upcoming festivities. Under a wistful sketch of a white bunny standing under the moonlight, she wrote, "I am awfully frightened to think of the screaming the day after tomorrow. Now I am going to Mama soon and then to bed." [26]

By Monday, the day before the ceremony, the skies finally began to clear. Olga and Michael played with their dogs in the garden and took each other's pictures. Nicholas, Alexandra and baby Olga joined them to announce that it was time to leave for the Kremlin, where they would all stay overnight prior to the ceremony. Olga, Michael and their mother got into the same carriage and rode off along the bumpy

streets of the city. Before long, Olga was terrified, declaring,
"We got into *such* crowds that we could hardly move and
the people cried hurrah so loud that I nearly got sick, I
mean deaf." [27]

On coronation day Olga awoke at six, already suffering
from "awful fears not to be too late." [28] Her frantic feelings
are conveyed best in her diary entry of that morning, which
states:

> While I tried to eat my breakfast not dressed
> yet, the hairdresser came to frizz it. When he
> finished me, Nana and I had to go down to
> Mamma to finish my toilet there. We had to
> press through crowds of gentlemen and every
> sort of people. At last I got there and was
> dressed in the bedroom. Misha was hurrying
> me all the time. We two went upstairs along
> the crowded corridors and into the St.
> Catherine's hall, just the room before where
> everybody was, an Indian Prince, Princess,
> Germans, even the Prince Victor of Monaco,
> heaps of gentlemen and all the ladies of our
> family. [29]

Once all the carriages had arrived at the Uspensky
Cathedral, the assembled guests, consisting of Romanov relatives, ministers of state and noblemen, waited until 8:45 for
the emergence of the Dowager Empress Marie, who was
dressed in a golden robe with ermine, and wore a diamond
diadem on her head. On one of her arms was Crown Prince
Frederick of Denmark, and on the other, Alexander III's
brother, Alexis. Xenia, dressed in a lovely gown of pink and

silver, was accompanied by "an awfully ugly fat old man"[30] in
Olga's words. Olga, who was wearing a blue dress with
roses, was escorted by the Prince of Saxe-Coburg-Gotha
down a carpet so unrelentingly red it hurt her eyes.[31]

After Marie was seated on her throne, with two members of the corps de page holding up her heavy mantle,
everyone waited three-quarters of an hour before Nicholas
and Alexandra finally appeared. Alexandra wore a dress of
white and silver brocade with nothing on her head, while
Nicholas was dressed in the uniform of the Preobajenski
Regiment, with the red cordon of Alexander Nevsky and the
plain collar of St. Andrew around his chest.

The couple took their places on the thrones and the five-
hour-long ceremony commenced. The reciting of prayers
was followed by the singing of hymns. Nicholas, pale and
tense, placed the crown on his own head and, as Alexandra
knelt on a cushion, he placed a smaller crown on her head
and hung the chain of St. Andrew around her chest. Then he
kissed her gently.

Soon after, he read a prayer to his people, and the officiating priest read a prayer to him. A mass was held and Com-
munion administered. When it was over, Nicholas slowly
descended the steps of the throne, approached his mother
and kissed her so tenderly and with such sad emotion in his
eyes that his mother recalled she nearly "burst from emotion
and compassion."[32]

With that, the ceremony came to a merciful close and
the participants filed out in the same order in which they
had arrived. Nicholas and Alexandra eventually walked to
the top of the steps of the Cathedral of the Annunciation,
where they paused and bowed three times to the people.

The imperial couple and the Dowager Empress were required to attend both an official luncheon and dinner. By 9:30 that evening they fell into bed too shattered from exhaustion to appreciate the dazzling explosion of fireworks that Olga watched from her bedroom window.

All week long there were balls, banquets and theatre performances for the imperial couple and other foreign dignitaries. Common citizens, however, were not to be ignored. Between eleven and twelve o'clock on Saturday, May 18, live animal shows and musical and theatrical performances were to commence on Khodinka Field just outside of Moscow. Afterwards the new Emperor was scheduled to address the adoring multitude from a pavilion especially built for the occasion.

The highlight of the day was to occur when the citizens received gifts on a first-come, first-serve basis. Four hundred thousand "gifts" were prepared. Each contained a pound of sausage, rolls, sweets, nuts, gingerbread and an enamelled cup bearing the Emperor's monogram and the year of the coronation, all wrapped up in a coloured handkerchief.

Shortly after dawn, catastrophe struck. During the night more than seven hundred thousand people, "more people than Napoleon brought with him to Moscow," [33] said an observer, lined up on the narrow approaches to the field to be among the first in line. Only a thin cordon of Cossacks stood between the multitude and the field.

Once daylight broke and the citizens got sight of the "pyramid of large cups" [34] awaiting them, they broke through the lines, ignoring shouted warnings concerning the "pits, mounds and abandoned trenches" [35] that lay ahead. A reporter who was present said, "The crush was terrible . . . many felt faint; some lost consciousness, having no chance to get out or even to fall: lacking sensation, with eyes closed, caught as in a vice, they jostled along together with the mass of people ... [a] tall, handsome old man, standing near me, next to my neighbour had long since stopped breathing: he suffocated in silence, died without a sound and his corpse had grown cold as it jostled along with us. Someone alongside me vomited. He could not even lower his head."[36]

The ones who didn't suffocate from the swell of people were trampled to death racing to the buffet tables where the cups were stacked. Hundreds fell into the open trenches, head first, one atop the other. According to official statistics 1,301 people were injured, 1,389 died. Weeks later, the broken bodies of those who had fled the scene were still being discovered on the streets of Moscow.

Nicholas called the event a "great sin." After lunch, he and Alexandra went to the field to address the sizable crowd that still remained. A surrealistic scene awaited them. Despite the presence of carts hauling away the wounded to hospital and the dead to morgues, the band continued to play the national anthem, "Be Glorified," as if in shock. Those who had received the gifts cheered.

Back at the Petrovsky Palace, where she had returned after the coronation ceremony of four days before, Olga was reaching the foot of one of the staircases when the visiting Grand Duke of Weimar dashed in, grasped her elbow, and steered her into the Dowager Empress's drawing room. "[He told us] about an awful accident that happened at the Khodinka Field with the crowds," Olga wrote in her diary. "Nobody knows how it began but there was such a squash that more than a *thousand* poor people were killed and over two *thousand* hurt, counting the dead! What an awful thing!"[37]

The tragedy was the main topic of conversation at a fete Olga and Michael were required to attend with their mother and the rest of the family later in the afternoon of May 18th. Michael and Olga rode to the party in the same carriage, which was quickly surrounded by schoolboys singing the anthem. "Then my page brought me a cup, a handkerchief, and two painted pictures, I mean papers about it all,"[38] Olga recalled.

On the same night of May 18, an elaborate French ball was hosted by Grand Duke Sergei, which Xenia and Sandro begged him to cancel. Grand Duke Nicholas Mikhailovich—Sandro's brother, and a liberal voice within the Romanov family—agreed and urged Nicholas to consider the resemblance of the event to Versailles during the French Revolution. "Do not let the enemies of the regime say that the young [Emperor] danced while his murdered subjects were taken to the Potter's Field,"[39] he argued.

Despite these pleas, Nicholas and Alexandra reluctantly attended the ball, even staying for supper when Grand Duke Sergei convinced Nicholas that leaving would make him look too sentimental. As soon as the couple left, they visited the hospitals, where the horribly mutilated people lay. Nicholas donated 1,000 rubles to each of the families of the victims, but did not reprimand Grand Duke Sergei for his disastrous organizational skills. The only person dismissed from his post was the chief of police.

Socialists abroad took advantage of Nicholas's leniency toward the organizers of the event by labelling him "Bloody Nicholas." Those closer to home accused him of being incompetent compared to his father, who had organized successful events on Khodinka Field without incident.

For Olga, the day ended with her challenging and winning "as usual"[40] foot races down the long corridors of Petrovsky Palace with Baby Bee, better known as Princess Beatrice, the daughter of the Prince of Saxe-Coburg-Gotha. Olga had learned from her father that looking back was one's downfall; she had learned early how to quickly turn the page.

CHAPTER THREE

A WEDDING

*H*AVING WITNESSED THE STRESSES placed on Nicholas during his coronation, Olga resisted entering into adulthood. Her fingernails were often caked with dirt, while her thick brown hair cascaded over her shoulders in a windtumbled mass. She abhorred protocol, preferred linen smocks over silk dresses, and sought every opportunity to rebel.

The Dowager Empress Marie blamed Nana for Olga's reluctance to take her place in society. Marie had a long memory and those chastising letters Franklin had sent more than a decade before were ticking time bombs set to explode. Franklin was "too indulgent" of Olga, "too cloyingly affectionate,"[1] insisted Marie.

In a fit of pique fuelled by a mixture of boredom, jealousy and the fear of losing the only daughter she still had control over, Marie summarily dismissed Franklin without notice and tried to replace her with a humourless British nurse named Mrs. Orchard.

This time it was Olga's turn to explode. After first securing her brother Nicholas's permission to allow Nana to stay on, she burst into her mother's apartments and threatened in a voice loud enough for palace servants to hear that if Nana went, so would she. "I will elope with a palace sweep," she exclaimed. "I will go and peel potatoes in someone's kitchen, or offer myself as a kennel maid to one of the society ladies in St. Petersburg. And I am sure that Nicky will be on my side." [2]

Declaring her daughter "willful," even "mad," Marie expelled her from the room, preferring in future to take out her punishment on Franklin by withholding Christmas gifts and monetary bonuses. [3]

Olga took charge of her life in other ways too. When she was barely a teenager, she became obsessed with finding a suitable husband who would not require her to leave Russia. A fellow Romanov like Sandro, her sister's husband, would be a perfect match, but there was a shortage of Romanov men young enough for Olga. Her sleep was troubled by nightmares about "waking up in a strange bed, in an unknown country, without all my dear little pets." [4] One night she tossed and turned so violently that she was soothed only when Nana Franklin got up and made her feel "all secure and safe again." [5]

Before any marriage plans could be drawn up, Olga's brother Georgy died at the age of twenty-eight from complications associated with tuberculosis. He was found lying beside his motorcycle near Abbas Tuman, a sanitarium located in the foothills of the Caucasus mountains, by a peasant woman, who cradled his blood-soaked face until he died.

Conspiracy theories surrounded his death, but came to naught. Olga believed the doctors had erred in not officially diagnosing him with tuberculosis earlier, so that more effective treatments could be implemented. What she may have ignored was that Georgy smoked half a pack of cigarettes a day. One bumpy motorcycle ride would certainly have been enough to induce fatal bronchial bleeding.

At Marie's insistence, the "tall, black-robed"[6] woman who had cradled Georgy's head visited with Olga and the Dowager Empress at Anichkov Palace, describing in gruesome detail the last moments of Georgy's life.

A few days later, accompanied by Nicky, Michael, Xenia, Sandro and the Dowager Empress, Olga attended Georgy's funeral in the chapel of St. Peter and St. Paul Fortress, in St. Petersburg. During the mass, the assembled gasped when Marie suddenly staggered and collapsed as the coffin was lowered into its tomb. On the carriage ride back to the palace, Marie clutched to her chest Georgy's hat which she had snatched from the top of his coffin.

As soon as the year of official mourning ended, the still-tomboyish Olga endured her Imperial Court-mandated coming-out party, consisting of a lavish reception held on the hottest day of the year on the grounds of Gatchina Palace. "It was a nightmare," recalled Olga. "In full court dress, with an unwanted lady-in-waiting hovering behind me, I felt as though I were an animal in a cage—exhibited to the public for the first time."[7]

By 1901, she had become a travelling aunt to the increasing number of nephews and nieces born to her sister, Xenia, and to Alexandra. Xenia and Sandro's daughter, Irina, was a particular favourite, as well as Nicholas's daughters: Olga,

Tatiana and Marie. Nicholas and Alexandra's fourth daughter, to be named Anastasia, was due in June.

Olga knew that the longer she waited to marry, the more intensely her family and the public would pressure her to choose an unsuitable husband just for expediency's sake. At least one strong incentive to marry early was Olga's fear that if she remained unmarried for long, she would be at her mother's beck and call forever. Ironically, deceiving herself into believing she was following her own heart, Olga impulsively chose a fiancé as bad as any that the public could have forced upon her.

With little fanfare and even less enthusiasm, in the late winter of 1901, she announced that she had found a mate. Her choice both stunned and amused those who received the news. Far from being the burly outdoorsman they expected her to choose, he was a spindly hypochondriac named Prince Peter (Petya) of Oldenburg, thirty-three years old to her nineteen, and an inveterate gambler. He had escorted her to the opera and theatre performances throughout the previous year and had been an attentive, if less than ardent, suitor. He was highly educated, and his amusing bons mots captivated an otherwise lonely Olga. What the couple came to share wasn't love, but it wasn't hate either. Best of all, his pedigree was suitable, and by marrying him Olga could stay in Russia.

The Oldenburgs were of German ancestry. Prince Peter's father, Prince Alexander, was a great-nephew of Tsar Nicholas I. He owned several properties in Russia and contributed large portions of his money to building schools, theatres, and hospitals in which victims of cholera could seek treatment. Peter's mother, Princess Eugenia of

Leuchtenberg, a close friend of the Dowager Empress, was a granddaughter of Nicholas I.

A completely flabbergasted Dowager Empress immediately wrote to Nicholas from Anichkov Palace, informing him of the engagement:

> Children are children no more! I am sure you won't BELIEVE what has happened. Olga is engaged to PETYA and BOTH are very happy. I had to consent, but it was all done so quickly and unexpectedly that I still cannot believe it; but PETYA is nice, I like him, and God willing, they will be happy. Don't talk about it yet, except to Alix of course, your agitated Mama.[8]

As Olga predicted, Marie's agitation was caused by her sudden realization that she might no longer have Olga to do her bidding. Nicholas's reaction was to burst out laughing. He wrote back to his mother:

> Though today is not the 1st of April I cannot believe Olga is actually ENGAGED to Petya. They were probably both drunk yesterday, and today don't remember all they said to each other. What does Misha think? And how did Nana [Franklin] take it? We both laughed so much reading your note that we have not recovered yet. Petya has just rushed in and told us everything. Now we shall have to believe it. But let's hope everything is for the

best—I am sure they will be very happy but it
all seems rather queer.⁹

As soon as Nicholas recovered enough to believe that
Olga was serious about her choice of a future husband, he
and the Oldenburg family, along with an officially appointed
committee comprised of various government ministers, rati-
fied a prenuptial contract ensuring the protection of Olga's
future assets. The agreement stipulated that Nicholas would
provide Olga with one million rubles, equivalent today to
approximately eight million Canadian dollars, whose annual
interest was to be distributed by a general administrator. "To
testify to his particular affection for his dear sister Olga," ¹⁰
Nicholas also bestowed an additional life annuity of one hundred thousand rubles a year.

The day after the wedding Peter was to give his bride
50,000 rubles, also deposited with the general administrator, from which she could draw interest. She was free to dis-
pose of that capital at her discretion. She also received one
million rubles as a legacy of Georgy's estate.

Meanwhile, according to the prenuptial agreement, the
Dowager Empress Marie promised to provide her "dear and
loved daughter" with a complete trousseau "conforming to
her birth and rank." ¹¹ It included a silver brocade dressing
gown, various skirts, blouses and nightgowns; a wedding
dress valued at 3,450 rubles; three fur coats, of ermine, fox
and polar fox; and diamond brooches, emerald necklaces,
tiaras of pearls and sapphires worth 340,000 rubles.

Finalizing the details of the trousseau reminded the
Dowager Empress that soon she would be truly alone. She
wrote to Nicholas, "I think with dread about my sweet

Olga's wedding which will already take place in a month! . . .
[It] will be horrible for me when she also leaves me, the dear
child, but one should naturally rejoice in the dear children's
happiness."[12]

*T*HE MORNING OF JULY 27, 1901 dawned fair and cool. At
eight a.m. five cannon shots from the St. Petersburg Fortress
in Gatchina announced the wedding ceremony of Grand
Duchess Olga Alexandrovna and His Highness Prince Peter
Alexandrovich Oldenburg.

Olga, who had awoken two hours earlier, curled under
her blankets, nursing a queasy stomach. At her feet lay her
white Maltese poodle, whom she gently picked up and began
to stroke. In a dresser drawer beside the bed she found a red
ribbon, just long enough to fit comfortably around the dog's
neck. The colour was perfect, since Olga's white wedding
dress included a velvet crimson mantle with ermine fur. With
that, the colour-coordinated dog became an unconventional
but very important member of the wedding procession.

At two-thirty, members of the Holy Synod and other
priests assembled at the Altar of the Palace's Church, along
with state counsel members and ministers, foreign ambassadors and representatives with their spouses. Other guests
and members of the palace's household were instructed to
take up positions in various galleries of the palace through
which the procession would walk. Women wore their finest
Russian-style gowns consisting of embroidered silk damask
and low-cut collars trimmed in animal furs, while gentle-
men wore ceremonial dress.

In yet another room, Olga and her ladies-in-waiting began the ritual dressing, whose origins dated back to the beginnings of the Russian culture. The bride's friends dressed her, starting with underwear, piece by piece, singing melancholy songs designed to express their sadness over losing their friend forever.

Nana Franklin brusquely directed the proceedings in between dabbing her eyes with a handkerchief. Halfway through the dressing, Olga took Nana aside and handed her an envelope containing 1,800 rubles, a gift from Olga on the occasion of the wedding. She embraced the only true mother she had ever known and tenderly kissed her cheek. Fittingly, it was Nana who had the final honour of placing the diamond- and turquoise-studded crown on Olga's head.

At the conclusion of the ritual, four chamberlains entered the room to begin the process of lifting various sections of the mantle's train. Each few feet of fabric was assigned to another chamberlain. The end was carried by the second highest ranked member of the Royal Court.

Twenty-one cannon shots announced the arrival in the Chinese Gallery of Nicholas and Alexandra. The procession out of the gallery toward the church was led by Nicholas, with his mother on one arm and Alexandra on the other. Olga and Peter were the last to emerge, smiling slightly.

At the entrance to the church each member of the family was greeted by His Grace Metropolitan of St. Petersburg, with a cross and holy water. Nicholas then led the betrothed couple to the altar, where the wedding rings were placed on golden plates by the master of ceremonies. The confessors accepted the rings from the arch priest and placed them on the trembling hands of the betrothed.

Once the crown-holders approached the couple, the cere-mony began. With the less-than-hour-long ceremony com-plete, Olga and Peter approached Nicholas, Alexandra, Marie, and Peter's parents to express their gratitude.

At the conclusion of the hymn "Our Praise Is to You, God," 101 cannon shots were fired. At seven p.m. a ceremo-nial dinner was served, accompanied by the court choir and orchestra, endless toasts, and enough cannon blasts to per-manently deafen the ears. Fireworks exploded throughout every courtyard of the city. All churches held services for the occasion and for two following days church bells chimed.

Unfortunately, rather than being moved, some witnesses to the wedding appeared amused, even cynical. Senator A.A. Polovtsev, a family friend, had this to say about Olga: "The Great Duchess is rather plain, her snub-nosed Mongoloid face is compensated only by extremely beautiful eyes, kind and clever, looking right inside you. Wishing to stay in Rus-sia she chose the son of Prince Alexander Oldenburg."

Peter did not fare much better. Polovtsev continued, "In spite of being high-born and extremely well off . . . [the] prince is rather undistinguished in all respects and his appearance is far less than undistinguished. Though he is young he doesn't have much hair on his head and comes across as a sickly person, lacking the ability of producing multiple descendants. . . . Obviously this match was made for reasons other than making this couple happy which will most probably lead to disaster."[13]

At nine-thirty in the evening, the newlyweds and their guests attended a performance at the Theatre Hall of Gatchina Palace. Afterwards, the Metropolitan of St. Peters-burg and the Governor General of Moscow publicly announced their plans to distribute to the poor the curious sum of exactly 7,103 rubles.

After such a harrowing day, neither of the newlyweds was disappointed to ride a horse-dawn carriage to the Baltic Railway Station. From there they travelled to the Voronez province to honeymoon at the estate of Her Royal Highness Princess Eugenia of Leuchtenberg, Peter's irascible mother, or as Olga came to call her with derision, "Princess Gangrene."[14]

Because of his delicate, almost aesthetic build, and because he generally preferred parlour games over blood sports, Peter was covertly considered by family members to be either homosexual or bisexual. And yet he was tentative and tender with Olga, and she with him. At dawn, neighbours watched the couple walking hand in hand across the roughly wooded terrain surrounding the estate, with Olga resting her head intermittently on her groom's shoulder.

One morning, while holding Peter's hand, Olga descended a muddy embankment, but lost her footing halfway down. Lacking sufficient ballast to steady his wife, Peter too began to slide. The two members of royalty, who only days before had been festooned in the finest fabrics and jewels money could buy, found themselves cartwheeling like kegs of nails toward a stream of icy water. By the time she reached the bottom, Olga was nursing a sprained ankle.

Possessed of more chivalry than strength, Peter scooped up his wife and stumbled over rocks and twigs toward his parents' home. By the time the couple burst awkwardly through the front doorway and Peter ingloriously deposited his bride in a chair by the fireplace, their faces burned with laughter.

All Peter's hitherto invisible imperfections emerged, however, during his and Olga's meals with his parents. A few nights into the honeymoon, Prince Alexander, raging at his son's profligate ways and passion for the roulette tables, dug a fork into the wooden dinner table, as his horrified wife looked on. Ignoring Olga's pleas, Peter shouted back at his father and, grabbing his wife's arm, bolted from the dinner table to their bedroom. After Olga retired to bed, he sat in a chair fully clothed staring coldly into the darkness for the rest of the night and on into the morning.

The protests of Peter's parents were well founded. A few months into the marriage Peter would manage to gamble away Olga's inheritance from her brother Georgy.

The symptoms of the strain of living with her in-laws did not take long to manifest themselves physically. Within weeks of her lavish wedding, Olga was brushing her hair in front of her vanity mirror when she noticed an abnormally high number of hairs in her brush. Hands shaking, she tentatively drew the brush across her scalp again and muffled a scream as strands of hair fell like streamers to the floor. Within days, she was completely bald. It was the first in a series of bad omens.

The couple tried to escape the unhappiness that had developed between them by travelling first to Biarritz, then to Sorrento. At the Hotel du Palais in Biarritz, Olga was dancing the foxtrot when the wig she had been wearing flew off her head and onto the dance floor, forcing the orchestra to abruptly stop playing mid-note. Olga turned "green" with embarrassment, as onlookers stared.[15]

Soon after, in the same hotel, a fire broke out in which Peter lost many of his most valuable uniforms and medals.

England's King Edward VII placed a yacht at the couple's disposal, in which they sailed to Sorrento off the coast of Italy, where they finally avoided mishaps.[16]

It slowly dawned on the couple that each had married the other to escape tyrannical parents. Peter resented having curtailed his freedom to roam throughout the gambling establishments of Moscow and St. Petersburg and retire to cigar-smoke-filled parlours with his male friends. And yet he respected and protected Olga, even loved her in his own way. When it suited him, he found her warmth a comfort during his frequent black moods. Nevertheless, Olga often lamented that her husband coddled her like a child when she wanted to be loved like a woman. The faster the couple tried to outrun their disenchantment with their mismatched personalities, the faster it caught up to them.

Once back in St. Petersburg, the consequences of their union manifested themselves, especially once they moved into 46 Sergievskaya Street, a 750,000-ruble wedding gift from Nicholas.

The gigantic two-hundred-room, four-storey house had its own church; servants' rooms; coach-houses; a two-storey brick gardener's shed; a one-storey brick yardman's house, where the laundry room and shed were located; and a greenhouse, where Olga indulged her love of flowers. Nana Franklin was the first servant to arrive at the home, and she soon settled into a comfortable room with its own studio attached.

But even though Olga was an independent married woman, her authority was curtailed. As owner, Nicholas retained authority over the great mistress and the manager of the household, each responsible for ordering in essentials

such as foodstuffs and linens as well as arranging for transportation. As far as the rest of the seventy-odd servants were
concerned, Nicholas granted Olga and Peter free rein to
"choose them, dismiss them, or call them back willingly."[17]

As mistress of her own home, Olga was obligated to host
lavish parties for a vast array of guests, including foreign
ministers and heads of state. The Emir of Bokhara, a
favourite of Olga's, one year presented her with, in Olga's
words, "an enormous gold necklace from which, like
tongues of flames, hung tassles of rubies."[18] Fresh-cut flowers were shipped in from the Caucasus for these evenings.
Most guests were entertained either in the dining hall or the
first of two living rooms.

The dining hall's walls were covered with finely worked
oak decorations with caryatids in Renaissance style. The
floor was marble, with ornaments, while the ceiling was
decorated with stucco mouldings and painted to look like
oak. An oak mantelpiece was decorated with four caryatids
and two doors with a carved design. The first living room's
ceiling of stucco moulding was in the style of Ludwig XVI,
with golden ornaments. In the centre of the ceiling was a
plafond of fine work with cupids.

No amount of ornamental cupids, however, could work
their magic on the romantic aspects of the marital home.
Olga and Peter maintained separate bedrooms from the day
they moved in, and though their marriage was almost certainly consummated, sexual relations were performed perfunctorily and perhaps not very successfully since it was
becoming an open secret throughout polite society that
Peter preferred the amorous company of men over women.

If Olga thought that marrying would free her from her

mother's grasp, she soon realized her mistake. Marie was in need of Olga's companionship even more now that Michael had joined the élite Blue Cuirassiers unit of the army and Xenia was busy raising her six children. Whenever the Dowager Empress decided, sometimes on the spur of the moment, to attend a theatre performance, she expected her younger, and childless, daughter to accompany her.

On these outings Olga at least derived some amusement from watching Hussars from her own Akhtyrsky Regiment or sailors from the imperial yacht *Standard* called upon to play the parts of warriors. "It was a riot to see those tall husky men standing awkwardly on the stage, wearing helmets and sandals and showing their bare, hairy legs. Despite the frantic signals of the producer, they would stare up at us with broad grins,"[19] she recalled.

Another stop in the social world of St. Petersburg was Princess Zinaida Yusupov's palace. The Princess was the mother of Felix Yusupov, who would eventually marry Xenia and Sandro's daughter, Irina. This palace, where crystal bowls full of uncut sapphires, emeralds and opals sat on drawing-room tables, was by far the grandest in St. Petersburg.[20]

There were also endless balls at the Winter Palace, which Olga loathed for its huge impersonality. Nicholas loved to dance but Alexandra, partly because of her disappointment that their fourth child was yet another girl, shied away from these extravagant social occasions. Olga shared her sister-in-law's dislike of grand balls and normally she and Peter left early in the evening to return to their quiet home, where Olga would paint or play the piano.

Perhaps out of pride, or fear of having their mutual weaknesses exposed, Olga and Peter became so adept at hiding their mutual unhappiness that even the Dowager Empress was fooled. Barely a year after the marriage she wrote of Peter: "He is such an excellent, splendid person, of whom I am really so fond, and they are both so happy that I can only thank our Lord for it."[21]

As 1902 approached, Olga and Peter left St. Petersburg, their winter home, to take up summer residence in an enormous villa named Ramon, which the couple inherited from Peter's mother. Olga suffered bouts of severe loneliness in the villa, despite its panoramic view of the vast countryside surrounding it. Her closest friend lived eight miles away in a neighbouring village and Olga would frequently arise at dawn to walk the entire distance alone, and at the end of the day summon a carriage to transport her home.

At Ramon, which was situated near Peter's parents' home in the Voronez province, Olga would stroll for hours in the fragrant countryside and climb steep hills overlooking the nearby picturesque town of Olgino. She also began visiting villages where she met peasants whom she described as "rich for all their poverty."[22]

Reinvigorated by her rural surroundings, she decided to try to save her marriage by building with her own money a villa for her and Peter not far from Ramon. The small white villa was to be named Olgino after the town and to become a place of peace for the careworn couple. Built atop a hill, the town of Olgino overlooked a monastery named after St. Tihon. Olga was so calmed by the sight of the gold-domed structure that she promised that her first-born son would be named Tihon.[23]

Any chance Olga and Peter had to plan a family, however, was shattered within weeks by a scandal created by an imprudent business deal that Peter's father, Prince Alexander, entered into in 1902. This time it was Peter's turn to bail out his father, instead of the other way around.

At the urging of Prince Alexander, members of the Russian aristocracy, unwillingly to pay the exorbitant costs to travel to spas abroad, had sunk enormous sums of money into the building of a health resort in Gagry. A hospital was also to be built, which would offer treatment for assorted ailments. Building materials for the hospital had been bought, excavations initiated and the foundations laid, when news arrived that the proper clearances had not been approved and it would have to be scrapped.

No amount of intervention on the part of Prince Alexander could save it and all the money had already been spent. As investors raged, the now elderly Prince suffered an emotional collapse. Rich as he was, he was not willing or able to compensate the investors for the enormous losses they incurred.

Because she was now a member of the extended Oldenburg family, Olga's name was dragged into the scandal, which caused her so much emotional distress that, with the blessing of her husband, she swiftly left Ramon to seek refuge with her mother back at Gatchina.

After she left, it was Prince Peter's obligation to try to compensate for his father's mismanagement. His letters to Olga during this period reveal the extent of the shame and regret he felt over the whole matter.

My Dearest, sweet Olga, I am writing this
short letter to you only to describe what happened after your departure. I miss you and our
house seems dead without you. I came into
your room, thinking about the time we spent
here together and I felt tears in my eyes. . . . [I]
am happy for you that you are in your beloved
Gatchina and that you had a chance to embrace
Mama and Misha and Nana. I am sending my
love and kisses to them and tell Mama that she
is often on my mind and that I am kissing both
her hands. . . . Papa seems to feel better. Yesterday I had a long conversation with him
about the internal situation in Gagry; he listened to me with great patience; *I am so sorry
for him* . . . [It] is not raining today and I think
of taking a walk to Olgino to have a look at the
construction . . . I am kissing you and hugging
you, my dearest Baby. God bless you.[24]

The next day he continued to worry about the Dowager
Empress's and Michael's opinion of him and pledged to Olga
that he and his father were "racking their brains to find
money," adding, "I am having nightmares about his business."[25]
Looking ahead, he said, "with excitement and anticipation" toward the completion of the building of Olgino, he
hoped that "with God's help" he and Olga would be able to
spend the coming fall "happily and quietly." His affection for
Olga is unmistakable: "It is so boring here without you; in
spite of your periods of melancholy you managed to cheer
up all of us, though you do not even realize it yourself. . . . [I]

kiss you passionately, my dear Baby. P.S. How is Misha doing in his new regiment? I kiss and hug everyone. How is Nana? My best regards to her and tell her that she shouldn't be so angry with me. I am not so bad." [26]

The next day Peter wrote yet another letter. The words portray a lonely, tortured man coming to grips with the realization that he alone must save his errant father from complete social ostracism. "Everything is such as mess that it is hard to describe. Papa is responsible for it *morally and financially*. I consider it to be my obligation to get him out of this mess." [27] He reserved his deepest worries over the ramifications the scandal might have on Olga's name. "My dearest Baby," he wrote, "I feel so concerned that you found yourself mixed up in this unfortunate business. . . . [Enjoy] yourself in Gatchina. You make me happy because I know you are happy. I am hugging you with love." [28]

There is no documented evidence that indicates how the crisis in Gagry was ultimately resolved. It is, however, likely that Peter called in some markers. By September the Gagry storm had subsided, if not entirely blown over. Best of all, Olgino was finally complete and he and Olga could at last settle in together in relative compatibility.

Olga resumed her lone walks, now daily visiting a hospital on the estate where she carefully studied all the procedures doctors and nurses performed. [29] If not a paradise, life in Olgino was certainly no purgatory either. In fact, in a letter Peter wrote to his mother in September 1902, he described his new house in Olgino as "absolutely wonderful and cozy; we lead a quiet and pleasant life here." Olga, whom he says "makes me very happy," appeared well and cheerful and occasionally accompanied him on wolf hunts. [30]

Despite the tranquility of Olgino, by the winter of 1902 or certainly the spring of 1903 it must have preyed on Olga's mind that as infrequent sexual companions, she and Peter would never bear children. Despite his promises to be a more responsible and loving husband, he again began his frequent trips into Moscow or St. Petersburg to gamble, leaving Olga alone to brood.

The couple continued to shuttle between St. Petersburg and Ramon and from one social engagement to the next. Olga had few friends, but many nieces and nephews on whom she lavished gifts. With no one in authority to instruct her otherwise, and partly from boredom, she began to spend money at a prolific rate. In addition to the Olgino house, bought at her expense, she paid each member of her staff and purchased gifts for them on birthdays and on religious occasions.

Whether obligated to or not, she even subsidized the education of staff members' children, who all wanted to be doctors and engineers.[31] The rest of her money was coaxed out of Olga by Peter, who immediately squandered it away at the crap tables.

Similarly, the free-spending good times of the dynasty were also drawing to a close. Competition involving the ultimate ownership of a Russian-controlled port in the China Sea was about to plunge Russia into a disastrous war with Japan. The war would ultimately cost the country thousands in men and millions in rubles.

On January 22, 1903, Nicholas hosted what would turn out to be the last *bal masque* at the Winter Palace in St. Petersburg's history. The participants dressed as historical figures from the seventeenth century. Nicholas was attired as Alexis, the second Romanov Tsar, in raspberry, gold and silver; while Alexandra was Tsarina Maria Miloslavskaya, Alexis's first wife. She wore a sarafan of gold brocade trimmed with emerald and silver thread. Xenia wore a gown covered with glittering jewels, the costume of a "*boyarina*," or member of the privileged aristocracy. In her hand was a Fabergé fan made entirely of peacock feathers and various gemstones. Sandro came as a court falconer, wearing a white and gold long coat with golden eagles embroidered on the back, a pink silk shirt, blue silk trousers and yellow leather boots.

It was Sandro who had the best perspective on the evening when he wrote, "This magnificent pageant of the seventeenth century must have made a strange impression on the foreign ambassadors: while we danced . . . [the] clouds in the Far East were hanging dangerously low."[32]

A$_S$ THE WINTER TURNED into spring, Olga dispiritedly attended one function after another. In April she was invited to Pavlovsk Palace to watch a military review given by her brother Michael's Blue Cuirassier Regiment.[33] While there, her admiring gaze fell on a tall, blond, twenty-two-year-old junior officer nicknamed God Apollo by his fellow officers, but better known as Nicolai Kulikovsky, a member of the gentry of Voronez province and a close friend of Olga's brother Michael.

At the conclusion of the parade, Olga begged Michael to arrange a luncheon where she and Kulikovsky could be casually seated together.[34] Michael complied, and it was at this luncheon that Olga experienced an instantaneous attraction.

Like Olga's father, Nicolai possessed a commanding presence, and as the descendant of a long line of military men, believed actions spoke louder than words. His grandfather had been a general in the Russian army when it successfully triumphed over Napoleon's army.

Despite his impressive military pedigree, Nicolai was neither an erudite man, like Peter, nor a particularly well educated one. Though the son of an aristocratic family, he was educated for free at Petrograde Real College of Gurevich and as an officer cadet at the Nickolai Cavalry College, where he received a degree. Physically he was not without his charms, possessing an athlete's slim, muscular build; a deep, even haughty voice; and ice-blue eyes.

Shortly before he met Olga, he was transferred to the Blue Cuirassier Regiment of Her Majesty the Dowager Empress Marie Feodorovna, where he studied marksmanship and light-machine-gun shooting. Like Olga, he adored animals, and during his youth on his family's two sizable estates in the Ukraine, he perfected an almost uncanny skill at training and riding Arabian horses.

Emboldened by her attraction to Nicolai, just a few days after the parade, Olga requested a divorce from Peter. He replied that he might reconsider the idea in seven years' time, but that currently, social appearances being everything, he considered the idea preposterous.

At the turn of the twentieth century in Russia a woman was not legally allowed to leave her husband to set up a separate residence of her own. If a husband committed adultery, a woman could be granted a legal separation pending a divorce, but if a woman committed adultery, she might be legally forced to return to her husband.

Peter almost certainly committed adultery first, but any attempt by Olga to prove it would have embarrassed her and potentially destroyed the reputation of the Romanov dynasty. "Even the loss of a dear person is better than the disgrace of a divorce," her mother was fond of saying. In spite of moral impediments such as these, Olga kept her eye on the future, and her heart firmly fixed on Nicolai Kulikovsky.

CHAPTER Four

WAR, MARITAL WOES AND A MAD MONK

*A*LEXANDER III'S CHILDREN HAD never known war and believed they would never have to. A conflict with Japan, a nation they had dismissed as being populated by "monkeys,"[1] was about to prove them wrong.

Sergei Witte, Foreign Minister under Alexander III, convinced Alexander to build a railway across Siberia that would link central Russia with the Pacific Ocean and China. In the late 1800s, permission was obtained from the Beijing government to stretch the railway to Port Arthur, located in Chinese Manchuria, with the proviso that Russia sign an accord recognizing China's sovereignty over the region.[2]

The ink hadn't dried before Russia violated the accord by posting numerous military units to the port as a prelude to annexation. By 1903 Nicholas decided to annex Manchuria. Japan, however, had its own eye on the region but made a proposal. In exchange for being allowed to lay claim to Korea, Japan offered to leave Manchuria to the Russians.[3] In response, Nicholas warned Japan not to try Russia's patience, or "else it could end badly."[4]

As soon as he realized that war might be in the offing, Sandro warned Nicholas not to toy with the Japanese, whom he described as "wonderful fighters"[5] when they were riled up. Nicholas lived up to Witte's assessment of him as a man who had "neither will nor character"[6] when he reacted to the news with annoyance. "The Japanese are not going to declare war on Russia,"[7] he replied testily. He was right. The Japanese didn't waste time declaring war; they bombed Port Arthur instead, an act that paralyzed Russia's Pacific fleet and ensured Japanese domination over the China Sea.[8]

The next day Xenia wrote in her diary, "War has been declared!!! May the Lord help us! It's so terrible, you simply don't want to believe it, or what it will bring with it."[9] When war with Japan broke out, Olga reflexively sided with her brother, insisting that Nicholas had never intended to go to war but had been "pushed into it by the so-called war party of politicians and generals who were so certain of a quick and sensational victory—to bring glory to themselves and to the crown, in that order."[10] The Dowager Empress Marie quickly telegraphed from Denmark where she was staying: "Greatly saddened by the news from the Far East, but the responsibility for this lies with them."[11]

This time the Dowager Empress was wrong and the general populace knew it. Reading the morning newspapers announcing the attack, the intelligentsia were shocked and began openly challenging Nicholas's effectiveness as ruler. Nicholas knew that overnight he had lost the trust of his people. Against the recommendations of his advisers he dispatched thousands of terrified soldiers on the seven-thousand-mile journey to the port along the newly built railway. The Japanese received advance news of the Russians' approach and were ready for them. As a result, few Russian soldiers returned home alive. Those who weren't shot died of scurvy and typhoid. Meanwhile, Russian cruisers sent to the port were swiftly destroyed by guns placed atop the banks of the China Sea.

Nicholas had at least one happy distraction from the tumult around him. On July 30, 1904 a 301-gun salute announced the birth of Nicholas and Alexandra's first and only son, Alexei. The pink-cheeked, apparently healthy baby weighed a hefty eleven pounds. The Act of Succession was optimistically altered to read that Alexei, not Michael, was now to be the heir-apparent to the throne.

The couple's elation turned to despair, however, when within six weeks of his birth Alexei was diagnosed with the "bleeding disease" or hemophilia. Nicholas confided to Olga that Alexei's condition convinced him that he was a marked man, forever to be pursued by the demons of fate. Rather than fight his despair, Nicholas, some say with the help of hallucinogenic Tibetan herbs supplied by Alexandra, entered a drug-induced Shangri-La, disinterested, even annoyed, by affairs of state.

Alarmed by their Emperor's disinterest in the disintegration of his own empire, representatives from all parts of Russia converged on St. Petersburg in 1904 to introduce a constitutionally representative body that would "offer the Tsar non-binding advice"—in effect to strip Nicholas of his autocracy and reduce him to an impotent figurehead. Nicholas procrastinated, hoping events in the Far East might improve. They did not. Disturbances in the cities were increasing. Grand Duke Konstantin Konstantinovich, a cousin of Nicholas's, observed that revolution was "banging on the door. A constitution [was] being almost openly discussed."[12]

Olga soon felt the public's rage first-hand. On Epiphany Day in 1905, she and her mother attended the annual Blessing of the Waters ceremony held on the frozen Neva River. On the ice, a dais had been built in front of the palace, which Nicholas, his retinue and members of the clergy ascended. The Metropolitan of St. Petersburg dipped his gold cross in a hole that had been cut in the ice and pronounced his solemn blessing.[13]

Immediately afterwards guns from the St. Peter and St. Paul Fortress across the river opened fire—not with their customary blanks, but with live ammunition. Bullets ricocheted off the pavement, mere inches from Olga's feet. Glass from shattered windows behind her flew into her skirt, hair and skin. A fatalistic Nicholas impassively recalled that one bullet literally "whizzed by" his head.[14]

Olga and her mother lay on the ground, their hands scraped, cut and bleeding. The courtyard was chaos. Police and military units rushed to protect the Emperor, who had not budged from his spot atop the dais. "I knew somebody was trying to kill me. I just crossed myself. What else could I do?"[15] he told Olga later. Nicholas confessed to an alarmed Olga that he was born on Job's Day and was resigned to accept his fate.[16]

The would-be assassin, who was able to sneak past the guards and load the guns with live bullets, was never found, fuelling rumours of an inside job. Paranoia within the palace was at its zenith.

As more and more money was wasted on the futile war

effort, and the lives of thousands of soldiers sacrificed to a hopeless cause, the mood of the citizens of St. Petersburg and Moscow quickly turned from ugly to violent. A local priest named Father Gapon organized several unions founded on Christian principles to fight for better working conditions in the plants. In December 1904, Gapon's union members were fired from the largest industrial plant in St. Petersburg. To protest, on January 7 of the following year, more than over 120,000 workers marched toward the Winter Palace to present Nicholas with a list of grievances. Just as the procession reached the palace, armed troops opened fire, killing 200 and wounding 800. The day became known as Bloody Sunday and it marked the beginning of the end of autocratic Romanov rule. Nicholas, who was vacationing at his country estate, in typically anemic style pronounced the attack "painful and sad."[17] Olga begged her brother to come back to St. Petersburg to speak personally to his people.

Russian citizens soon reacted to Romanov incompetence more violently. Within weeks a Moscow extremist tossed a bomb into the carriage of Grand Duke Sergei, the organizer of the infamous Khodinka Field catastrophe. Unlike many of the victims of Khodinka Field, he was killed instantly. Critics said the retribution was long overdue.

In May 1905, Russia finally capitulated to Japan when Witte signed a peace treaty ending the Russo-Japanese conflict. It wasn't enough to save the reputation of the monarchy. By October, Russia was being attacked internally by massive nationwide strikes. Essential services were cut off. Indispensable goods such as butter, milk and sugar were no longer produced. Rallies were held in university lecture halls calling for the violent overthrow of the Tsar.

Bowing to the inevitable, Nicholas finally signed a manifesto that guaranteed freedom of speech, conscience and association to citizens. It also· paved the way for the first elected legislative parliament, called the Duma. Nicholas's diary entry for that night read, "After such a day, the head is grown heavy and thoughts are confused. May the Lord help us save and pacify Russia."[18]

Reaction among Nicholas's family members was more decisive. Sandro, who immediately resigned as Minister of the Merchant Marine, concluded that Nicholas had "consented to divide his authority with a band of plotters, political assassins and undercover agents of the Department of Police," and concluded with dramatic flourish that Nicholas's actions meant "the end of the dynasty and the end of the empire."[19]

Olga agreed with Sandro that the manifesto had satisfied no one but the extremists. She and her mother sat in the front row of seats on the first day of the newly formed Duma where they observed sullen-faced peasants and workmen looking upon them with hatred. Back at home on Sergievskaya Street, Olga seethed at the hypocrisy shown by what she called the "pampered liberals" within the aristocracy, who dined with her at exclusive clubs then went home to plot ways to destroy her brother.

Indeed, the signing of the manifesto and the creation of the first Duma did not immediately quell the political unrest. It was only with the appointment of the liberal-minded Prime Minister Stolypin in 1905 that the populace temporarily calmed down.

Conditions inside Olga's house had degenerated to pure misery. Her meetings with Nicolai, usually at Michael's home, were becoming less discreet and more dangerous. Peter did not notice his wife's absences since he spent most of his time with his cronies and betting at card games and craps. Over the years, he had lost all interest in displaying anything more than perfunctory affection toward his much younger wife.

Once he was promoted to captain with the Blue Cuirassiers, Nicolai had to endure being posted to other provinces of the country, and as a result, being separated from Olga. For months, the only contact the couple had was through letters. Ever cognizant that some of his letters might fall into the wrong hands, he never addressed Olga by name, only as "my dear friend," and rarely included a signature.

By 1906 he was writing to Olga several times a week, self-consciously apologizing for his weak style, explaining that he was "not a good letter writer and [I] still have to get used to writing to you."[20] The letters are boastful, even slightly tiresome accounts of barracks life with his ribald fellow soldiers. In one he tells a story of a mutual friend who, after getting drunk on guard duty, got into a mishap in which he cut his hand, then when he tried to "syringe it," couldn't find salts and had to rush to St. Petersburg to get some, only to become hysterical when he couldn't find a cab. One can only surmise that Olga, never the hearts and flowers type, was one of the few women who might have chuckled heartily at these tales of drunken male misadventures.

It is not hard to understand why Nicolai was attracted to Olga. Despite her plainness, she could be a bold, flirtatious charmer. One little-known example of her teasing self-assurance occurred between her and an overly sensitive twenty-year-old soldier named Vladimir Trubetskoy at a railway station in St. Petersburg. While waiting for a train bearing his relatives to arrive at the station, Trubetskoy noticed a "rather small lady," whose face "was not beautiful but rather lively."[21] He passed by the woman but failed to recognize or salute her as Grand Duchess Olga Alexandrovna. Once he realized his mistake, an embarrassed Trubetskoy inched his way over to the far corner of the platform.

After greeting two officers, Olga unexpectedly waved Trubetskoy toward her. The youth approached the Grand Duchess, removed his cap, and kissed her hand. When he tried to withdraw his hand, however, Olga, he thought, smiled "provocatively," gently pressed his fingers and without releasing his hand started talking to his friends. The soldier wrote:

> According to etiquette, I could not withdraw
> my hand and I felt I was blushing. I felt
> ashamed for myself and for Olga Alexandrovna
> a little, as I knew that the Great Duchess
> should not behave so free and easy in public...
> [There] was something vulgar and provocative
> in her behaviour as she was pressing and shaking my hand harder and harder ... [22]

At last, Olga released the soldier's hand. Trubetskoy wondered what had motivated Olga's odd behaviour. "Was it her punishment for me for not saluting her or was it a game of a sophisticated woman with an inexperienced youth?"[23] he asked himself years later.

At last, to make Olga happy and perhaps to conceal his own sexual activities, Peter allowed Nicolai to move into their Sergievskaya Street home as his personal adjutant.[24] Olga's brother Michael drew up the paperwork that facilitated the transition. That Nicolai buried his pride to accept such a position shows the intensity of his devotion to Olga.

When Olga and Nicolai finally did live under the same roof, General Bernov, commander of Kulikovsky's regiment, was delighted, theorizing that his soldier's "success" with the Tsar's sister made the regiment "even more fashionable."[25] But before long the intensity of the couple's public displays of physical affection elicited growing gossip among members of the staff and military. Society started to gossip openly as the couple was viewed walking hand in hand, driving in a cab through Gatchina, or strolling arm in arm through public parks.[26] One of Olga's ladies-in-waiting and Michael often went along on these trips as camouflage, but instead of acting merely as disinterested observers, they plunged into a torrid affair, one that ultimately resulted in the lady-in-waiting's banishment from Russia.

Around the same time that Olga's romance with Nicolai was heating up, a new enemy of the people arrived in her brother Nicholas's court. His name was Grigory Rasputin and he would attempt to insinuate himself not only into the souls of the imperial couple and into the politics of the country but eventually into the affections of a horrified Olga.

One of the earliest recorded visits by the peasant from Tobolsk to Nicholas and Alexandra's palace of Tsarskoe Selo occurred in October 1906. "He made a remarkably strong impression both on her Majesty and on myself, so that instead of five minutes our conversation went on for more than an hour,"[27] Nicholas wrote that night.

Rasputin's first recorded "healing" of Alexei occurred a few weeks later. After a fall, Alexei began experiencing high fevers and hemorrhaged badly from weak leg veins. Olga was summoned to Tsarskoe Selo to comfort Alexandra, who was out of her mind with worry. For hours the child was racked by excruciating pain. As far as Olga was concerned, the doctors were "just useless" and looked "more frightened than members of the family itself."[28] Late in the evening, Olga retired to her rooms. While she was away, Alexei's condition worsened and Alexandra sent a telegram to Rasputin in St. Petersburg. As soon as he received it, he took a cab to the palace, arriving just after midnight.

In spite of his agony, Alexei smiled at Rasputin the moment he saw him. As Alexandra and the rest of the family knelt and wept in prayer, Rasputin placed his hand upon the boy's forehead. Almost immediately the tsarevich smiled slightly and looked around the room, first smiling at Rasputin and then his mother.[29] By the time Olga arrived in the boy's room she noted that he had made such a rapid improvement that his fever had vanished, the swelling in his leg had subsided, and he was strong enough to sit up in bed. "The horror of the evening before became an incredibly distant nightmare,"[30] she recalled later.

Nicholas and Alexandra were so overwhelmed with their "saint"'s powers that shortly after Alexei's "healing," they sang his praises to Prime Minister Stolypin. Revolutionaries had recently bombed Stolypin's home, leaving his fourteen-year-old daughter Natalya with badly smashed feet and the imperial couple was sure that Rasputin could help. The

Stolypin family received Rasputin, but no healing occurred. After he had left, Natalya sprinkled her bedroom with eau de cologne to mask the "prophet"'s stale odour.[31]

Shortly after the healing, Olga was invited to join Nicholas and Alexandra for dinner at the palace. It was important to the couple that Olga not only like Rasputin, but fervently believe in their "friend"'s mystical power to heal. In keeping with her character, Olga observed Rasputin with an open mind.

Though much had been written about Rasputin's magnetic eyes, Olga's first impression was that they rolled about in a "frightening manner," and contained a "vulgar inquisitiveness" which she described as "unbridled and embarrassing."[32] After dinner, Alexandra and Nicholas invited her to visit the children's bedrooms, where Olga was initially startled to see an unsupervised Rasputin cavorting with the female pyjama-clad children, while Alexei "hopped around like a rabbit."[33]

After a short while, Rasputin took Alexei's hand and led him to his bedroom. Alexei stood praying beside his bed, gazing up as if transfixed by the "giant" hovering over him. "It was all most impressive," said Olga, initially convinced of Rasputin's "utter sincerity."[34]

Once Alexei was tucked into bed, Rasputin slowly walked with Olga, Alexandra and Nicholas into Alexandra's mauve boudoir. There, Olga's opinion of the seemingly pious holy man changed dramatically. He wasted no time in staring into Olga's eyes, his pupils contracting and expanding like those of a cat. He mumbled disparate biblical quotations in an attempt to impress her with his religious knowledge. But Olga soon realized his knowledge of religious doctrine was no more vast or deep than that of any average "*strannik*," or lay pilgrim, of a type frequently castigated by the Orthodox hierarchy.[35]

Rasputin may have possessed an ability to heal but he possessed an even greater ability to instill paranoia in members of the imperial family, many of whom had skeletons to hide. Olga was one of them. The man she came to refer to as "vulgar and uncouth" began to ask unseemly questions about her life at home with Peter. What was the nature of their relationship? Were they "happy"?[36] Smiling to hide her nervousness, Olga inwardly quaked at the possibility that the inquisitor was going to exploit the gossip circulating about her and Nicolai. Had he guessed about the depths of her passionate longings for this man who lived under her roof?

As Rasputin continued to cross-examine her, Nicholas and Alexandra shifted uncomfortably in their seats, frowning at each other. When the evening was over, Olga nearly tripped over the hem of her own skirt racing for the train station. Once she sat down in her private train for St. Petersburg, she thought, "Thank God he hasn't followed me to the station."[37]

Olga encountered Rasputin a second time at Tsarskoe Selo during one of Nicholas and Alexandra's picnic lunches on the palace grounds. Anastasia, the couple's six-year-old daughter, whom Olga called Shvipsik, had pulled out an easel and paints and was painting an image of her Aunt Olga with broad brush strokes. Nicholas had been called inside on business, while Alexandra and Rasputin were tending to a sickly Alexei, who was resting in his bedroom.

The sun was blazingly hot. Olga began nodding off to sleep on her divan when she felt a tickle against the back of her neck, which she assumed was a mosquito or fly. As she drowsily reached back, her fingers gently brushed against the flesh of another hand. In her half-dreaming state she had imagined the hand to be Nicholas's but a millisecond later her eyes snapped open to reveal the spectral-like figure of Rasputin standing over her, grinning as if with satisfaction.

"Look, swans," Anastasia blurted out, pointing a chubby finger toward the inhabitants of a small pond nearby. In the time it took Olga to awkwardly respond to her niece, Alexandra and Nicholas had rejoined the group, and Rasputin sat back in his chair staring slyly at her from the corners of his eyes. Olga was too startled and upset to complain. The luncheon proceeded without incident, with Alexandra and Nicholas sipping tea as their friend spouted what Olga called "his inanities." [38]

Returning by train that night, Olga had yet another discomforting experience that added credence to other people's assertions that Rasputin could teleport or materialize in more than one place at a time. As she sat looking out at the night sky from her train window, reviewing in her mind the disquieting events of the afternoon, she could have sworn she saw "that grinning licentious face" [39] staring back at her in the glass.

A third encounter steeled her against the so-called monk. One evening Anna Vyrubova, an intimate friend of Alexandra's, invited Olga and her brother and sister-in-law to her small cottage. When they arrived, they were startled to find Rasputin already there to meet them. "He seemed very pleased to meet me again," [40] said Olga. After Nicholas and Alexandra left the drawing room, Rasputin immediately walked over to Olga, boldly wrapped his arm around her shoulders and began stroking her arm. She pulled herself away violently, admitting later that "I'd had more than enough of the man, I disliked him more than ever."[41]

As soon as she returned home later in the evening, she recounted what had happened to Peter, who took her indignation more seriously than she thought he would and advised her to avoid meeting Rasputin in the future. "For the first and only time I knew my husband was right,"[42] she recalled.

A few weeks after the ill-fated evening, Vyrubova arrived at Olga's home to ask if Olga would receive a contrite Rasputin into her home. Despite Vyrubova's insistence that Rasputin wanted to see Olga, Olga refused to let him enter her home and thereafter only met him on chaperoned social occasions. In private circles, her hatred of Rasputin was well known.

In public, Olga knew her countrymen remained unaware of Alexei's illness, so she supported Rasputin, adding that neither Nicholas nor Alexandra "had been duped by Rasputin, or had the least illusion about him."[43] Michael parroted much the same line. In private, though, he often broke down weeping over his brother whom he thought "seemed indifferent to his fate, leaving everything in the hands of God, but under the influence of Rasputin, God had assumed a strange shape."[44]

Whenever the Dowager Empress Marie came into contact with Rasputin, she left with grave misgivings about his powers, and openly worried about his talents for persuasion, especially toward the vulnerable Alexandra. She had been struck and somewhat repulsed by what she described as his "ponderous yet catlike tread."[45] When she realized the extent to which the imperial couple had come to rely on him, she wrote, "My poor daughter-in-law does not realize that she is ruining both the dynasty and herself. She sincerely believes in the holiness of some trickster and we are all powerless to ward off misfortune."[46]

Between 1906 and 1914, when he wasn't at his sparsely furnished flat in St. Petersburg, or travelling back to Tobolsk to visit his wife and two children, Rasputin visited the imperial couple with increasingly regularity. Every time Alexei suffered an attack of bleeding, Alexandra would be frantic until she received a telephone call, telegram or personal visit from Rasputin reassuring them that all would be well. Her and her husband's public appearances became less frequent, and on the few occasions when they did appear at an event they looked grim and put-upon, the last thing an unhappy populace needed to see.

Meanwhile the "humble" Rasputin, who Alexandra insisted gave every penny he made away to the poor, profited nicely from his association with the family. He achieved such a high profile that businessmen needing favours paid Rasputin to speak to the imperial couple on their behalf.

Rasputin's activities outside the palace were less than chaste. In response to rumours circulating among the upper classes of St. Petersburg, police surveillance teams trailed Rasputin almost nightly into dimly lit taverns where he got drunk, jumped up on tabletops and boasted of his conquest of Alexandra, whom he called "the old girl." One night he showed an embroidered waistcoat he was wearing and bragged, "The old girl made me this waistcoat . . . I can do anything I like with her."[47]

Even after they received news of these events, the imperial couple chose to focus their wrath on Rasputin's accusers rather than Rasputin himself. Finally in 1911 Rasputin's lewd conduct was seen first-hand by the imperial couple when several photographs were taken in nightclubs showing Rasputin surrounded by a bevy of nude women.[48]

Since these photographs could fall into the public's hands, Nicholas reluctantly sent Rasputin on a four-month pilgrimage to Jerusalem until things cooled off. Olga, who visited the palace almost every day now, or had her nieces over for tea parties and tennis matches at her house, believed that because of the scandals, the reputation of the Empress in particular was irrevocably harmed. Nevertheless, she did not feel it was her place to interfere. "I felt that their friendship with the man was their private concern and that not even I would have been justified in interfering."[49] Bearing in mind her own experiences with the insolent monk, she was alarmed when her niece Olga admitted that she had sought Rasputin's advice concerning a young man she had been sexually attracted to in church. There is no record, however, of what the details of Olga's attraction were, or of what specific advice Rasputin gave her.

A few months after his return from Jerusalem, the storm that Olga feared was hovering over Alexandra and her daughters finally broke. Catastrophically, handwritten copies of some of the Empress's and Grand Duchesses' letters to Rasputin were distributed throughout town. They were intimate in the extreme. In one Alexandra referred to Rasputin as an "unforgettable teacher, saviour and guide." She spoke of "kissing his hand," "sleeping on his shoulder," "feeling the balm of his presence." The girls, meanwhile addressed him as a "dear," "priceless," "true" and "unforgettable" friend.[50] For all intents and purposes the letters signalled the end of

Nicholas's patience with Rasputin, but the man described (by a minister in Nicholas's government named Alexis Khvostov) as an "Armenian peddler with an ace of diamonds up his sleeve"[51] had one more card to play.

During a vacation at Spala, the family's hunting lodge, Alexei injured his lower abdomen while jumping into a boat. The family physician, Dr. Evgeny Botkin, tended to the boy in Rasputin's absence and all seemed to be well. One day Anna Vyrubova and Alexandra took Alexei for a carriage ride that aggravated the earlier injury and nearly ended his life. Every bump in the road caused him excruciating pain; the colour drained from his face; he began to sweat profusely. By the time they returned to the lodge, he was delirious. Dr. Botkin could do little. It was an unstoppable internal hemorrhage. In just a few hours, the boy grew so thin and pale that his eyes looked like small black coals.

Against Nicholas's express wishes, Alexandra contacted Rasputin, who sent back a telegram that stated: "God has seen your tears and heard your prayers. Do not grieve. The Little One will not die. Do not allow the doctors to bother him too much." By two p.m. that afternoon, the bleeding stopped. It was just the "miracle" Rasputin needed to get back into the imperial family's good graces. But not for long.

Shortly after Alexei's latest brush with death, Olga returned to her peaceful villa of Olgina, where reports of Rasputin's misconduct reached her, along with alarming reports that German troops had mobilized to invade France, an action that would eventually precipitate Russia's entrance into the First World War.

Rasputin was now openly sitting in the front row of the Duma, forcing security men to remove him. He insisted to people that he had "an intense, almost mystical conviction that Russia must avoid war at all costs."[52] He sent a telegram to Nicholas stating that he vehemently opposed a war and predicted it would destroy the empire. Viewing the telegram as evidence of "unprecedented interference in affairs of state,"[53] a highly irritated Nicholas ignored it.

Around the time that Rasputin sent the telegram, a high priest by the name of Georgi Shavelsky, who was connected with the Russian army and navy, visited Olga to see if she might be willing to persuade Nicholas to banish Rasputin permanently. Describing her as the "most approachable, democratic and simple in her ways of the whole Emperor's family," he brought up the issue of Rasputin and his increasingly dangerous influence on the affairs of state. The following is his transcript of the conversation in which he begged Olga to speak to her brother about the dangers surrounding him and his empire:

> We all know about it—she said—It is our family grief which we cannot do anything about . . .
>
> You have to talk to the Emperor firmly, your Highness—I said.
>
> Mother has spoken to him, but nothing helps—she said.
>
> Now you must try and talk to him. I know that his Majesty loves you dearly and trusts you. I hope he will listen to you—I insisted.

I am ready to do it, Father, but I know nothing
will come of it . . . It will take him [Rasputin]
only two words to demolish all my arguments
and to make me feel confused—she replied,
with suffering in her voice. [54]

For several days after the priest's visit, Olga anguished
over whether or not to approach her brother, finally dismissing the idea when Peter pointed out that any criticism of
Rasputin to Nicholas would not only be angrily repudiated
by Alexandra, but might seriously damage Olga and
Nicholas's relationship.

CHAPTER *FIVE*

*L*OVE ON THE *B*ATTLEFIELD

*I*N THE MONTHS LEADING up to the First World War, Olga periodically asked Nicholas to permit a divorce but wisely did not press the matter. Like his mother, Nicholas had little sympathy for divorces and morganatic marriages. At the turn of the century he had angrily banished from Russia his first cousin Grand Duke Cyril when, against Orthodox rulings, Cyril married Victoria-Melita, the divorced wife of Grand Duke Ernst of Hesse-Darmstadt. Nevertheless, because Cyril had performed heroically during the Russo-Japanese war, Nicholas eventually allowed him to return.

Olga's chances of success were further hampered by Michael's surprise 1912 marriage to Natasha Wulfert, the twice-divorced daughter of a Moscow solicitor, who had already borne Michael a son, George. For this marriage, Michael, the heir presumptive, the next in line to the throne after Alexei, was banished.

"How many times did he promise me that he would not

marry her," wrote an enraged Nicholas, shortly after the wedding. "[At] a time, too, when everyone is talking of war, and when the tercentenary of the Romanovs is due in a few months! I am ashamed and deeply grieved."[1]

Olga was also "angry beyond words" that Michael was foolhardy enough to marry a twice-divorced commoner while rumours of war were in the air and public loyalty to the family was low. Olga's anger had somewhat of a double standard to it, however. Just as Michael had accepted Olga's passion for Nicolai, Olga had initially supported Michael's relationship with the then still-married Natasha, even though Natasha was a divorcee and the wife of Vladimir Wulfert, an officer in Michael's Blue Cuirassiers Regiment. Indeed in 1908 and 1909 Olga, often accompanied by Nicolai, frequently visited Natasha's home, where she fussed over Natasha's daughter, Tata. Tata remembered Olga as "a very charming simple women, nearly always dressed in a white jersey and a beret." Captain Kulikovsky, who, she said, was a "marvel at mending toys," was a "man of some mystery," whose relationship with Olga generated a great deal of gossip among servants since everyone knew Olga was married to a "Germanic princeling."[2]

A famous 1909 photograph shot by Natasha's husband, Vladimir, shows Natasha and Michael sitting close together on a grassy bank. A little farther up the hill behind them is Olga, accompanied by a semi-reclining Nicolai. At the time the photograph was taken the photographer was not yet aware of the relationship growing between his wife and Michael. By the summer of 1909, Michael, Natasha, Olga, Peter and Nicolai were lunching openly on Michael's yacht *Zernista*, with the cuckolded Wulfert becoming a distant memory.[3]

Given their mutual indiscretions, it is particularly tragic that Olga did not take Michael's side. It was a snub that Michael could never forgive.

After Michael's sudden elopement, the Oldenburg dinner table in the opulent house on Sergievskaya Street in St. Petersburg became so silent one might have confused it with the catacombs. Guests were few. As servants removed the china after the completion of each course, the quiet was broken only by the wind rattling the mansion's windows which had solid gold grates. Worse, whenever Olga raised her eyes, she faced, sitting at her husband's elbow, the man with whom she wished to spend the rest of her life.

There were times when Olga wondered whether Peter's slavish adherence to convention actually allowed him to derive perverse pleasure from watching her and Nicolai repress their ardour. Certainly, Peter gave every indication that he was content with the status quo and saw no necessity to end a marriage that distracted the public from taking an undue interest in his late-night activities.

Olga had few if any intimates to turn to. Xenia was already married and the mother of seven children, one of whom, Irina, had just married Felix Yusupov, a scion of one of the great houses of Europe. Olga's mother, with whom she never exchanged her innermost fears, lived the cloistered life of a former Empress, leaving her home only for official occasions and parties and for the most part distracting herself by playing card games and receiving visits from foreign dignitaries. Marie did not approve of Olga's growing dependence on Nicolai and for many years adamantly refused to acknowledge him as a fixture in her daughter's life.

Most isolating of all, Olga stopped writing to Michael, at first out of anger and later because her letters were intercepted and returned by a bitter Natasha. Nicholas suffered a similar fate when he tried to write to Michael. He wrote:

> Poor Misha is evidently not responsible for his own actions at the moment; he thinks and reasons as she tells him, and it's utterly useless to argue with him. . . . Mordvinov [Misha's former ADC] has very much asked us NOT TO WRITE to him AT ALL, as she not only reads any telegrams, letters and notes, but takes copies which she shows to her people and then keeps in the bank together with the money. She's such a cunning, wicked beast that it's disgusting to even talk about her.[4]

Nineteen-thirteen and -fourteen brought with them civil unrest and government skirmishes with striking workers as well as a growing threat of war. More than ninety per cent of the Russian population remained illiterate and in low-paying jobs in factories. No longer able to sustain themselves through merely agrarian means, farmers flooded into Moscow and St. Petersburg, hoping to find work but finding only more poverty.

Rumours of war were ignored by members of the nobility, who responded by hoisting champagne glasses and participating in frenzied spates of partying. Nicholas meanwhile fidgeted, smoked cigarettes incessantly and sought respite in the arms of his loving nuclear family, including Alexandra, and through her, his family's most dangerous outside adviser, Rasputin.

Fearful of Germany's potential to lay waste to western Russia, in its ravenous quest to force Russia into acting as an economic colony created to supply Germany with inexpensive labour and raw materials they could use to dominate the European continent,[5] Russia responded to Germany's threats to invade France with idle warnings of armed retaliation, which were not backed by any realistic strength, either in manpower or weaponry. Even the general populace seemed to believe that the combined powers of Austria and Germany were simply baring their teeth and that soon everything would be forgotten. Their complacency would prove to be a suicidal mistake.

Olga faced estrangement at every level of her life. Her country was being torn apart, her nuclear family was shattered, and her marriage was a sham. The strain of sharing a roof with the man she loved, yet could approach only in the most furtive ways, exhausted her physically and mentally.

Visiting Sandringham in England with the Dowager Empress shortly before the war, she suffered a nervous breakdown, describing herself at the relatively tender age of thirty as feeling "shelved . . . [desperately] old."[6] During a later visit to Buckingham Palace, Olga felt overwhelmed by the tensions in her life. "All the time I had an odd foreboding that something would happen," she said. "One evening, I went to the theatre with my dear friend, Lady Astor. There I was taken ill."[7] Olga's breakdown at this time very much resembled the one she suffered after her marriage to Peter, when she had gone bald with stress.

While accompanying her brother Nicholas to the Romanovs' 1913 tercentenary celebrations, Olga eerily predicted the end of the Romanov dynasty: "As I watched all those illuminations in honour of the dynasty, and went from one ball to another, I had an odd feeling that though we were carrying on as we had done for centuries, some new and terrifying conditions of life were being formed by forces utterly beyond our control."[8]

Adding to Olga's unhappiness in 1913 was the sudden death of her beloved Nana Franklin, who was buried on the grounds of Olga's childhood palace of Gatchina. Needless to say, Marie did not attend the funeral.

"For me she was the closest and most loved person. With her everything felt so cozy and I trusted her in everything. She lives in my soul always and everywhere,"[9] cried a bereft Olga.

DURING THE EVENING OF JULY 19, 1914, Olga accompanied Nicholas and his children to church and then proceeded to the villa of Alexandria for dinner. Before the group could finish removing their coats the news arrived: Germany had officially declared war on Russia.

Pale and distraught, Olga returned to St. Petersburg. A few days later she received even worse news. Nicolai's regiment was going to be one of the first called to the front.

Olga was at a crossroads. Much as she would have liked to, there was no way to exempt Nicolai from his military duty. Yet the idea of being separated from him was almost unendurable. The only alternative was to appeal to her brother to be allowed to travel close to the fighting, where she could practise the nursing skills she had picked up in Olgino. Nicholas reluctantly agreed.

Next, Olga boldly informed Peter that no matter what the consequences, she was leaving him for good, by all accounts a threat he took with disbelieving equanimity. Without a trace of sadness, she packed away her party dresses and gem-encrusted necklaces for the last time and filled a small suitcase with undergarments and a few other essentials.

After wrapping a bandana around her head, she threw a warm overcoat over her simple nurse's smock, and clutching the suitcase in her hand, boarded a carriage to the railway station. There was general turmoil at the station, with trains coming and going filled to capacity with troops and supplies. Virtually no one had time to notice, amid clouds of steam, the slim woman holding a bulging suitcase close to her chest. Finally, a soldier with one of Nicholas's regiments noticed Olga. He bowed and asked if he could be of some assistance. Olga exclaimed excitedly that she wished to catch the next train to Rovno, near the Polish-Austrian border, where a makeshift army hospital had been set up and her Akhtyrsky Regiment was stationed. Clearing a path through the throngs of soldiers gathered on the platform, the soldier escorted Olga to the first train heading south. As the shrill train whistle blew, she hopped on board, drawing her coat around herself protectively.

Huddled on open freight trains, wrapped only in blankets to shield her from the elements, Olga rumbled toward Rovno, 1550 miles south of St. Petersburg. On the way out of St. Petersburg, she passed fatherless families standing in line for hours for scraps of food to feed their starving children. She knew the eyes of the Russian citizens were now turned toward the family whose expenditures of money on armaments was bringing economic calamity upon the country.

Upon her arrival at the army hospital, Olga was introduced to the rest of the nursing and medical staff, who had been informed in advance not to treat her with any undue deference. Afterwards, she was led to a small, cluttered room that resembled the room she and Xenia had slept in as children at Gatchina. It contained a cot and small wooden table with a kerosene lamp on it. A religious icon hung from the wall. Between smudges and clustered bugs on a tiny window, Olga could see rows of men on stretchers laid out on the grass to get some sun. Music from a gramophone in the main recreation room drifted up through cracks in the floorboards. After a brief lunch of assorted fruits and vegetables, Olga was put to work.

Within days Olga was assisting during operations, stitching wounds and injecting medications. With every new arrival of wounded, the atmosphere in the hospital was one of controlled chaos.

Sometimes the wind outside blew doors open so violently that towels, papers, letters and maps of war action flew around the room. Often, after soldiers were laid down, bullets spontaneously popped out of wounds. Limb amputations were commonplace. Many times Olga attempted to comfort men whose deaths were mere seconds away.

The suffering of one young soldier particularly moved her. His gunshot injuries were so grave that his body was already starting to decompose. Propped up on a stack of pillows, he opened his eyes and tried to smile at Olga as she entered his hospital room. She stood by his bed, and tried to restore warmth into his ice-cold hands by rubbing them between hers. All at once his eyes lit up and he asked, "Sister, can you hear the church bells ring, how beautiful they sound?" Olga heard nothing. The soldier asked her to open the windows so he could hear the bells better. When Olga returned to his bed, he sighed deeply and his face stiffened into a happy expression Olga described as resembling that of someone "who had seen something wonderfully beautiful."[10]

At the front, the grim reality was that Russian soldiers were outmanned three to one, in some cases fighting the armed enemy with only sticks in their hands. Within weeks of Olga's arrival, the approaching enemies had driven the hospital back four hundred miles to Kiev.

Olga, who now shared a small room in Kiev with another nurse, started work at six a.m. Many soldiers, especially officers, were initially embarrassed to have their wounds dressed by a Grand Duchess. Some averted their faces and blushed. In every face she saw that of Nicolai, or "Cuckooshkin" as she had come to affectionately call him, and how much she wanted and needed him in her arms, safe. She confessed in a letter to Nicholas that "knowing and seeing so much suffering going on doesn't stop human nature from thinking of its own wishes—which makes me angry."[11]

In the few hours she had off in the late evenings, Olga read by kerosene lamps, swatting small flies and gnats away from her face. One night she came upon what she referred to as one of those *new* books. After reading a few pages, she disgustedly tossed it on the floor. "It's called 'Hussar,'" she wrote Nicolai, "and describes his intimate relationship with a whore . . . and then he gets a certain disease which is even named! And then it describes his suffering from this disease—a very frank book! I won't read it any more, it makes me feel dirty. I'd like to be clean. It's impossible, of course, because I am too 'human.'"[12]

As the weeks passed, she wrote many letters, including those to her brother Nicholas, who eagerly welcomed any familial communications to distract him from almost certain military defeat. In one letter of July 4, 1916, Olga wrote:

> Just now we have so much work that for more than a month I did not get out neither for a walk nor for a ride. There are so many wounded, nearly 500 beds. [13]

Near the same time, she wrote to her niece Grand Duchess Maria:

> I went just now to a military hospital where I spent the morning talking to the sick and wounded and there were two from your Kozantzi regiment. One had been wounded in the arm and leg and the other was dying from a deep wound in his stomach. His wound already has an odour. He told me about the battle of July 28, when they attacked the Austrian infantry. They were machine gunned. From the first squadron and from his 3rd platoon, only two people were left. He was breathing with difficulty. I'm so sorry for him, he has big suffering blue eyes. [14]

The passion between the Olga and Nicolai was unmistakable to all who witnessed their unrestrained kissing and embracing in the hospital corridors, whenever Nicolai, usually mud-splattered and with several days' growth of beard, dashed in.

Olga mentioned in a letter to her niece Maria how "rough" Nicolai's manners had become in her presence since he began fighting at the front. She recounted an incident that occurred as the couple walked down the street one day. The couple met two young soldiers. One of them saluted Olga without taking the other hand out of his pocket—and as Olga described, was "honoured with Nicolai's encouraging words—'Take your hand out of the pocket, ass!'" [15]

Approaching the age of thirty-five, Olga ached to share with Nicolai her long-repressed instinct to bear children. Even Xenia's daughter, Irina, had given birth to a daughter, prompting Olga to remark to Nicolai, "I have become a *Grandma* not being a mother. It's scary, I wish it could be vice versa... I miss you so much that I can't bear it! (it's not true, I can bear it as long as God wants it)." Envisioning a possible marriage to Nicolai, Olga ended the letter on a passionate note. "I am covering you with kisses! I see you in my thoughts and admire you. I see your loving eyes, suntanned face, your smile—and kiss your lips—the lips that belong only to me! My own Baby, dearest Baby! I love you, I love you, I love you... God bless you. Yours, yours, yours, loving wife, bride, sister and baby." [16]

Emboldened by her exposure to freedom, Olga continued to prevail upon her brother to grant her a divorce so she could marry Nicolai. Nicholas had resigned himself to Olga's decision to leave Oldenburg, since the family now had much more to fear than merely the loss of its reputation. Shockingly, it was not Nicholas this time who protested her request, but his wife, Alexandra, who saw Olga's desires as another example of the misplaced romantic impetuousness of the Romanovs. "I cannot tell you the bitter pain it causes me for you, your own sweet sister doing such a thing," she wrote to Nicholas in a March 26, 1916 letter.

In the same letter she admitted that for years she secretly, even "wickedly perhaps" hoped that Peter would not give Olga a divorce because it would force Nicholas into "acting wrongly." She could understand Olga's longing for freedom and happiness, but at the same time accused her of flouting family laws and being responsible, along with Michael, for destroying society's moral values: "How shall we ever stop the rest from similar marriages? It's wrong she [Olga] puts you into this false position and it hurts me it's through her this new sorrow has been inflicted on you. What would your Father have said to all this?"[17] she argued, unable to relax protocol, even in the waning days of her husband's empire.

Olga harboured no illusions about her sister-in-law Alexandra's straitlaced moral nature and disapproval of Nicolai. Due to the prolonged psychological and physical distress she suffered over her hemophiliac son, Alexei, Alexandra malingered in an emotional time warp in which she imagined the ornate protocol of the grandest days of the Imperial Court prevailing over the anarchy that was about to overtake the life she had known.

By contrast, Olga, living alone amid the horrors of the war, grew determined to "make haste and be happy," as egotistical as she admitted it sounded. She swiftly went over Alexandra's head and appealed directly to Nicholas. In a letter dated May 16, 1916, she wrote:

> Do tell me once upon a time what you really think. I had no time to speak with you and only spoke with Alix, who seemed strongly

against it [the marriage] all for your sake and
also for the children's I think . . . [Don't] you
think that to finish with the divorce now during the war while all eyes and minds are occupied elsewhere—and such a small thing
would be lost in all the greater things—would
be better? If you don't think so I'll say no
more—but don't you?[18]

As an added stress to Olga, political tensions within the
army hospital began to mount as quickly as Russia's military
fortunes fell. The polite camaraderie that had existed
between her and some members of the nursing staff began
to evaporate as Bolshevik sympathizers imagined their first
taste of freedom from the clutches of imperialism. Gradually
the more anarchic members of the hospital staff refused to
speak with Olga, averted their eyes when she tried to meet
their gaze, and declined to assist her on her rounds.

Even the presence of Olga's Cossack regiment in town
could not prevent an assassination attempt against her. One
night a nurse who was working at Olga's back raised an
enormous jar of Vaseline and would have struck Olga with
it had Olga not turned in time to scream and run away.[19]

Meanwhile, sensing the gathering storm approaching St.
Petersburg, the Dowager Empress swiftly closed up
Anichkov Palace to flee to Kiev to be with her daughter.
Upon her arrival, she settled at the Maryinsky Palace on the
banks of the Dneiper River.

The Dowager Empress was soon to learn, however, that
the political climate in Kiev was becoming equally unstable.
Initially, she went about town as if all the citizens were as

loyal to the monarchy as they had ever been. "Mama enjoys everything—beginning with the view and ending with the birds singing in the trees," wrote Olga to Nicholas, adding, "she is busy running about Kiev—thinks the whole town belongs to her—I try quietly to dissuade her but she clings to this idea."[20]

Before long, though, Bolshevik-backed police, nick-named "the green men" by Olga, stopped both women in the street for questioning. Whenever this occurred, Olga waved imploringly to a Cossack to come to her rescue. "If this lasts long, I shall fall ill from the emotion!"[21] she admitted.

Finally, the stress grew so intense that Olga wrote to Nicholas, pleading with him to station Nicolai permanently at her side in the city of Kiev and away from the constantly shifting front. "It gets harder and harder to separate," she wrote. "If something were to happen to him, it would be enough to go mad. Oh! I don't want to lose him just when we might belong to each other—the idea haunts me."[22]

No doubt the permanent stationing of Nicolai to Kiev was a relief to some of his fellow soldiers as well, who complained to Olga about Captain Kulikovsky's harshness. One officer in particular, named Jury Kazanovich, wrote Olga a letter whose contents she shared with Nicolai. A note of sarcasm crept into her voice as she mockingly chastised her lover for mistreating Kazanovich, "He started telling me that he participated in two military campaigns—that is why my Baby [Nicolai] should listen to him, as he is more experienced—instead my Baby picks on him—for being late (or something like that) and that my Baby builds his authority by intimidating others—which is not good—and that soldiers and officers resent it."[23] Olga gently chided her love, "Don't you ever intimidate my dear soldiers, or else! . . . But don't you worry," she added, "I don't believe a word of [Kazanovich's] because *we* know each other much better than he thinks and I know that my Baby takes care of his boys as *no one else*. . . . [Please] don't be cross with him. I am sorry for him as I would be sorry for a trapped animal who bites because there is no one to pet him."[24]

Despite her seeming bravado, Olga fretted that her love affair with Kulikovsky would upset the refined and highly moral sensibilities of her four nieces: Olga, Maria, Tatiana and Anastasia. "Do your daughters know about me?" she asked Nicholas in a July 4, 1916 letter. "I never told them. May I write or do they know? I hate hiding things from them as I love them so."[25]

Confirmation that the daughters accepted the relationship arrived from Alexandra a few weeks later. A clearly relieved Olga wrote back to Nicholas, "Oh! I'm so glad 'the daughters' know about me. I hated hiding it from them and yet I couldn't write—in case Alix hadn't told them or didn't want to."[26]

Xenia's husband, Sandro, soon followed Olga and the Dowager Empress to Kiev, living on board his personal train at the Kiev station. Sandro, whom Nicholas had placed in charge of the air forces, had predicted the inevitable failure of Russia's ill-equipped army in the face of Germany's massive strength and Nicholas's inept leadership. Like many liberals and monarchists alike, he felt the monarchy needed to be saved from the monarch.

Like a juggernaut, the German army had successfully invaded France and vanquished Belgium and Poland. The borders of Russia now beckoned.

The end came when Nicholas took Rasputin's advice, given via his wife, to replace his uncle Grand Duke Nicholas Nicholaevich at the still-retreating front. Under Nicholaevich's leadership the army had lost at least two huge divisions of highly trained soldiers in Poland. Army materiel had become virtually nonexistent. Bitter infighting had erupted among military commanders.

Nicholas hoped that his presence at the front would rekindle the troops' sense of patriotism. His scheme worked briefly, but was overshadowed by the economic crisis back home in St. Petersburg. The fact was that Russia was virtually broke. In St. Petersburg alone, inflation was making most goods, including foodstuffs, unaffordable. Even more distressing, Rasputin was now dictating to Alexandra which government ministers should be fired and which retained. Sensing a leadership vacuum, citizens of St. Petersburg started to revolt in favour of what they hoped would be a people's government run by the people.

Remaining at the front, the dreamy Nicholas daily awaited military and political advice from his wife in the form of four letters a day. In the fall of 1916, she insisted Nicholas appoint a man named Protopopov as the new Minister of the Interior because their "Friend" liked him. "'Our Friend''s opinions of people are sometimes very strange," Nicholas tried to argue, adding, "All these changes make my head go around."[27] Of course, Alexandra won out. Nicholas could not prevail when his wife's feelings were this strong.

The nation's hatred of Rasputin only increased when citizens discovered he had tried to prevent his own son from being drafted. When his son was assigned to medical services, instead of active duty, many enraged citizens concluded it was probably a favour bestowed upon Rasputin by his lover, Alexandra. Crude posters of the two were hung on buildings throughout St. Petersburg, a city now described as resembling "a person just recovering from a drunken bout."[28]

*I*N 1915, NICHOLAS LIFTED MICHAEL'S banishment and allowed him to return to Russia. Because of what Michael viewed as Olga's betrayal of him and his wife, he pointedly did not visit her, a slight she did not overlook. "Just imagine, Misha was here again. Sandro asked him to visit me but he said that I had been so mean to him all these years that he didn't want to hear about me! What a bitch she [Natasha] is and what could she tell him about me to make him think that way? It hurt me deeply—when I saw his letter with my own eyes,"[29] she wrote to Nicolai. By the following year, though, Michael finally agreed to visit Olga at the army hospital, where with pained formality they shared childhood reminiscences.

The Dowager Empress Marie was overjoyed that her two youngest children had apparently reconciled. "At last he [Michael] has made it up with poor Olga," she wrote. "I am SO happy and have shed tears of joy! Thank God that is now settled and I can die in peace!"[30] But appearances were deceiving; in truth, Michael never truly forgave Olga for her repudiation of Natasha. After 1912 her name was never mentioned in his personal diaries.

In September, a shockingly thin and wan Nicholas arrived at Olga's Kiev hospital from Mogilev to inspect injured troops. Olga accompanied him as he strolled past bed after bed of dying and seriously wounded young men, many of whom had professed their disillusionment with Nicholas's reign. The actual sight, however, of their once-beloved Emperor reduced them to tearful silence. One boy, court-martialled and condemned to death, admitted to Nicholas that he had deserted the front. Nicholas absolved him, and in gratitude the boy pathetically leapt out of bed, knelt on the floor, wrapped his arms around Nicholas's knees, and wept.[31]

Nicholas's visit lasted only a few hours. As they walked toward the train that would take him away from Olga forever, he took both her hands in his, kissed her tear-stained cheeks, and informed her that in spite of Alexandra's feelings, he would present to the Holy Synod the matter of her divorce from Peter Oldenburg.

Now closer than ever to marrying the man she had loved for thirteen years, Olga was never as far away from the brother she had adored for thirty-five. Alone in her room that night, she unsealed a letter Nicholas left for her, written on simple vellum paper. He wrote:

> My darling Olga, You have my permission and all my *blessing* for your upcoming wedding. May N.K. [Nicolai Kulikovsky] be worthy of you, dear, and may he give you all you deserve and expect from him! . . . It was a great treat to have seen you twice, but I am nevertheless sorry it was not more than just a few minutes. I leave this evening at 10 most contented with my visit to your Moxma [Mother] and to her and my Kiebr [Kiev] . . . God bless you darling Olga! I shall think of you and pray for you

more than ever . . . I hug you lovingly . . . Your
old brother, Nicky.[32]

As soon as she read his letter, Olga dashed off a postcard
to Nicholas requesting his permission for her and Nicolai to
wed on November 5, which Nicholas gave as soon as the Holy
Synod officially rendered its decision to grant the divorce.

Olga recorded that she was "awfully touched" that at the
last minute the Dowager Empress agreed to attend the ceremony, but added that Marie was "deranged because she
didn't want the police there."[33] Sandro, who also attended
the wedding, instructed the Governor of Kiev that "not one
policeman was to be placed near the church."[34]

The excited bride was dressed and coiffed by nineteen
fellow nurses, who all squeezed into the same small room
with her. She emerged wearing a veil of orange blossoms in
her upswept hair. Her simple silk dress, covered with hand-
embroidered roses, was made by a local designer. Around
her neck she wore the single strand of pearls her father had
given her when she was a child and which she never removed
for the remainder of her life.

The wedding she had awaited for fifteen years was conducted in small, dark Kievo-Vasilievskaya Church on
Triokhsviatitelskaya Street (Street of Three Saints), not far
from a monument of St. Olga and a statue of the Russian god
Perun, god of wind and rain. Olga chose the church because
of its cozy sensuousness and because it was "out of the way,
old and pretty—not very big, very high and dark."[35] A choir
sang "God Have Mercy," Olga recalls, one singer's voice
"rising in the sky like a lark," as the "slave to God" Olga was
united with the "slave to God" Nicolai.

The old priest who married the couple read the scriptures with one eye fixed nervously on the Dowager Empress Marie, whose presence intimidated him. When it came time for him to greet Marie at the conclusion of the ceremony, Olga was amused to see that, though it was very cold in the church, he had big beads of perspiration on his face.

Even the usually cynical Sandro rejoiced for Olga, of whom he was immensely fond. He wrote: "It was an exceedingly modest, almost a secret ceremony: the bride, the bridegroom, the old Empress, myself, two Red Cross sisters and four officers of Olga's own Akhtyrsky Hussar Regiment. An elderly priest officiated in a thin voice, which seemed to be coming from far beyond the half-lighted chapel. Our faces beamed."[36]

The snow was softly falling outside as the couple exited the church and boarded the motorcar that would take them to the army hospital where the reception was to be held. At the entrance to the hospital, several nurses and doctors pelted the newlyweds with handfuls of hops and oats. They were joined by those members among the wounded who were strong enough to walk.

The Dowager Empress, who along with Sandro stayed for supper, presented Olga with an ornate jewel-encrusted silver icon as a wedding present, with a simple expression of love written on the back.

At about eight o'clock the Dowager Empress, Sandro and the members of the Akhtyrsky Regiment left. The clinic doctor played the piano, as Androvsky, the local druggist, filled everyone's glasses with brandy. After a few swigs, the assembled started dancing on tabletops.

A young black doctor, who had drunk too much brandy,

was "killingly funny" in Olga's words. "He danced—rocked about and fell over the chairs and onto the tables." A few hours later the doctor was found on Olga's bed feeling very ill. With the assistance of a few strong men, he was half-carried down to the infirmary, where he spent the rest of the evening "being sick into a sky-blue enamel pot—while a sister—who is very fond of him, sat by his side changing a wet towel on his chest and stroking his head."[37]

Just prior to their departure, Olga and Nicolai visited the infirmary to say goodbye to their poor, sick friend, who in Olga's words "kissed us both lovingly—again assured me he was not a bit tipsy—and absently kissed my husband's hand!"[38]

Despite her joy, Olga must have been pained to notice that one member of her family—her brother Michael—was conspicuously absent, and, even more significantly, no wedding present was ever sent.

The couple's motorcar sped them to the train station from which they embarked on a two-week honeymoon. From there they were invited to stay at a cozy old farmhouse filled with handwoven tablecloths and floor coverings in the town of Podgornoye. The house had once belonged to friends of Nicolai's family named Lupovinov. Most of the family members were away except the owner's thirty-nine-year-old daughter whom Nicolai referred to as an "old maid." The porcine woman served fattening meals to Olga, who she thought had grown too thin from overwork. To Olga's delight, the woman had an affection for animals, so every table and chair in the house teemed with all breeds of dogs, especially greyhounds, and cats.

Every morning, Nicolai drove from the house to an eight-hundred-acre piece of tree-covered hilly land where the couple hoped to build their dream house. Curiously, the house was not to be built from scratch, but out of the pieces of a previously standing house. "Here one does such things all the time, buys someone's house, takes it to pieces—and puts it up in one's own estate,"[39] wrote Olga.

In a letter she sent to Nicholas during the honeymoon, Olga thanked him again for helping her realize her dream of marrying Nicolai, reiterating her disappointment that the two could not speak alone during his recent visit to Kiev. The interfering Alexandra pointedly never received a similar letter of thanks. Instead Olga asked Nicholas to pass on to Alexandra the letter Olga wrote to him, using the excuse that she was "too lazy" and "can't write this all over again."[40]

Returning to Kiev at the conclusion of their honeymoon, the couple stopped off for a day at the town of Kharkoff, where Nicolai's parents and grandmother lived. Nicolai's half-blind grandmother, a tall imperious women who had never met Olga before, took Olga's shoulders in her hands and turned her toward a light so she could see her, saying, "I want to have a proper impression of what you look like before I go quite blind."[41]

Before they had left for their honeymoon, Olga and Nicolai had arranged to rent a small home within walking distance of the army hospital. The day they returned home, all the tables in the dwelling had vases of flowers on them, along with overflowing baskets of fruit, courtesy of what Olga described as her "war buddies" at the hospital.

left: Tsar Alexander II,
murdered by a bomb
in 1881.

below: The most devoted
royal couple in Europe,
Tsar Alexander III
and his wife
Marie Feodorovna.

Tsar Alexander III and his family.
From left: Michael (Misha), wife Marie, Nicholas, Xenia and George.
Olga is in foreground in father's arms, circa 1887.

above: Alone, as usual, Olga with her dolls in corridor of Gatchina Palace. (Photo: Joel Clark)

below: Olga's first brush with death, the Borki train wreck (1888).

above: A rare photograph showing Olga with both her husband Prince Peter of Oldenburg (rear centre) and Nicolai Kulikovsky (far right). At Olga's left is Nanny Franklin. (Photo: Joel Clark)

below: Courting scandal: a relaxed Olga seated beside a reclining Nicolai Kulikovsky. In foreground, Olga's brother with lover Natasha Wulfert (1907). (Photo: Pauline Holdrup)

left: Nursing a wounded soldier at Kiev army hospital, circa 1915.
(Photo: Joel Clark)

below: Tsar Nicholas II inspecting injured soldiers at Kiev army hospital six months before his arrest— the last time Olga saw her brother (1916).

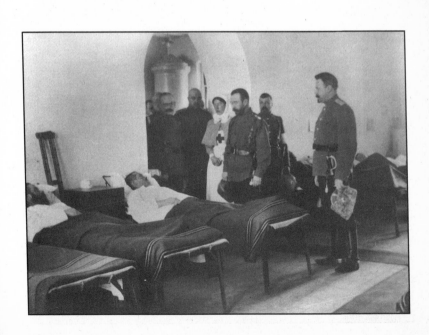

above: Olga's wedding party, Kiev, 1916. From left: Dowager Empress Marie, Olga, Nicolai. (Photo: Joel Clark)

below: From left: Maria, Olga, Anastasia, Tatiana, Olga's nieces, under house arrest, Tobolsk, 1917. (Photo: Joel Clark)

above: Hvidøre in Denmark.

below: Olga and sister Xenia, Denmark. (1920s).
(Photo: Joel Clark)

left: Guri and first wife, Ruth.

below: Tihon and first wife Agnete.
(Photo: Agnete (Kulikovsky) Petersen)

*T*HE BLUSH WAS BARELY OFF the cheeks of the wedding celebrants when on December 17 news reached Kiev that Rasputin was dead, murdered by Felix Yusupov, the husband of Sandro and Grand Duchess Xenia's grown daughter, Irina, and by Grand Duke Dimitry, one of Olga's cousins. The murder was brutal. After being poisoned, bludgeoned and shot, Rasputin finally drowned in the Neva River, where he had been thrown by the unrepentant murderers. The two men involved in the plot to eliminate Rasputin thought that it was their last chance to save tsarism from toppling.

Rasputin had known he wasn't going to die a natural death. "I see a sort of black cloud over our St. Petersburg house,"[42] he told his daughter as 1916 wound to a close. A series of mysterious telephone callers warned him, "Your days are numbered!" or "As for you, you will shortly die like a dog." Employing what some believed to be "second sight," he composed a blood-chilling letter in which he accurately predicted that he would not survive the New Year, and added this warning:

> Tsar of the land of Russia, when you hear the sound of the bells telling you that Grigory has been killed, you must know this: if your relatives carried out the murder, then not one of your family—that is none of your children or relatives—will remain alive for more than two years. They will be killed by the Russian people.[43]

Olga condemned Rasputin's murder, though she had no personal affection for the lascivious monk. "There was just nothing heroic about Rasputin's murder," she said years later. "What did they hope to achieve? Did they really believe that the killing of Rasputin would mend our fortunes at the front, and bring to an end the appalling transport chaos and the resulting shortages? I've never once believed it."[44]

Nicholas, indecisive about what type of punishment to mete out to men viewed by the general populace as heroes, banished each: Felix Yusupov to his estate at Rakitnoie, near Kursk, and Dimitry to the Persian front.

The starving peasants of St. Petersburg were wild with revolutionary zeal. Breadlines lengthened, food rotted at the sides of railway stations. Munitions workers struck. Sandro and Michael begged Nicholas to agree to support a new and independent provisional government to avert a bloody revolution. Nicholas refused.

Even in the jaws of defeat, Alexandra and her family never grasped the true seriousness of the situation, choosing instead to elevate Rasputin to the status of martyr and to believe that the most recent peasant revolts would pass as had all the rest. What she hadn't predicted was that her husband's own generals would go over to the other side. With that, the three-hundred-year-old Romanov dynasty quickly unravelled.

CHAPTER SIX

ESCAPE

ST. PETERSBURG TEETERED ON THE brink of collapse. With Rasputin's murder and Nicholas's absence at the front, the citizens smelled blood and began to demand the immediate overthrow of the monarchy.

By March, as he had done previously, Nicholas boarded the imperial train in Mogilev to take him to Alexandra's side at Tsarskoe Selo. This time he did not make it. Less than one hundred miles from St. Petersburg, his train was stopped by members of his own army who told him that revolutionary troops were blocking the entrance to the city. The train immediately turned around and headed seventy miles in the reverse direction, then an additional couple of hundred miles west to Pskov station. The retreat was in vain. Waiting for Nicholas at the Pskov station were ministers of his own government bearing a manifesto calling for his resignation. The message was clear. Not even Nicholas's own government, nor the generals in the field, were prepared to support the continuation of his reign.

Among the traitors in his own family were his uncle Nicholas Nicholaevich, who retaliated for being removed from commanding the front by urging Nicholas to abdicate. Grand Duke Cyril, whom Nicholas had once banished for marrying a divorcee, had signed the Manifesto even before it arrived at Pskov and pledged his allegiance to the Duma, or provisional government, that sought to overthrow the monarchy. Surrounded by those he viewed as traitors, Nicholas signed the abdication papers, naming as his successor, not his ailing son Alexei, but his younger brother Michael. The date was March 2, 1917.

After signing the Manifesto, a despairing Nicholas ordered the train back to Mogilev station. Halfway through the journey he suddenly awoke from sleep, remembered that he had not yet informed Michael of his less-than-good fortune to be named the new Emperor and immediately fired off a telegram to his brother that began, "To His Majesty the Emperor Michael: Recent events have forced me to decide irrevocably to take this extreme step. Forgive me if it grieves you and also for no warning—there was no time."[1]

News of the abdication was greeted among his family members in Kiev with angry silence, then bitter disbelief. "I shan't say anything of all we feel because it isn't to be expressed," said Olga. "Such changes that I thought I was going mad and can't sleep till now and when I do—all the events go on in dreams."[2]

Sandro concluded that Nicholas must "have lost his mind," adding, "since when does a sovereign abdicate because of a shortage of bread and partial disorders in his capital? . . . [He] had an army of fifteen million men at his disposal!"[3]

The Dowager Empress Marie vacillated between bouts of hysterical laughter and tears. Accompanied by Sandro, she boarded a train immediately for the Mogilev station, where shortly after it pulled in, Nicholas's train had been detained by soldiers from his own regiments who had crossed over to the Revolutionaries' side.

For two hours, with Cossacks stationed outside, Marie and Nicholas remained sequestered in the privacy of her train. By the time Sandro was invited to join them, Marie was sobbing, while Nicholas rocked back and forth like a small boy, periodically smoking and gazing at his feet. "The calmness of his demeanour showed his firm belief in the righteousness of his decision,"[4] Sandro concluded.

Treason surrounded Nicholas. Over the next three days he met with Sandro, the Dowager Empress Marie, and various generals, officers and personal attendants. At night he and the rest of his disgraced family were forced to listen to crowds of citizens outside the railway station shouting and hooting in celebration at the fall of the dynasty.

On their final day together, Nicholas covered his mother's face with kisses and a few minutes later, waved and smiled wanly from behind fogged windows as the train slowly pulled out of the station. Once he was allowed to return to his beloved Tsarskoe Selo, his health, especially his mental health, rapidly deteriorated. Deep lines etched themselves around his eyes and mouth.

Nicholas's Manifesto of Abdication was hastily published throughout Russia. In the section of the Crimea still controlled by White Russians, particularly Livadia, citizens celebrated Michael's accession. Nicholas's portraits were stripped from shop windows and portraits of Michael hung in their place. Complacent citizens eagerly anticipated that a constitutional monarchy would spare their country further bloodshed.[5]

Before Michael considered accepting the offer of succession, he asked about Nicholas's health, and was reassured that it was fine. The next order of business was to consider the consequences of the burden placed upon him so unexpectedly.

Had he accepted his right of succession, Michael almost certainly would have become a politically impotent tsar, with no government to support him and only mutinous troops to track him down and kill him. Civil war would have been inevitable. Michael theorized that the war with Germany could be won only if the Provisional Government restored order and confidence to the nation.

Therefore, after struggling with the enormous decision thrust upon him by his brother, Michael carefully drafted a manifesto stipulating that he would agree to become tsar only at the will of the people and if the new moderate Provisional Government worked with him. In other words, Michael was prepared to be tsar if he were elected to the position. It was a clever document, leaving open the possibility of a monarch continuing to reign, but under more democratic conditions.

Hardline members of the Duma, who did not wish to see a constitutional monarchy in their future, decided to interpret the document as a statement of abdication. An ungenerous, even disgusted Nicholas, who had started all the problems in the first place, interpreted the document the same way,[6] remarking in his diary, "Misha, it appears, has abdicated. His manifesto ended by kowtowing to the

Constituent Assembly, whose elections will take place in six months. God knows who gave him the idea of signing something so vile."[7]

By the time the Dowager Empress Marie returned to Kiev, the imperial train platform was barred and no Cossacks arrived to greet her. The red flags of the Provisional Government had been hung at each end of the platform and around town. Citizens sympathetic to the Revolutionaries took to wearing red armbands.

Olga, pregnant with her first child, rushed to comfort her distraught mother. In her haste, she fell face first out of Sandro's motorcar onto a curb, hurting her left knee, leg and worst of all her pregnant "tummy." Pains shot through "one area then the other,"[8] she said. For the rest of the day she worried whether she might have seriously injured her unborn child.

Anarchy reigned, as discontent among hospital workers turned into outright violence. Olga rarely dared to venture near the hospital any more, and complained that "uncertainty is always the most trying thing for one's nerves. Mine are in a bad state."[9] Compounding her stress was having to watch her mother drift into and out of denial. "Poor mama doesn't quite realize all—her position, her life to be—but little by little—as we speak of it all—she first gets furious and then quiets down and begins to put up with the idea."[10]

Making life even more unbearable for Olga was wondering if or when she might be arrested. One afternoon Olga and her mother were sipping tea and gazing out of the front window of Olga's living room. Suddenly, Olga's eyes widened, as the cup she was holding slipped out of her fingers and crashed into pieces on the floor. Her mother traced Olga's horrified gaze outside to the road leading up to the house. At that moment, just yards away, a strange motorcar containing four students with guns and an officer sped through the gates, then braked abruptly near the front door. "What's next?"[11] Olga gasped. This time there was neither Nicolai nor any sympathetic policemen to summon to her rescue.

The purpose of the intruders' visit soon made itself known. As the two women continued to look on, a general who had been residing with Olga was brusquely hauled away and placed under arrest. The women never saw him again.

On the final Sunday of her life in Kiev, Olga attended church. After the service, she reminisced about the good times in Gatchina with many of the Cossacks and soldiers who still remained loyal to the Romanov name. "I wonder what will become of them," she thought sadly. In a letter she wrote to Xenia soon after the service, she confessed that her faith sometimes came close to deserting her and she agonized over how many "good friends and good people" had already been killed, adding, "One is taught to believe and I still try to, but it becomes difficult, doesn't it?"[12]

Meanwhile, back in Moscow and St. Petersburg, monuments erected in honour of the Romanovs were dismantled and plaques bearing the Imperial Eagle torn from buildings. When Marie tried to assuage her pain by visiting with injured soldiers in Kiev, her carriage was rudely turned away and hospital gates slammed in her face.

Finally even she realized that the time to flee had arrived. Sandro chose the Crimea, where he and Xenia, who was travelling from St. Petersburg to join her husband, owned an estate named Ay-Todor. Olga's decision to join them in the Crimea was dependent on whether her "beloved" Nicolai might be sent back to the front. "Right now I have no idea what and where I shall be," she remarked, adding, "he hopes not to have to go back to fight—who for?"[13]

Within mere weeks, the question became moot as Nicolai was officially "retired" from the army by the conquering Bolsheviks. Though he was allowed to leave the army with the rank of lieutenant-colonel, he had to endure the disgrace of no longer being allowed to wear his uniform.

Wrenching reports emerged about the ultimate fate of Nicholas. Some suggested that members of the British royal family had offered to grant the former Emperor and his family asylum. Olga prayed that the reports were true. "If only one could be quiet as to the fate of Nicholas and the children . . . I won't feel quiet till they are on English soil,"[14] she wrote.

By this time, there was no possibility that a Romanov could leave any regular train station without fear of being arrested on the spot. Complicating their departure was the presence of hundreds of other people desperately looking for a way to get out of town. As a result, under cover of a bitterly cold night, with the stars fairly crackling overhead, the family silently boarded a train located on a deserted siding that Sandro had arranged for through friends and other private contacts. A small unit of loyal sappers agreed to guard the train on its perilous journey to the Crimea.

Olga, shivering in only her flimsy nurse's uniform, clutched the same small case containing all her worldly possessions that she had brought from St. Petersburg almost three years earlier. She said, "I remember the moment when, looking upon that small case and my crumpled skirt, I realized that I owned nothing else in the world."[15]

Mimka, Olga's maid of many years, was the only member of the imperial retinue to stay behind. She promised her mistress that she would walk if need be back to St. Petersburg to rescue some of Olga's jewels from the Sergievskaya Street home. The Dowager Empress, fortunately enough, had had the foresight to already bring a large number of her jewels to Kiev.

In spite of her resolve, actually persuading the Dowager Empress to leave Kiev took Herculean effort. She had to be dragged almost bodily. Where Olga accepted their leaving as "god's will," her intransigent mother did not wish to board any train that would take her even farther away from her adored Nicholas.

At last the train chugged toward Ay-Todor and at least the illusion of freedom. The entire journey took three days and two nights. There were so many outbursts by citizens lining the tracks that normal rail traffic was periodically halted and any minute Olga expected her train to ram into another train that might have previously been abandoned on the tracks by personnel who feared proceeding under such dangerous conditions. At each stop, a group of sappers stood watch at all the doors to ensure that the train wasn't stoned by Russian citizens. At Sevastopol, the party transferred to cars provided by the Military Aviation School where Sandro had been Chief. Were it not for the presence of the sappers, bayonets drawn, the family might have been annihilated by the mob of angry sailors who faced them at the station. Men with whom Olga had once exchanged pleasantries during her inspections of troops glared and raised their fists in contempt.

Overnight Olga's train climbed steep hills and thundered through dark mountain passes. By daybreak, the family had finally reached the flat lands and as she gazed out her window, Olga saw the Black Sea glittering in the morning sun like thousands of diamonds.

At first the family believed they had escaped what Olga called the "witches brew" in Kiev and found an oasis at Ay-Todor. Though only March, the weather was mild and the trees were in full bloom. Xenia (who with her children had travelled from St. Petersburg to join the family) and the Dowager Empress took daily walks to unwind from their hasty journeys. Olga and Nicolai decided to stay in a small room on the main floor of the house. The Dowager Empress lived on the first floor. The rest of the family moved into an old house next to the manor house.

The family's idyll was shortlived, however. At daybreak one morning, Olga and Nicolai awoke to the sound of someone knocking violently on their bedroom door, the cocking of a firearm and an angry voice ordering them to lie still and put their hands in plain view over their blankets. Moments later, a heavily armed soldier, who identified himself as the Special Commissioner of the Soviet Government, entered the room, walked over to a chesterfield and impudently sat down, resting his head on the side of his gun barrel. More confused than frightened, Olga and Nicolai lay silent, and glared at their intruder.

"If I were you, I would get dressed," the Commissioner said quietly after several minutes. "Don't worry about me, I'll close my eyes." [16]

The couple rose and dressed and sat on the edge of their bed. As time passed, they heard a commotion in the room above them where the Dowager Empress had been sleeping. Gathering up their courage, Olga and Nicolai demanded to know why the Commissioner was on the property. He informed them that an expedition corps had been sent on behalf of the Sevastopol Soviets to locate secret radio transmitters rumoured to be hidden at Ay-Todor, as well as find any arms possibly stashed on the property. He then added that the family members were to consider themselves prisoners and were restricted from travelling beyond the perimeter of the 175-acre estate.

Like Olga and Nicolai, Sandro and Xenia were also awakened by the sound of guns being cocked. Soldiers rifled through their correspondence and accused them of conspiring with enemies in anti-revolutionary activities.

Even the Dowager Empress's rooms were ravaged by thugs, who ripped up floorboards, tore down curtains, and emptied dresser drawers in front of the tiny, nightgown-clad woman but failed to notice the presence of a jewellery box sitting in plain view on a bedside table, the same jewellery box whose contents eventually sustained the family finances for years to come.

Of more value to the intruders was the "anti-revolutionary" Bible the Dowager Empress had brought with her from Denmark when she first came to Russia. Marie offered some of her jewels in exchange for the return of the book, but in vain.

For several months following the initial searches, life at the estate settled into a semblance of order. Soldiers were posted at all the entrances and exits and permission had to be obtained before anyone was allowed to enter or exit buildings.

Olga was soon to discover that because she had married a commoner, she was no longer considered a Romanov and therefore was eventually allowed to venture beyond the grounds of the estate. Taking advantage of her liberated status, Olga and her husband rode a dilapidated pony-cart out to the seashore where they secreted deep in a rock hole a cocoa tin containing Dowager Empress Marie's precious jewels. A dog's skull was placed in front of the hole to mark the spot.[17]

One day they arrived to find the skull lying on another part of the beach. Frantically plunging their hands into myriad rock holes, sweating with fright, the heavily pregnant former Grand Duchess and her once-proud husband at last pulled out from a hole the rattling metal box that contained their future livelihoods.[18]

On August 12, 1917, almost nine months to the day after her marriage, Olga gave birth to Tihon, named as promised after Olga's most beloved saint. She enjoyed knitting him clothes and listening to his small breaths as he lay sleeping in one of the family's heirloom cribs. In the evenings, she and Nicolai, gently cradling the baby against his chest, lay on lounge chairs on a veranda overlooking the sea. Newspapers were forbidden, so Olga suffered increasing anxiety about the fate of Nicholas, Alexandra and their children.

JUST DAYS BEFORE THE birth of Tihon, Aleksandr Kerensky had decided "to remove the ex-Tsar from the political chess-board while there was opportunity to do so."[19] Plans were developed to move the entire imperial family from Tsarskoe Selo, near St. Petersburg, to Tobolsk, Siberia. At this time, Kerensky disbanded his Provisional Government and proclaimed himself the Supreme Commander of what he termed a "democratic republic."

Michael was allowed to visit Nicholas one last time before the latter's departure. Five months had passed since Michael had last seen his brother. Kerensky followed Michael into Nicholas's study and pretended to read as the brothers talked privately.

Sadly the once affectionate and loving siblings could utter nothing much beyond pleasantries. Occasionally one took the other's hand or fiddled with a button on his uniform. After ten minutes Kerensky deemed the meeting over. Nicholas remained stoic, but as Michael left, he wiped tears from his eyes.[20] His diary entry that night was as usual extraordinary in its restraint. "I found that Nicky looked rather well"[21] was all he wrote.

Though Michael was eventually allowed to obtain permits to emigrate to Finland or England, he chose to stay in Russia, still believing that free elections might liberate his tortured land. It was a romantic notion, and it ultimately doomed him. The Russian people he believed in did not reciprocate his loyalty. With the emergence of the hardline Bolsheviks during that fall of 1917, his opportunity to escape was revoked and his fate was sealed.

The atmosphere at Ay-Todor meanwhile was a mixture of bitterness and regret. Half-hearted theories were exchanged about how the family members might have averted their fall in stature. White bread, butter, tea, coffee and especially milk became scarce. Olga's breast milk became so depleted that she was forced to milk the few underfed cows still roaming the property. Acorns were ground into coffee, while rosebuds brewed in hot water provided a pleasing tea. The Dowager Empress, grateful that the family was at least reasonably safe for the time being, noted that Nicolai no longer acted like a stranger in the family's circle. "He is quite nice," she wrote her brother Valdemar, "and what is most important, [Olga] is so happy with him, thank God."[22]

Olga's ex-husband, Peter, was also suffering privations. While Olga was at Ay-Todor, Peter wrote that he was living "in a small town in a house abandoned by Jews"[23] near Lvov. There was a great shortage of essentials in the town, including matches and candles. Neighbours exchanged eggs for salt. As time passed, he was forced to move from house to house, unable to send or receive telegrams or letters, as the Bolsheviks razed the countryside.

In September, just after Russia was proclaimed a Democratic Republic, Dowager Empress Marie suffered a near-fatal bout of influenza, prompting Sir George Buchanan, the British ambassador to Russia, to inquire into her welfare.

Lenin seized power from Kerensky in October and almost immediately conditions worsened at Ay-Todor. A six-feet-four-inch soldier named Zadorojny was sent by officials to intimidate the Ay-Todor prisoners. Every morning, after cocking his revolver, he would order the prisoners to pass review in front of him as he read their names from a list. From the beginning, the Dowager Empress refused, and with the shyness of a recalcitrant schoolboy Zadorojny holstered his gun and agreed to conduct roll calls without her. Profiting once again from their perceived status as commoners, Olga's and Nicolai's names were dropped from the roll call list.

A reign of terror descended on villagers as the Bolsheviks

pillaged house after house, assaulting and murdering citizens in their path, particularly those from the privileged classes, who huddled in their once luxurious sanctuaries like trapped animals.

The Dowager Empress Marie was able to confirm from the few letters smuggled to her by a sympathetic Russian peasant that the Bolsheviks had followed through with their plan to transfer Nicholas and the rest of his family to a house in Tobolsk. In her last letter to Nicholas, she wrote, "I live only in my memories of the happy past and try as much as possible to forget the present nightmare . . . God bless you, send you strength and peace of mind . . . [and] may He not allow Russia to perish."[24]

Yalta and Sevastopol Soviets meanwhile were in direct competition over the ultimate fate of the Romanovs. Zadorojny insisted that the Sevastopol Soviets alone ruled over the Bolshevik government of the Crimean region, and that the Yalta Soviets were a group of murder-happy braggarts, intent on usurping the authority of their fellow Bolsheviks in the Crimea. Each Bolshevik faction argued over who should get the honour of either shooting or beheading the prisoners at Ay-Todor, and when.[25]

Every few weeks, truckloads of machine-gun-toting members of the Yalta Soviet arrived demanding the Romanovs' immediate execution. Zadorojny insisted on delaying any executions until he received definite orders from Lenin. To gain better control over his prisoners, he moved them, including Sandro, Xenia and their children, to the town of Dulbert, where Grand Duke Peter Romanov and his family's well-fortified villa was located. In a wry bit of irony, it was here that the unhappy family caught up with

Grand Duke Nicholas Nicholaevich, who was rewarded for his participation as one of the prime architects of Nicholas's Manifesto of Abdication, by himself being arrested.

Olga and Nicolai, separated from the main group, were allowed to stay at Ay-Todor, coming and going through the town with as much ease as could be expected of those still under the surveillance of the Soviet Bolsheviks. After a few weeks, the loneliness of the house, and its painful reminders of once happy times, convinced the couple to leave. They soon found a couple of rooms in a building located near Dulbert. Olga wasn't allowed to visit the rest of her family at the Dulbert estate, but when she and Nicolai climbed up a particular hill they could wave to the family as they worked in the estate's garden.

Gradually, a strange love-hate relationship developed between Zadorojny and his prisoners at Dulbert. In his memoirs, Sandro recalled assisting Zadorojny in supervising a new set of fortifications added to the line of machine guns and in editing his daily reports on the activities of his imperial prisoners to the Sevastopol Soviet. Sandro also helped Zadorojny install searchlights along the rocky waterfront to spot enemy submarines both men knew could not possibly land in the shallow depths of water surrounding the property. So absurd was the situation that Xenia suggested with disgust that Zadorojny might eventually ask Sandro to load the guns of their firing squad.[26]

On March 3, 1918, the Brest-Litovsk Treaty was signed, which gave the Germans the right to occupy western Russia, specifically the Crimea. In response, the Yalta Soviet issued immediate orders to "liquidate" the Romanovs before the Germans arrived. Zadorojny conducted anxious phone calls with contacts in Sevastopol, in search of reinforcements to fight off the five trucks full of Yalta Soviets speeding toward the Romanov prisoners.

Zadorojny instructed his prisoners not to go to bed, promising that he might still be able to save their lives. What he hadn't told the group was that the Germans were also steadily making their way to the Crimea, and that soon the tables might be turned and he and his men would no longer be the political predators, but the prey.

Not far from Dulbert, Olga was alone in her room with Tihon. Terrified, she heard trucks rumbling by, filled with men firing their weapons into the sky. A neighbour ran past the dwelling and shouted through a window, "Disappear as fast as possible!"[27] Olga knew then that the Yalta Soviets had already arrived. As fast as she could, she snatched up Tihon from his crib and jumped out of the window, straight into the arms of Nicolai, who had returned from a town meeting. The couple quickly ran up a mountainside and sought shelter in a neighbour's home.

All night, gunshots shattered the quiet streets of Dulbert as women and children fled for their lives. At dawn the shooting abruptly stopped. Soon after, excited voices announced that the prisoners at Dulbert were free. Slowly and tentatively, Olga, Tihon and Nicolai walked back toward Dulbert. There, lying by the side of the road, was a neighbour—bayoneted.[28]

Overnight, Zadorojny had succeeded in repulsing the first wave of Yalta Soviets to attack the Dulbert estate. However, before the Yalta Soviets could regroup to batter down the only gateway separating them from the Romanovs, German soldiers arrived at the estate and chased off the

Soviet attackers. The Dowager Empress Marie, haughty to
the end, refused to meet the German officer who routed the
Soviets and saved the family from being shot. It was a trembling Zadorojny this time who pleaded with Sandro to prevail upon the Germans to spare his life, which Sandro,
grateful for Zadorojny's good treatment, did, to the profound befuddlement of the German occupiers.[29]

For the next few months Olga and the rest of her
extended family lived in relative peace at Harax, the estate
of Grand Duke George Mikhailovich, which was south of
Dulbert. Shortly afterwards, Germany ordered the Crimea
evacuated. Despite pleas from senior British officers, the
Dowager Empress Marie refused to leave Harax on board
any of the British ships placed at her disposal, clinging to
the hope that all the talk of a revolution would pass and
soon she and her daughters would be able to return to their
looted homes.

I_N THE EARLY MONTHS OF 1918, orders were given to
move first Nicholas and Alexandra, followed by their children, from Tobolsk to Ekaterinburg, in the Urals. Their destination was a house owned by a local businessman named
Ipatiev. The family's new residence was ominously nicknamed The House of Special Purpose by the Bolsheviks.
That special purpose, as it turned out a few months later,
was the murder of the entire family, as well as the servants,
including the maid Demidova and the imperial physician,
Dr. Evgeny Botkin, who heroically volunteered to follow
the family to their deaths.

One by one Nicholas's family's privileges were cut off. Much of their staff was dismissed. Food became scarce. Unsupervised walks were forbidden. An enormous fence was built around the property so sympathetic onlookers could not gape. Windows were painted to prevent the family from looking out, or signalling to possible sympathizers. Letters could neither be sent nor received. The prisoners were now effectively cut off, alive, but no longer living, estranged from everything but each other and God.

Shortly before Nicholas and his family were transferred to Ekaterinburg, Olga had a chance to write him a final poignant letter in which she lamented the fact that her brother had never seen Tihon, her first-born son. It is unlikely Nicholas ever read the letter. Olga wrote:

> It is really terrible how I miss you all. I would love to show Tihon in all his appearances. He is the sweetest in his bath in the morning when he wakes up. He is always happy and smiling. Most of his smiles go to the ceiling, with which he has a very good relationship. He talks with it a lot in a language only understandable to them. Together with Nicolai, we sing him different soldiers' songs. He is delighted. Just now he fell asleep listening to the old march of the regiment of Chasseur.[30]

Any relief Olga might have gained at believing Nicholas could eventually end up safe on English soil was dashed by her cousin Georgie, now King George V. The King initially offered the family asylum, then in part fearing civil unrest over the arrival of the German-born Alexandra, swiftly reneged.

By the fall of 1918, unconfirmed rumours about the fates of Michael and Nicholas arrived at Harax almost daily, each one more contradictory than the last. Olga and the rest of her family could not have known that by now both Michael and Nicholas were dead. In June 1918, Michael, Olga's "dear darling Floppy," was rounded up and driven out to a secluded wood in Perm along with his faithful manservant. Both were shot in the head at point-blank range.

On the seventeenth day of the following month, Nicholas, Alexandra and all their children were awakened and informed by their captors that they would have to be moved somewhere else since the White army was approaching Ekaterinburg. Believing they were going to be taken on a trip, the family dressed and descended the stairs to the basement where they were told they would be greeted by men in charge of arranging their transportation. Within moments, Jacob Yurovsky, the Bolshevik leader assigned by Lenin to liquidate the Romanovs, told Nicholas: "Your relations have tried to save you. They have failed and we must now shoot you."

Nicholas was shot first, in the head, at point-blank range. Alexandra was next. Their daughters did not have time to make the sign of the cross before being pinned to the walls by bullets. Soon everyone, including the servants, lay dead. At dawn the next morning their bodies were wrapped in sheets, loaded onto trucks and taken to the Four Brothers Mine Shaft, where they were chopped up, burned, doused with acid, and thrown down into the shallow waters of the shaft. Hours later, fearing the location was too conspicuous, the men retrieved the remains and transported them to a deeper burial spot.

A bounty was now on the head of any Romanov. Olga thought the area around the Crimea was a "mouse-trap" ready to snap shut on the family at any moment. Fearing renewed violence and a potential retreat of the protective German army, she could stay with her mother no longer, and informed her she was fleeing with Nicolai and baby Tihon to the Caucasus, where the Red Army had been beaten back by the Whites. Marie impulsively kissed both of Olga's hands then just as suddenly burst into tears, accusing her daughter of betrayal.

A dreadful scene erupted, with Nicolai the "commoner" getting all the blame for tearing a daughter from her mother's arms. A few hours later, after exhaustedly packing what few possessions they retained, the small party left to catch a steamer for Novorossiysk. The couple was crammed into a small cabin with some of Nicolai's officer friends. They were on board yet another ship, heading for yet another temporary home, with the murderous Bolsheviks still in hot pursuit, and, complicating matters, Olga was again pregnant. The seas ahead were littered with mines. The first night out, the steamer had to remain stationary until dawn so that the morning sun could burn off the dense fog enough for the mines to become visible.

Rumours of the family's arrival in Novorossiysk mysteriously preceded them. Not long after docking, they were met by General Koutepov, an old family friend, who offered his private wagon to take them into a Cossack town named Novo-Minskaya, located a few miles away. The evening they arrived in the town, admirers invited them into their homes for meals of duck, chicken and assorted vegetables. After the privations of the Crimea, this variety of food proved irresistible and for the first time in her life Olga ate almost an entire duck by herself.

Soon Olga and Nicolai, with baby Tihon, rented a small house in the town consisting of four rooms and a kitchen. A fruit garden outside extended down to a shallow river. On April 23, 1919, Olga bore her second son, Guri, named after Guri Panaev, a fallen officer in Olga's Akhtyrsky Regiment. Three weeks after Guri's birth, Olga helped Nicolai hoe the fields, although she was unused to hard physical labour. Guri slept in a straw-filled manger, while Tihon mischievously ran between Olga's and Nicolai's legs, impeding their progress.

A young woman named Marushka arrived to help out in Olga's house. She was a highly superstitious woman who believed in omens. A few weeks after she arrived, Olga and Nicolai had an eerie experience. Olga's tiny white poodle had gone missing. Two nights after the dog's disappearance, Olga and Nicolai felt something scratching and pushing at their bed. Olga called out to the dog but received no response. The couple immediately got out of bed and struck a match, but saw no sign of the poodle. As soon as they returned to bed, the scratching and pushing resumed. When Marushka arrived the next morning, she warned the couple that the phantom scratchings were made by a house spirit telling the couple they must leave the house. At the time, Olga laughed. Within weeks, however, admittedly without any logical reason, she and Nicolai developed the instinctive feeling that there was danger afoot and it was time they moved on.[31]

Originally the couple, with their children, planned to travel north, but an officer friend convinced them to travel south to Rostov, where they stayed for a week in the home of a wealthy widow. Unwilling to intrude upon the woman any longer, the couple soon found shelter in a ransacked and abandoned Armenian monastery a few miles out of town. Most of the monastery's windows were smashed. Since it was winter, the couple stuffed hay-filled burlap sacks into the holes in the windows to keep out drafts. Wooden doors, already dangling from their hinges, were broken up and used for kindling. Once the sun set, the couple kept watch against the marauding bands of thieves that had infiltrated the town.[32]

One morning in December, the couple received word that the town would soon be evacuated. With no time to lose, they packed their bags, wrapped the boys in warm shawls and boarded a horse-drawn sleigh that Nicolai always kept ready. Nicolai was perched on the driver's seat with a gun strapped across his shoulders, while Olga huddled in the back, nestling her small boys against her chest. A few miles into their journey, the sleigh struck a bump in the road, catapulting Nicolai's gun barrel across the bridge of Tihon's nose. Tihon retained the scar for the rest of his life.[33]

Just as the sun set, the couple arrived in Rostov. The roads were already jammed with citizens looking for a way to flee the town. Streetcars were filled with wounded soldiers. After considerable searching, the couple found a train whose compartment they were forced to share with soldiers suffering from typhus. There was so little room in the compartment that the soldiers had to lie flat on the floor. By now, both boys were sobbing from exhaustion and hunger and yet Olga knew that if she and Nicolai left their compartment, even momentarily, their seats would be taken by others. The family sat for hours, almost giving up hope that personnel would show up to run the train. At last, the wheels began to squeal, and the train slowly chugged out of the station. Olga gazed out a grimy window as the Rostov station shrank to a tiny speck in the distance. It was only then that she remembered it was Christmas Eve. Images of the lavish and high-spirited Christmases of her youth passed quickly through her mind. Despite feeling grateful that she and her family were still alive, she nevertheless considered this the strangest and most dangerous Christmas of her life.[34]

The Kulikovskys rode the train to a nearby Cossack town, where they disembarked and stayed for two weeks. The townsfolk fed them and gave them fruits and vegetables to take on the rest of their journey. All too soon, the couple and their children had to board another train heading back to Novorossiysk, by now the only safe port out of Russia. To Olga's horror, the family's compartment was filled with bugs. During the day the bugs disappeared, but at night they fell out of cracks in the walls, crawling over the slumbering children. To make matters worse, only three of the train's four brakes worked. In desperation, some soldiers hooked a petrol car to the rear of the train to try to slow it down. Every time the brakes screeched down a hill, Olga thought the family's days might be numbered.

Soon after the tired family's arrival in Novorossiysk, Danish Consul Thomas Schytte invited them to take shelter in the Danish embassy, where the couple were finally able to wash themselves and feed the children nourishing meals. Due to a lack of space, the couple was assigned two cots, in which each slept holding one child close.

Within a month, Schytte arranged for the family to obtain passage out of Novorossiysk aboard the passenger ship *Hapsburg*. The day-long trip was uneventful and Olga appreciated being able to use the ship's kitchen to make her sons' meals.

The ship docked at the Dardanelles, where the family was immediately quarantined. The men, who were placed in one line, and the women, who were placed in another, were ordered to walk single file into cold wooden shacks in which they had to strip off their clothes and stand under warm disinfecting showers. Once they emerged from the shacks, the couple was handed back their crumpled clothes, which were still damp from the steam kettles used to fumigate them. Children under three years of age were curiously exempted from the disinfection process.

For the rest of the day, the family sat outside in the sunshine. That evening, they boarded a barge that carried them to the nearby island of Prinkipo. There they shared three small rooms for two weeks with eleven other adults. The adults, a number of them mothers who had lost their children, told Olga terrible stories of the death and destruction they had left behind in Russian villages.

Through the assistance of a contact in the British High Commission, Olga and her family were allowed to sail to Constantinople, then ride on to Belgrade where they were met by King Alexander, who tried to persuade them to stay permanently. Though Olga was exhausted enough to be tempted by the offer, she was anxious to confirm reports that her mother and other family members had arrived safely in Denmark. And so the family ultimately travelled by sea to Copenhagen.

Olga must have resented the comparative ease with which her mother and sister, Xenia, journeyed toward exile. Intransigent almost to the end, the Dowager Empress and Xenia were allowed time to load all their belongings and valuables on board the British ship *HMS Marlborough*, before it sailed from Harax to Malta on April 20, 1919. Afterwards, another British ship, the *Lord Nelson*, took them the rest of the way to England. On board there were champagne lunches and dancing.

A general atmosphere of gay frivolity prevailed as Marie and Xenia remained staunchly convinced of the truth of rumours that Nicholas had escaped the Bolsheviks and was being hidden by a seventeenth-century religious sect in a monastery in the north of Russia. Crew members complained about the unruliness of Xenia's children, who ran wild along the decks, kicking crewmen in the shins. Their father, Sandro, was of no help, since he had sailed for France in March 1919 on the pretext of informing the heads of the Allied Governments on the status of the situation in Russia.

Marie and Xenia's arrival in England was low-key. There were no spectators or dignitaries to crowd around the once-exalted Empress and her daughter. Luckily, the Dowager Empress never learned that, because he wanted to keep Russia allied with Britain in the war against Germany, King George had refused to grant Nicholas and his German-born wife similar asylum. Queen Alexandra, who was Marie's sister and King George's mother, helped to conceal the truth of the shameful way England had doomed Nicholas II and his family.

The Dowager Empress and her sister nevertheless shared an emotional reunion. Michael's wife, Natasha, who through arduous efforts had also reached exile in England, was briefly allowed to join the group of exiles, along with Michael's son, George.

By the summer of 1919, however, Marie decided to return to Denmark and her childhood summer villa, Hvidøre, located on the shores of the Baltic Sea. Once there, she took up her regime as though recent events were a thing of the past and the past was a thing of the present. Very quickly she resumed her active social life, entertaining guests for tea.

Sentries from the Royal Danish Life Guards stood outside the gates of the villa and two armed Cossack bodyguards escorted her around town. Queen Alexandra often came to visit and the two chatted, still avoiding the painful topic of the possible fate of Nicholas and his family.

Xenia and the youngest of her children remained at Sandringham, where she had decided to live. She separated from Sandro, who remained in France to raise money by selling off his collection of rare coins.

As soon as the Dowager Empress heard of Olga's arrival from Turkey, she summoned her to Amalienborg Palace, where she had moved once the winter came. On Good Friday 1920, Olga and her mother were finally reunited amid a flood of tears and excited embraces. A thatch of Tihon's blondish brown hair poked out from behind one of Olga's knees. The little boy had no memory of the imposing woman who stood before him. Guri, wrapped in blankets, slept peacefully in Nicolai's arms. It was a delighted Marie's first chance to meet her second grandchild by Olga. As she leaned forward to look at the child, she bestowed an unexpectedly cordial kiss on Nicolai's cheek, a man she had once claimed to despise.

Relations between the Dowager Empress and Nicolai, although initially improved, degenerated within weeks when he protested against Olga's fetching things for her mother like a hired servant. Tempers within the home flared. Although the Dowager Empress refused to face it, money was short. As if that realization wasn't painful enough, she also had to soon learn that even the Danish royal family was no longer anxious to roll out the welcome mat to the mother of such a famously disgraced monarch.

CHAPTER SEVEN

EXILE AND A WOMAN NAMED MISS UNKNOWN

FROM THE MOMENT SHE joined her mother at Hvidøre, Olga was consumed with regrets. "I have such a longing for my native land—it is such as strong feeling," she wrote. "I live so much in the past that sometimes I am frightened, maybe I am missing my life now, like that between my fingers."[1] Like her mother, Olga "longed terribly" to return to Russia, holding out a "gleam of hope" that "the dear, sweet Duma," as she sarcastically called it, might be disbanded and life restored to its pre-Revolutionary glory.

With its caryatids gazing impassively out to sea, Hvidøre, situated atop a grassy hill, resembled a wedding cake more than a home. It was built in 1873, an era that later architects described as one of "stylistic confusion, hypocrisy and lack of originality,"[2] combining English and Italian Renaissance styles. Inside, the enormous checkerboard-tiled entry hall on the main floor led into several airy drawing rooms filled with a clutter of mementos of Imperialist Russia. The highlight of the second floor was a glassed-in pergola from which, on melancholy evenings, the Dowager Empress could watch ships sailing toward Russia.

Olga and her husband in typically modest fashion inhabited a small corner room on the ground floor, with their sons Tihon and Guri sharing another room a short distance down the hallway. A hospital nurse who had worked with Olga in Russia served as a nanny to the children.

It took time for Olga and Nicolai to adapt to living under her mother's roof. On fragrant summer evenings, they tried to escape their sadness by walking hand in hand along an underground tunnel leading to the seashore.

Comforting a brooding Nicolai became a full-time job for Olga. Unable to attain the rank of colonel that he had so hoped for and stripped of his uniform, Nicolai replayed the events of the past over and over again. Some nights Olga awoke to find him slumped on a drawing-room sofa, chin in hands, gazing at nothing but the dark outlines of the busts of Alexander III and Nicholas that Marie had managed to smuggle out of Russia.

The reputation of the Romanovs had taken a severe beating. Although it took time for Olga's mother to realize it, the family had become *personae non grata* to their embarrassed European counterparts. Those crowned heads of Europe who remained in power secretly hoped that the Romanovs' fate was not, in Sandro's words, "a contagious disease."[3]

It was therefore up to the inhabitants of Hvidøre to create a lavish interior world that compensated for the austere world on the outside. The first step was to staff the house with servants. A surly, somewhat deaf old footman named Jorgensen, who had waited on Marie's father, King

Christian IX, was sent to serve the family meals and see that their clothes were cleaned and pressed. Among his jobs was to cut from the daily papers any reference to current events in Russia, and particularly articles about Nicholas and his family's fate. Marie conveniently ignored these gaping holes in her daily paper and continued to insist to Jorgensen and the rest of her family that "my son is not dead, he is in a monastery in Siberia."[4]

Because Hvidøre was primarily a summer home, the family moved to Amalienborg Palace in the winters, where King Christian X, a sympathizer of liberal causes and grandson of the late Christian IX, held court. The palace, which consisted of four huge wings encircling a vast courtyard, proved too cramped both physically and politically to successfully house the members of two royal households. Before long, the King decried Marie's "profligate ways."

Olga recalled that one evening while she and her mother were sitting knitting in their living room, a footman, sent at the King's behest, arrived to complain about the number of lights blazing in the palace and about the excessive monthly electrical bill. The deeply humiliated Dowager Empress retaliated by ordering one of her own servants to light up the entire palace, in Olga's words, "from cellar to attic!"[5] Further such mishaps were avoided when King George came to "dear Aunt Minny"'s rescue with a yearly allowance of £10,000. Despite the King's help, however, money remained short.

A few months after Olga arrived at Hvidøre, she was joined by Mimka. Miraculously, the hearty servant had sewn Olga's gems into the hem of her skirts, and at the height of the revolution, walked all the way from St. Petersburg to Copenhagen, stopping at temporary lodgings along the way.

The trip had taken her more than two years to complete.

By the early 1920s, the initial onrush of reporters seeking exclusive stories about the Tsar's fate ceased. The family gradually became old news. As a result, its marketability began to suffer. Engaging in what Sandro called "a series of childish attempts at salesmanship and shrewdness,"[6] family members such as Xenia hired third parties to sell off pieces of jewellery. As soon as the jewellers saw the pieces, they immediately recognized them as ones they themselves had sold to members of the imperial family many years before, and they lowered their prices. News of the family's attempts to sell off their jewellery spread quickly throughout the capitals of Europe. In the end, the owners were lucky if they received twenty per cent of each gem's original value.

Like her mother, Xenia had a hard time believing that she no longer had almost unlimited money at her disposal. And her business acumen was non-existent. In short order, two con men persuaded her to pawn some of her finest pieces of jewellery in order to subsidize what they promised to be a profitable photographic printing business. The business was a sham, and by the time the two men were arrested, the money was spent.

To protect Xenia's interests, King George finally placed her on a yearly allowance of £2,400 and invited her to live permanently in free lodgings, referred to as a grace-and-favour house, named Frogmore Cottage, as well as the house next door, located on the grounds of Windsor Castle. Feted and fussed over by her royal relations, it was easy for her to imagine that life had not changed so much after all. Her letters to her cousin Georgie are almost obsequious in their gratefulness.

Dearest Georgie, I have just heard that you have kindly placed the cottage next door to Frogmore Cottage at my disposal. Really, it is *much too much* and good of you and I can't say *how* much I appreciate this new work of kind affection and *how touched* and grateful I am! Why should you do it? I feel *quite shy* . . . and don't deserve all this kindness. . . . [I] don't know how I can ever thank you enough.[7]

By contrast, Olga lived frugally with her family and mother at Hvidøre; shopping for groceries; tending the garden; painting, which she did at five o'clock every morning; and handling her mother's correspondence. Tihon and Guri, too young to comprehend the death and destruction left behind them, squealed with laughter as they chased each other in and out of airy drawing rooms, played tennis, and swam in the sea, their high-spirited play often taxing the patience of the aging Dowager Empress.

When the time came, the two boys were assigned private tutors and completed their lessons at the villa. No longer royalty, yet not commoners, the children seemed out of place in the public school system, so, like their mother, they were deprived of the chance to grow close to other children.

Letters arrived at the villa from the "murderer" Grand Duke Dimitry and the "traitor" Grand Duke Cyril, who was vying to become successor to the Romanov throne. Marie ignored their letters, maintaining until the end of her life that Nicholas was still alive and in doing so thwarting any moves toward succession on the part of anyone else.

Queen Olga of Greece became a frequent visitor, along

with her grandson, the "wide-eyed youngster" Prince Philip, who later married Princess Elizabeth—the future Queen of England. The presence of a commoner in the house became particularly evident around tea time, when Olga was invited to join her mother in private, while Nicolai was left outside to fend for himself.

Despite the bitterness surrounding their divorce, Olga was grateful to discover that her first husband, Peter, and his mother (his father had died) had successfully escaped Russia for France, where they lived in part off the income derived from the jewels Olga returned to the Oldenburg family following the divorce.

*I*N ADDITION TO ADJUSTING TO life as exiles, the Dowager Empress and Olga were indulging in a strange mixture of stoicism and denial. In late 1918, while still in the Crimea, the two along with Xenia instructed Captain Paul Bulygin, an officer with the Imperial Life Guards, to attempt to find out what had become of the imperial family. Soon after his appointment, Bulygin linked up with a White-army-appointed investigator named Nicholas Sokolov. Despite her insistence that the imperial family was still alive, Marie schizophrenically paid 1,000 rubles to Sokolov to continue his work to find out the true fate of the family.

Sokolov's report, completed by the end of 1919, was so devastating that Marie was instructed not to read it. Shortly after the imperial family's murder, and while the White army had temporarily overtaken Ekaterinburg, Sokolov managed to locate a pile of ashes and other debris at the Four

Brothers' Mine Shaft, not far from the home where Nicholas and his family were murdered.

Scattered amid the ashes were horrific reminders of the once illustrious family, including a pair of false teeth, a lady's shoe buckle, burned corsets, fragments of sapphires and diamonds, a jewelled cross, earrings, a human finger (believed to be Alexandra's) and the corpse of a small dog, later identified as Anastasia's pet, Jemmi.[8] The items were identified, itemized and placed in a suitcase-sized box for transport to the Dowager Empress Marie and her daughters. When the Dowager Empress heard of the nature of the contents, she urged Sokolov not to come to Denmark.

It is rumoured that for a brief time in 1920 or 1921, Olga accepted receipt of the box in Denmark and, allegedly without opening it, believed that it contained the remains of her brother and his family. The word "allegedly" is important here, since many years later, while exiled to Canada, Olga told at least one person that a small matchbox beneath her bed contained "something macabre,"[9] implying that it was ashes and bits of bone from Sokolov's box. The box then apparently made its way to King George of England, who, without opening it, passed it to the Russian Orthodox Church of St. Jobs in Brussels, whose staff currently denies its existence.

IN 1920, SHORTLY AFTER OLGA and her mother settled in Denmark, a woman jumped from Bendler Bridge in Berlin into the freezing Landwehr Canal. Rescued by police, the small frightened woman, who refused to admit her identity, was taken to Dalldorf Asylum, where nurses addressed her as Miss Unknown.

By the summer of 1921, the virtually mute woman suddenly announced that she was none other than Her Imperial Highness Grand Duchess Anastasia Nikolaevna, Olga's favourite niece. Because of her particularly intimate relationship with Anastasia, Grand Duchess Olga was in the best position to put that claim to the test.

Anastasia, literally meaning "resurrection," had been born on June 5, 1901, one month before Olga's marriage to Prince Peter of Oldenburg. After the birth Nicholas, disappointed that Alexandra had not borne him a boy, took a long walk. Olga, the black sheep of the family, filled the breach by taking an instant liking to the "somewhat lumpy" but "quick-witted" child.

As she grew, Anastasia, sometimes accompanied by her sisters, became a fixture at Olga's Sergievskaya Street house, where she sipped tea, sketched, and played tennis every Sunday afternoon. By early evening, the girls and their aunt danced to gramophone records. Forbidden treats like cakes and cookies were served. When Anastasia grew older, these gatherings sometimes included young men.

Like Olga, Anastasia, whom Olga affectionately nicknamed Shvipsik (little one), was tomboyish and fearless. She was not afraid to get her hands dirty, and when her parents arrived by carriage to take her home, she could be found dressed in her Sunday best, dangling from the branch of a tree, while her Aunt Olga sat painting her likeness on canvas.

When Anastasia visited Olgino, she and her aunt rode horseback while Olga, Marie and Tatiana sat demurely under parasols to escape the sun. Just as Olga as a child had liked to sink her bright white teeth into the arm of her brother Nicholas, Anastasia frequently abused her older sisters. Once, she pitched a snowball at Tatiana's head, knocking her out cold, for which she received a slap from Olga.

By the time Olga left for the army hospital in Kiev, Anastasia was thirteen and already shared Olga's down-to-earth sense of humour. Olga's letters were filled with "naughty" stories only the two could appreciate. In one, she joked about how much she suffered from "headaches and hemorrhoids, and everything that starts with 'h,'" adding that even while nursing she was caught up in selecting a soldier to be Anastasia's husband. One "appetizing" boy in particular seemed a prime candidate. Olga teased: "I am not going to take [him] away from you for two reasons: 1) Because he is not my type. 2) Because, as I am old now, I won't be able to do it."[10]

In another letter, Olga related an amusing anecdote about a visit made to the hospital by Queen Olga of Greece: "In the morning, Aunt Olga went with me to put on bandages because she didn't want to keep me away from work; a young soldier came with a wound on the right side below the stomach, so he took off his pants without any hesitation—Aunt Olga jumped and started looking at a stain on the wall, but continued talking to him in a very sweet manner,"[11] she wrote.

Despite Anastasia's *joie de vivre*, Olga always had "a presentiment that she would not live long."[12] On two occasions Olga grew "cold with terror" when she saw her niece's life endangered. The first time occurred during a carriage ride when the horses bolted, nearly tipping Anastasia, then an infant, into a lake; the second, during a swim the family was enjoying while in the Crimea in 1906. A giant wave rolled in, submerging Anastasia for several minutes. As a frantic Olga watched from shore, Nicholas dived into the water, grabbed his daughter by her long hair and dragged her to shore.[13]

It is notable that despite gunshots, freezing cold, lice and near starvation, Olga managed to smuggle out of Russia among her possessions the few items Anastasia had given her, including a "tiny silver pencil on a thin silver chain, a small scent bottle, and a hat-pin surmounted by a big amethyst."[14]

By 1925, the rumours that had been circulating throughout Russian émigré colonies for years concerning the true identity of the woman in Germany claiming to be Anastasia, finally reached the court in Copenhagen. The messenger was Herluf Zahle, the respected Danish Ambassador to Berlin appointed by Empress Marie's brother, Prince Valdemar, to look into the patient's claims. Remarkably, after only two or three meetings, Zahle was convinced of the claimant's authenticity and urged Olga to visit with her.

For the first two years of her hospitalization Miss Unknown, who had been diagnosed, according to hospital records, with "simple psychic disturbance" characterized by the habit of "building castles in the sky," maintained a tantalizing air of mystery. When she finally decided to speak, both nurses and fellow patients concluded that her manners were "very grand" and consistent with a "lady of the highest Russian society."[15] Her knowledge of European history was impressive, as was her grasp of politics. For a working woman, which she claimed to be when she arrived, her hands were "very refined" and soft, and her "Eastern accent" thought to be Russian.

Many cheap illustrated magazines lay throughout the hospital containing articles about the Russian imperial family. Staff members eventually informed the patient that she resembled at least one of the Romanov grand duchesses, either Tatiana or Anastasia. Intrigued by the notion, the patient soon tucked under her mattress a tattered copy of the *Berliner Illustrierte* containing pictures of the imperial family, which she studied over and over again.

Either alone, or aided by the staff's overactive imaginations, the patient eventually decided that the Grand Duchess she resembled most was the youngest, Anastasia. Once word got around, myriad Russian émigrés associated with the monarchist society, some with links to the imperial family, began to flock to the hospital, eliciting fewer tidbits than they inadvertently supplied. They noted that the patient resembled the Grand Duchess, specifically in the blue colour and "intensity" of her eyes and in her imperial manner.

Later visitors included Captain von Schwabe, a former staff captain of the personal guard detachment of the Dowager Empress Marie, and Baroness Sophie Buxhoeveden, maid of honour to Empress Alexandra, who had known the four Grand Duchesses very well. The former came away utterly convinced; the latter, an utter skeptic.

Before long, the patient began to recount an improbable version of her rescue from Ekaterinburg. According to her, when he had seen the bayoneted Grand Duchess was still alive, a "merciful" Bolshevik murderer named Alexander Tschaikovsky carried her by cart to safety in Bucharest. Months later, still drifting in and out of consciousness, she nevertheless managed to bear him a son, also named Alexander. Marriage followed. The family lived for a time on the proceeds from the jewels she had sewn into her corsets before the night of the murders. It was apparently during his attempt to sell some of these jewels that Tschaikovsky was murdered. Soon after, the patient fled Bucharest for Germany, leaving her child with Tschaikovsky's parents.

In Germany, she planned to arrive unannounced at the door of Alexandra's sister Irene, but changed her mind when she realized that her dramatically altered appearance might make her unidentifiable. With few options left to her, she walked forlornly to the railing of Bendler Bridge. Minutes later police fished her out of the Landwehr Canal.

Before Olga would take Zahle's advice to visit the claimant, she needed more definitive proof. She asked Pierre Gilliard, the former tutor to the imperial children and his wife, Alexandra Tegleva (nicknamed Shura), Anastasia's childhood nursemaid, to travel to Germany to also check out the claimant's story. Pierre and Shura Gilliard were highly qualified to accept or reject the woman in the German hospital bed. Unlike Olga, they had been in day-to-day contact with Anastasia throughout her imprisonment in Tobolsk and were forced from her side only when she was transferred to the House of Special Purpose in Ekaterinburg. Olga wrote a letter to Shura in which she said,

> Please go at once to Berlin with M. Gilliard to see the poor lady. Suppose she really *were* the Little Girl. Heaven alone knows if she is or not. It would be such a disgrace if she were living all alone in her misery and if all that is true. . . . I implore you again to go as soon as possible; you can tell us what there is in this

story better than anyone else in the world....
May God grant you his aid. I embrace you
with all my heart.

P.S. If it is really her, please send me a wire,
and I will come to Berlin to meet you.[16]

On July 27, 1925, the Gilliards arrived at St. Mary's
Hospital, where the claimant, Mrs. Tschaikovsky, had been
transferred. They entered her room and took seats beside
her bed. Tschaikovsky, covered to her neck in blankets, was
clearly extremely ill, almost hallucinating. After an hour
Shura asked if the blankets might be rolled down so she
could observe the patient's feet. Once this was done, Shura
gasped and exclaimed, "The feet look like Grand Duchess's .
.. with her it was the same as here, the right foot was worse
than the left."[17]

What Shura was referring to was a fairly common foot
condition called *hallux vagus*, in which a bony part of the big
toe protrudes outward. The condition was common to both
Anastasia and Tschaikovsky. Other physical characteristics
the claimant shared with Anastasia were a scar from a mole
that had been removed from her shoulder and irregularly
shaped fingers, in which the middle finger was noticeably
longer than the index and ring fingers.

Their curiosity now inflamed, Pierre Gilliard and his
wife asked to see Mrs. Tschaikovsky alone, but they were
informed that the patient was too sick to answer questions.
"We will both come back when the patient's condition
improves,"[18] Pierre said. That night, after the Gilliards
had left, Tschaikovsky fell into a delirium in which she cried
out for her Aunt Olga Alexandrovna, who she thought was

standing outside the door laughing at her because of the
depths to which she had succumbed.

After the Gilliards' visit, Tschaikovsky was taken to yet
another clinic, where, at the expense of Herluf Zahle, she
was operated on for an infected arm to avoid amputation.
On the strength of his own intuition about the true identity
of the patient, Zahle agreed to pay for the patient's care, at
least until her identity could be proved once and for all.

Zahle was convinced of Tschaikovsky's authenticity
because of what he cited as her "inborn distinction," her facil-
ity at conversations about music and painting, and her ability
to correct her entourage on the finer points of royal etiquette.[19] On one of their excursions out of the Berlin hospital, Zahle was moved when Mrs. Tschaikovsky, following royal
tradition, bowed to acknowledge the waiters who served her.

In October 1925, on the strength of the reports of Pierre
and Shura Gilliard's visit, Olga finally decided, over the
impassioned objections of Nicolai and her mother, Marie, to
travel to Germany to visit the woman still referring to herself as Anastasia. Pierre and Shura Gilliard were to meet her
at the Mommsen clinic, where the recuperating claimant
now resided.

Before Olga arrived, however, Pierre, ushered into the
room by Zahle, made an unannounced visit with
Tschaikovsky. In Zahle's words, the appearance of an unfa-
miliar person "affected her strongly and rendered her
speechless for a couple of hours."

"Do you know my face?" Pierre finally asked, to which
Tschaikovsky responded, "I know the face, but there is something strange about it."[20]

After Gilliard left the room, Tschaikovsky confessed to

Zahle that the only reason she had not immediately recognized Gilliard was because he had shaved off a goatee she claimed to always have remembered him wearing. Despite this meeting, Pierre Gilliard was still far from convinced of the claimant's authenticity.

At 11:30 a.m., Grand Duchess Olga and her husband were scheduled to arrive in the sickroom. Zahle fretted before Olga arrived that she would have made up her mind to reject the claimant before she had all the evidence at her disposal and felt that since Olga had not seen the claimant since long before the departure for Siberia, she was not as qualified as the Gilliards to judge her. "I do not know the Grand Duchess' mentality, but I hardly doubt that she arrives firmly convinced that if it is not a question of a swindler, which is thus absolutely out of the question, then perhaps a hysteric, which is possible. I shall do everything possible to see that the Grand Duchess' visit lasts until she in my opinion has been able to form a true picture,"[21] he wrote in a letter to a friend.

At the appointed hour, Olga, accompanied by Nicolai and Zahle, and dressed in a purple velvet cloak, swept into the room. To disguise her identity, Zahle recounted that he "treated the Grand Duchess in the sick room exactly as if it could have been Shura, walked ahead of her in and out through the door and outwardly took no notice of her."[22] Despite his ruse, in his opinion the claimant's sparkling eyes revealed that she almost immediately recognized her aunt.[23]

Harriet Rathlef-Keilmann, a writer who had taken up Tschaikovsky's claim, and had nursed her for many months, watched as the Grand Duchess walked straight to the claimant's bed and, smiling, extended her hand.

"How is Grandmamma?"[24] the claimant asked in German. Olga replied in Russian that her mother was fine. A lot of small talk ensued, including Olga asking about Kiki, a cat of Tschaikovsky's that roamed the hospital room.

After a couple of hours, Olga left the room for a few minutes, at which point Zahle asked Tschaikovsky if she knew who the woman was.

"Papa's sister, my Aunt Olga," she replied.

"Why didn't you address the Grand Duchess right away by name?" Zahle asked.

"Why should I have done that? I was so happy I could say nothing," Mrs. Tschaikovsky replied.[25]

Olga stayed that first day until early evening. As she left, she bent down and kissed Tschaikovsky's forehead. In response, Tschaikovsky unexpectedly "sat up as far as it was possible with the injured arm and kissed the Grand Duchess' hand, a gesture she had never made before,"[26] noted Zahle. After Olga left, Tschaikovsky turned to Rathlef-Keilmann and asked, "Will everything be all right now? Do I never again need to be afraid of being put into the street?"[27]

At nine o'clock the next morning, Olga visited once again. This time she brought pictures of Tihon and Guri to show to Tschaikovsky. An awkward situation ensued when in response to Tschaikovsky's questions about Olga's sons, Olga asked Tschaikovsky about her own child, which she said had been fathered by Alexander Tschaikovsky, the man who ultimately rescued her from Ekaterinburg. "I would rather the earth had swallowed me up than my aunt should have asked me that,"[28] she said. The atmosphere lightened considerably when Tschaikovsky spontaneously recalled that her aunt had called her Shvipsik. "Yes," cried the Grand Duchess, obviously moved.[29]

Sometime during the morning, according to a later account of Tschaikovsky's, Olga got around to questioning her about money. On an earlier occasion Tschaikovsky had allegedly told Zahle that Nicholas II had deposited money with the Bank of England before the war, but that the funds could not be found since it was not known in what name the deposit had been made. Olga wanted to hear more details, whereupon the claimant recounted a conversation her "father" and "mother" had in Ekaterinburg, in which he discussed the sum of twenty million rubles, to be divided among the four girls. The money was supposedly deposited under a German sounding name with an "a" in it.[30]

Following a luncheon at the Danish Embassy, Olga returned for a third time, this time accompanied by Shura, whom Zahle accused of having a heart that was "stronger than her head."[31]

"How are you?" Shura asked in Russian, to which the patient merely stared, open-mouthed.

"Now," said Olga, "who is that? Won't you introduce me?"

"Shura," said Tschaikovsky, to which Olga clapped her hands in delight chanting, "Verno! Verno!"[32] Afterwards Olga insisted that Tschaikovsky speak Russian, a request that fell on deaf ears.

Shura was overwhelmed when the claimant suddenly grasped her bottle of eau de cologne and poured it into Shura's hands, asking her to moisten her forehead. It was a gesture the real Anastasia had performed on many occasions, and the request left Shura deeply shaken.

According to Rathlef-Keilmann, shortly after the perfume

incident, an excited Olga led her onto an adjoining balcony, where she said, "If I had any money, I would do everything for the little one, but I haven't and must earn my own pocket money by painting. . . . [I] am so happy that I came, and I did it even though Mama did not want me to. She was angry with me when I came. And then my sister [Grand Duchess Xenia] wired me from England saying that under no circumstances should I come to see the little one."[33]

By the time Rathlef-Keilmann and Olga returned to the sickroom, it was filled with people, including Nicolai, who sat grimacing in a corner. "He wouldn't say a friendly word to the invalid and you could plainly see what a bad mood he was in,"[34] said Rathlef-Keilmann.

The next day, just before she left the clinic, Olga confessed to Zahle, "My intelligence will not allow me to accept her as Anastasia; but my heart tells me that it is she. And since I have grown up in a religion which taught me to follow the dictates of the heart rather than those of the mind, I am unable to leave this unfortunate child."[35]

After the initial flush of excitement, Olga returned home to Denmark to an irate Dowager Empress. Without hearing her daughter out, she categorically denied the authenticity of Tschaikovsky, saying "What do they think? That I would sit here in Hvidøre and not rush to my granddaughter's side?"[36]

In spite of her mother's suspicions, Olga wrote to Tschaikovsky at least five times over the next couple of months. "Don't be afraid. You are not alone now and we shall not abandon you,"[37] she said in one letter. "Thinking of you all the time,"[38] she wrote in another. Her most intriguing letter contained the words, "My thoughts are with you—I am remembering the times we were together, when you stuffed me full of chocolates, tea and cocoa."[39] It is unclear whether the times Olga referred to are those she spent visiting Tschaikovsky at the hospital, or those prior to the Revolution, adding further fuel to the controversy.

Intimate gifts accompanied the letters, including a beautiful rose-coloured silk shawl, six feet long and four feet wide; one of Olga's hand-knitted sweaters; and an album containing childhood photographs of Olga and Michael, with captions handwritten by Olga.

By December 1925, however, the letters stopped, and within a month a shocking new development occurred. A January 1926 issue of Denmark's national paper, *National Tidende*, contained a statement released by Olga's family that, despite visiting with the claimant, Olga had found not the slightest resemblance between her and her niece Anastasia. It was a stunning about-face, undoubtedly precipitated by pressure from the Dowager Empress and Nicolai, who felt his wife had been manipulated by parties on both sides of the issue.

Letters Olga wrote provide strong evidence that she initially accepted the possibility that the claimant was her niece, but for the sake of peace, and possibly problems involving the inheritance of any newly discovered Romanov assets, took the safer route. Her change of heart was not, however, without personal pain. Even as late as 1958, a still-tortured Olga told at least one acquaintance that she believed the woman in Germany was her niece, "because she knew the pet name for my dog,"[40] but had been forced to change her mind by persuasive family members.

Any early attempts Olga had made to convince her mother of the authenticity of the claimant were stymied by the November 1925 death at the age of eighty of the Dowager Empress's sister, Queen Alexandra. Overnight, the atmosphere at Hvidøre became funereal. It is not surprising then that Olga, in order not to further upset her distraught mother, decided to drop the issue of Anastasia altogether.

Tschaikovsky was shattered by Olga's sudden repudiation of her. The blame fell on Gilliard, who maintained he had never been fully convinced of the woman's identity and pointed out that Tschaikovsky and the real Anastasia did not even remotely resemble each other. He made much of the point that the claimant did not speak Russian, though many observers, including Olga, noted that she had no trouble understanding the language.

In the spring of 1926, Olga stressed in a letter that Tschaikovsky had never said anything new and only spoke of trivialities. "Whenever we would ask her something about the past, she fell silent and covered her eyes with her hand," she wrote.[41] She argued that ultimately the claimant was interested only in the alleged Romanov fortune kept in foreign banks abroad, which Olga insisted had all been withdrawn by Nicholas to help the war effort in 1914. Eventually Olga became so distressed over the whole matter that she told a member of the family that she never wanted to hear "another word about it."[42] And with that, for the time being, the emotional affair came to an inauspicious close.

QUEEN ALEXANDRA HAD BEEN Marie's last link with life. Since their youth, the two sisters had written letters to each other every day, even throughout the dark days of the

Revolution. Alexandra's sudden death in November of 1925 loosened Marie's last tenuous grip on the outside world. With the air of someone lost in the woods [43] the Dowager Empress soon took to her bed, demanding Olga's presence in her bedchamber almost continually. For hours she examined photos of Nicholas and his family, which she had spread out across her coverlet.

She became obsessed with fears that her much prized jewellery box would be stolen and that her girls would have nothing to live on. The value of the box's contents had been further enriched by a staggering cache of jewels bequeathed to her by Alexandra. "There was certainly no Romanov gold in any bank in England, but there was a sizable fortune in my mother's bedroom at Hvidøre," [44] noted Olga.

King George suggested that the box be sent to England for safe keeping, an offer Marie found easy to refuse, although she did allow George to safeguard a copy of the box's key. King Christian X of Denmark also sniffed around the box, implying that he should be entitled to at least a portion of its contents due to his generosity in allowing Marie political asylum in his country. Even Sandro advised Marie to pawn the jewellery so that the family could open a paper factory. Considering the level of greed around her, it is small wonder that Marie sought respite in the past. More and more she cast her mind back to the glory days of the Russian Empire. She was now empress only of her own household.

Two years earlier she had proved how little she understood the permanent consequences of the destruction of Nicholas's government. In Christmas of 1924, she wrote to Sandro in Paris complaining that her yearly cheque from the Department of the Russian Imperial Estates had not arrived.

In his memoirs, Sandro admitted that he did not have the heart to tell her that "the much-lamented Department was now occupied by a club of communist youth." Instead he wrote a cheque to his mother-in-law, enclosing his "fervent hopes that Christmas would be exceedingly merry."[45]

Finally on October 13, 1928, the last living Empress of all the Russias died. "In her death, [she] suddenly recaptured what she had lost on the day of her son's abdication: the center of the stage,"[46] said Sandro, as a state funeral was arranged at Roskilde Cathedral, which was attended by ambassadors, heads of state and what royalty still remained in Europe. Grand Duke Cyril, who in Olga's opinion "should have had the sense to stay away,"[47] also appeared. Both Olga and Sandro bristled when some European royals hypocritically lamented that Marie's inordinate pride had prevented her from seeking help from them, when the truth was that they intentionally had no help to give.

Her body lay in state at the Alexander Nevsky Church in Copenhagen, the church her husband had built for her as a wedding present. Zoya Alexeyevna Lopetina, a young Russian émigré, alone volunteered to keep vigil over the late Empress's body overnight. "I wasn't afraid in the least," she said. "I read from a prayer book standing up and looking now and then at the Empress, a little pallid old woman with grey hair combed smooth. You might have thought she had fallen asleep with fatigue."[48]

At ten o'clock the next morning, Olga and the rest of her family arrived with Grand Duke Cyril and King Christian X. Father Kochev, Marie's private confessor, conducted the hour-long service. There was barely a dry eye at the end of the service as he knelt in front of the coffin, took a bow, and said, "Your Majesty, the whole of Russia bows to the ground before you."[49]

The Dowager Empress was eventually laid to rest in Roskilde Cathedral, a few miles outside Copenhagen. (No Soviet leader saw her tomb until 1993, when Prime Minister Victor Chernomyrdin paid a state visit to Denmark and bowed before her remains.)

The next morning, Marie's will was read to Olga and Xenia and their husbands. Everything had been left to the two girls. The jewellery box was now fair game, and before the last funeral bell could toll, at least one member of the family would begin to plunder its assets.

$\mathscr{F}$IRE $\mathscr{S}$ALE

Olga's and Xenia's future livelihoods depended to a great extent on how much money they could raise from the sale of the contents of their mother's jewellery box. First they had to take a pre-emptive strike against the false Anastasia, known as Miss Unknown or Mrs. Tschaikovsky. Less than twenty-four hours after the Dowager Empress Marie's death, they, along with other members of the family, released to the press a document entitled "The Declaration of the Russian Imperial Family Concerning the Tschaikovsky Affair."[1]

Drafted by Sandro, and subsequently signed by twelve of the forty-four-member Romanov family spread throughout Europe, the declaration was touted as representing the family's "unanimous conviction" that Miss Unknown was not the daughter of the Tsar.[2] The undue haste of its release was no doubt intended to act as a warning to Mrs. Tschaikovsky not to expect a share of any profits from the sale of the family jewels.

The declaration was viewed by many as an overreaction to a non-existent threat. Prior and later events, however, proved that line of thinking wrong. On several occasions Olga had seen the Anastasia pot simmer down only to be stirred up again months later by some new person claiming he or she recognized Tschaikovsky as the Tsar's daughter.

A few months prior to the Dowager Empress Marie's death, in fact, Olga had received an impassioned, one might even say desperate, letter from her first cousin Grand Duke Andrew Romanov, in which he begged her to reconsider her repudiation of Tschaikovsky. He wrote:

> Dear Olga . . . Once again, and probably for the last time, I am writing to you about Anastasia Tschaikovsky, because I feel I must carry out my duty to the end . . . [You] do not know, Olga what I went through in those days, sitting beside her, looking at poor Anastasia— but so ill and careworn. If you had seen her lovely smile, still so childlike, her eyes filled with sadness and suffering, your heart, like mine, would have been broken . . . [But] I am going to pray to God that she does survive, that she recovers her health and comes back to us from that distant land, not, this time, as a hunted and persecuted creature, but with her head held high and with the strength of spirit to pardon those who have brought her so much misfortune.[3]

When Olga received Andrew's letter, the Dowager Empress was already suffering from what would prove to be her fatal illness. As a result, Olga, undoubtedly one of those whom Andrew accused of bringing Tschaikovsky "much misfortune," never responded to her cousin's letter.

Back in England, King George, with Xenia's blessing, acted swiftly to secure possession of Marie's box. He rushed Peter Bark, the former Russian Finance Minister under Nicholas II, now the adviser to the Bank of England, to Denmark. Soon after his arrival, Bark insured the box for £200,000 (£5 million now) and, after binding and taping it, enlisted a messenger to transport it to Buckingham Palace, where its contents would eventually be itemized and evaluated.

Preoccupied as she was with comforting her sons and being an attentive wife to Nicolai, Olga did not discover what her sister had done until the day after their mother's funeral. It would not be the last time Olga was left out of a decision that had long-term ramifications for her life. "I knew nothing at all until the next day when Xenia told me that the box was already out of Denmark," she said. "I was given to understand that the matter could not concern me very closely because I had a commoner for a husband."[4]

In fact, Xenia, the daughter who boasted that she was there in sprit for her mother, was rarely there in body. That role was assumed by the more practical Olga, and as a reward, she was treated as a slightly second-rate member of the family. Despite what must have been palpable tension between the sisters, Xenia remained in Denmark.

Any bitterness Olga felt had to be repressed as she and Xenia faced what Xenia called the sad "ordeal" of "picking to pieces with our own hands our last home"[5] in preparation for the biggest and most elegant garage sale in the history of Denmark—the sale of the contents of Hvidøre. In her typically torrid prose, Xenia poured out her grief in a letter to Queen Mary:

> You know how we loved our Mother, how we clung to her always and now in these cruel years of exile. She was *all* that was left to us— everything was centered in her—our home, our country, all the dear past. We all looked up to her and it was through her and in her that we her children and our countrymen found courage to bear our heavy burdens! She was so wonderfully brave and such a help in every way. The light of our life is gone and we feel so miserably lonely and miss her quite terribly![6]

Tableclothes, towels, designer gowns and silver serving sets were sorted and tagged. Hundreds of letters, papers and belongings were divided between the two sisters.[7] Within a month the siblings would have to part, as Xenia returned to England and Olga began her life for the first time as an independent married woman.

In the meantime, King George wrote to Xenia reassuring her that "The parcel which M. Bark sent from Copenhagen has arrived all safely and is in my safe at Buckingham Palace, where it will remain until your return or until I see M. Bark and he tells me what your wishes are about it."[8]

On April 9, 1929, a four-day public auction began. Rasmussen's, the most prestigious antique and collectible shop in Copenhagen, produced a lavishly illustrated auction book that itemized the treasures of Hvidøre room by room. Each time the gavel fell it took another piece of Olga's past with

it. Seven hundred and fifty-four items were snapped up,
including rare paintings, crystal and hand-painted Russian
porcelain.

Hvidøre itself was the last to go. The house was originally
co-owned by Marie and her sister, Queen Alexandra, who
became renowned for beachfront cocktail parties from
which, thanks to the acoustics of the sea, the tinkling of
champagne glasses could be heard halfway to Copenhagen.
After Alexandra's death, her share of the house reverted to
her son, King George, and other royal relations, including the
Princess Royal, Princess Victoria and Queen Maud of Norway. All handed over their shares to Xenia and Olga, and to
Michael's son, George, who lived with his mother, Natasha,
in London. George also received a Belleville motor car.[9]

The sale of Hvidøre and its contents raised more than
200,000 kroner. The equivalent, a cheque for £11,704, was
immediately sent to Westminster Bank, payable to Peter
Bark to invest in a joint trust for Olga and Xenia.[10]

Consistent with her tender nature, Olga's main priority
was not her mother's jewels, but those items of truly sentimental value, including a small marble sculpture of King
Christian IX, which Marie carried in her purse at all times.
Ernst Bodenhof, a captain with the Royal Danish Guards, who
had regularly dined with Empress Marie at Christian IX's
table, greatly admired the sculpture. Shortly after Marie's
death, Olga personally delivered the sculpture to Bodenhof
along with a signed card that read, "This is for you, because
you were so fond of my Mother!"[11]

Barely a month after her mother's death, Xenia returned
to London. On May 22, 1929, Sir Frederick Ponsonby, the
Keeper of the Privy Purse, who had been entrusted with

keeping Empress Marie's box of jewels safe, finally revealed its contents to Xenia, King George and Queen Mary in a drawing room of Buckingham Palace.

Anticipation was high as Ponsonby slowly stripped the tape from the old box. As the process commenced, the King cleared his throat and tried to lighten the atmosphere by making innocuous comments about the unseasonably mild weather. Xenia sat primly in a chair, folding and unfolding her small hands, a nervous smile playing with her lips. The Queen, however, stood close to the table where the box had been placed, peering at it like a bird of prey.

At Ponsonby's request, the King stepped forward and inserted the key into the lock and turned it slowly until he heard the barely audible click. A collective gasp arose from those assembled as the King slowly raised the box's lid. Inside was a jumble of gems so dazzling they made the eyes water.

In his memoirs, Ponsonby recounted that "ropes of the most wonderful pearls were taken out, all graduated, the largest being the size of a big cherry. Cabochon emeralds and large rubies and sapphires were laid out."[12] Included were ruby and diamond bracelets, diamond brooches of all sizes and shapes, and tortoiseshell hatpins.

There were seventy-six items in all. Reduced to silence after viewing the contents, the group walked outside and sat in a garden. Queen Mary may have been already tallying up in her head the number of gems she wished to acquire for her personal collection. But first an official valuation had to be conducted. As soon as the group dispersed, Ponsonby turned the box over to Mr. Hardy, the senior partner of Bond Street jewellers named Hennell and Sons in London.

A week later, Hardy returned to the palace bearing a preliminary valuation of the gems at £144,000. Though Hennells neither confirms nor denies it, it is generally understood that because Hardy was aware of the financial straits of the two sisters, he advanced them £100,000, which was distributed to them by Sir Edward Peacock, the Canadian-born director of the Bank of England, who was an executor of Empress Marie's will and a trustee of the Grand Duchesses' trust.

For unknown reasons, Xenia got £60,000, while Olga got only £40,000. In the end, because of the 1929 stock market crash, the total sum realized by the sale of the jewels was only £137,000. Years later, thanks to statements made in Sir Frederick Ponsonby's memoirs, *Recollections of Three Reigns*, this sum would come under serious scrutiny, resulting in muffled allegations of fraud against none other than Queen Mary.

*F*REED FROM EMPRESS MARIE's often tyrannical demands, Olga and Nicolai began the most bucolic years of their lives. As soon as Hvidøre was sold, the couple set about finding a home just for them, their rambunctious boys and their two maids: Mimka and Tatiana Gromova, a former nurse to Grand Duchess Anastasia, who escaped Russia through Finland before joining Olga in Denmark.

The family's finances improved when Nicolai was elected to the board of a Russian insurance company located in Copenhagen, a position for which he received a yearly salary. Olga supplemented the family's income by accepting commissions to paint delicate watercolour flowers on sets of Danish porcelain.

The small family resided briefly at Amalienborg Palace before moving to the town of Holte near Klampenborg, where they leased a house for several months on the estate of Gorm Rasmussen, whose auction house had handled the sale of Hvidøre. Finally in 1932 they settled into a twenty-room semi-modern farmhouse named Knudsminde, fifteen miles north-west of Copenhagen in the picturesque town of Ballerup.

The decor was a jumble of badly worn furniture and family heirlooms. Photographs from the princely parties in Russia's days of glory stood on rickety tables alongside lots of small elephants, from dime-size to the size of a chicken egg, carved in gem stones.[13] Guests who stayed overnight slept on sofas or pushed-together chairs, or if there were too many people, were forced to lie on the floor with cushions.[14]

The house stood amid 185 acres of farmland and featured an enormous circular gravel driveway, a creek, servants' quarters where Mimka and Gromova stayed and stables. Horses, pigs, cats, dogs, rabbits, chickens and geese roamed the property. Corn, tomatoes, potatoes and other vegetables were harvested. Nicolai, who now had to wear an iron-boned corset because of a spinal injury he received during the war, daily inspected his crops and oversaw the work of several farmhands from a specially constructed pony-drawn cart. Once he nearly got into fisticuffs with a young farmhand who was breaking the tails of cows as he shoved them into barns.

Nicolai and Olga were always in bed by nine and up by five. Shortly after rising, Olga carried a folding chair and easel out to the pasture, where she spent several hours painting. Two or three hours a day were reserved for letter writing. The rest of the time, she threw herself into the same kind of chores performed by thousands of other Danish farmwives: washing, mending and gardening.

No amount of skin cream could soften the rough working woman's hands and weathered face she developed from spending hours in the sun, yet she never wore makeup, and she swept her hair up in a loose bun, and was free of vanity.[15] Unlike most women her age, she welcomed the appearance of wrinkles, stating, "I do know they are getting deeper and deeper. Well, I am proud of them . . . for they make me look like a Russian peasant woman."[16]

Donning rubber boots or sneakers and long skirt, usually purchased at Daell's Warehouse, a local discount store, she bicycled into town two or three times a week for groceries, which she stored in the farm's giant icebox. The trip often took well over an hour since along the way she made frequent stops to check up on her neighbours' health, to babysit, or to run errands.[17] Mushrooms picked during the summer were made into soup. Illustrious visitors were often startled to see Olga perched on her haunches using a tree branch to stir a giant cauldron that she had placed atop a stack of stones and twigs.

Members of royalty were less enthusiastically received at the farm than commoners. One day Olga was busy shovelling the floor of the hen house when Mimka rushed out to inform her that the King of Norway had arrived to see her. "He'll have to wait," Olga reportedly replied, finishing her work before she went indoors to greet her guest.

Olga and Nicolai's loyalty toward Mimka and Gromova,

their two old maids from the imperial days, meanwhile, was touching. "If one had to buy a pair of shoes in Copenhagen, it was discussed at great length in the family, where they would be bought, and where they would be the cheapest, and when she arrived home, the shoes were very meticulously examined by the whole family,"[18] noted a family friend.

In 1933, Danish newspapers announced that Sandro had died in his modest apartment on the Côte d'Azur with his daughter, Irina, and her husband, Felix Yusupov, by his side. He had been eking out a living in France selling his rare-coin collection and some pieces of his wife's jewellery. Pride prevented him from accepting offers to stay for free with wealthy friends.

To honour the man who had been such a support to her, Olga planted some forget-me-nots in a nearby field. She did not attend his funeral in France, but sent a letter of condolence to her sister, Xenia, who had never stopped loving Sandro, despite their separation.

Not long after Olga and Nicolai moved to Knudsminde all kinds of visitors began to arrive at the house, including destitute officers and Russian princesses. Russian exiles seeking sanctuary also began to drift to Olga's home. A few years later, Olga donated a small piece of land in the northeastern area of Ballerup to young exiles who built a wooden summer cottage where they met to share news about political developments in Russia. There can be little doubt that by the late thirties at least some of these exiles saw Nazi Germany's invasion into Poland as a precursor to the destruction of Bolshevik Russia and the eventual restoration of the monarchy. Just as Churchill admitted that despite his hatred of Bolshevism he would welcome the Devil as an ally against the Nazis, so in turn White Russian exiles welcomed the Nazis.

*T*IHON AND GURI WERE GROWING harder to discipline with each year. By the mid-1930s each had received by mail his graduation certificate from the Ecole Secondaire Russe in Paris and was preparing to enter the Danish Royal Guards.

In their mid-teens, both were slightly plump and unathletic. Tihon was the less cerebral, though the more passionate and artistic of the two and was extremely close to his mother, who adored him. Guri, whom a family member insists Olga gave birth to so "Tihon would have someone to play with,"[19] was quick-witted and jealous of his older brother. They fought continually.

For his birthday one year, Olga gave Tihon an old sword. Guri became so jealous that Nicolai had to compensate by giving him his own sword from the Imperial Horse Guards, which Guri promptly used to cut the heads off Olga's flowers. With Olga doting on Tihon, Guri turned to Mimka, who spoiled him by laying out his clothes for him and tidying up his room.

The two boys often visited nearby houses to gamble at cards. Once Tihon won, he would pocket his money and hurry home. Guri, on the other hand, kept on betting until all his money was spent. One of Guri's favourite pastimes was attending the cinema at the Tivoli Gardens. To finance his trips, he reputedly stole money from his mother's purse.[20]

In order to finish six months ahead of his brother, Guri entered the less prestigious cavalry division of the Danish Royal Guards, while Tihon entered the infantry. In addition to focusing his mind on a worthy pursuit, the army had the added bonus of transforming the once-plump Tihon into a slim and strikingly handsome man. By the end of training, he had grown several inches, eventually towering over six feet, with broad shoulders and the same kind of winning smile as his mother.

The summer before he left for training, he had begun dating Agnete Pedersen, the statuesque daughter of a Danish shopkeeper. The two had broken off partly because Agnete thought him a bit dumb and unattractive. By the end of officers' training when he came back "half the size,"[21] the two resumed their courtship.

Soon after graduation, Tihon decided that he would like to become a shopkeeper, an ambition Olga supported wholeheartedly, suggesting that he begin his training at the store of a man named Nielsen in Ballerup. According to Ernst Bodenhof, a family friend who was convinced that "shopkeeping wasn't exactly an excellent patronage for the Tsar's grandchild" prevailed upon the chairman of the International Chamber of Commerce in London, Mr. Watson, to make Tihon a "travelling ambassador for the company."[22]

Because of Tihon's royal connections, Watson thought the idea a good one and invited the family friend to present the idea to Olga. In light of her overprotective relationship with Tihon, Olga's response was amusing and typical. She looked at the friend "with her kind eyes" and said, "How nice it was of you to think of it, but I would much rather have him at Nielsens, for then he can come home for lunch every day."[23]

In his relentless bid to one-up his brother, Guri was the first to propose marriage to a girl. She was a delicately boned sixteen-year-old, with luxuriant black hair and liquid brown eyes, by the name of Ruth Schwartz, the daughter of a local farmer. The two dated for three years, before announcing their engagement in 1939. To please her future mother-in-law, Ruth learned to speak Russian and converted to Russian Orthodoxy.

She and Guri married in May 1940 at the Alexander Nevsky Church in Copenhagen, from which Empress Marie had been buried twelve years before. "The day was as if cut out of a fairy tale,"[24] Ruth said, adding that she could only hope that their marriage would be as happy as Olga and Nicolai's. "I don't think I ever saw a happier couple than those two. They simply couldn't live without each other."[25]

As a wedding gift, Olga gave Ruth a brooch consisting of dozens of fiery red rubies and diamonds. Guri and Ruth lived happily in Knudsminde, where Ruth was treated like a daughter of the house. "I always called Olga Mama, and she was like a mother to me, right from the first time I came into her and my father-in-law's house," she says.[26] Before long, Ruth was presented to King Christian X and Queen Alexandrine, with whom she ended up on a first-name basis.

In June of 1940, barely a month after Ruth and Guri's wedding, Danish soldiers stationed in bunkers by the seashore awoke at dawn to see German soldiers striding up a hill with carbines over their shoulders, and pistols jammed in their belts. The German invasion of Denmark had begun. The evening before, for reasons the soldiers did not yet understand, the King of Denmark had ordered all military firearms to be confiscated because he knew the Danish army could not win against the German military might poised against it. As a result, having only sabres left to defend themselves with, the Danish soldiers were forced to surrender. Many soldiers openly wept. Shortly after the invasion, the King made a radio announcement asking everyone to keep his dignity and to go to work as usual.

Guri's and Tihon's later boasts that they worked for the Danish underground were wildly exaggerated. Though a photograph shows Tihon stomping a German military helmet into the ground, he did not participate in any overtly anti-Nazi activities. Like all other members of the Danish Royal Guards, the brothers were forced to spend time in a German-run POW camp, but in this case the camp consisted of a downtown Copenhagen hotel, and the imprisonment lasted no more than two months. The Germans encouraged visits from wives and children because it was one of the few opportunities they got to share home-cooked meals.

Though admittedly never in love with Tihon, Agnete was ultimately worn down by his ardent pursuit of her. When the two became intimate, she worried that she might become simply his good-time girl, and sought to break off the relationship again. As soon as he thought he might lose her for good, Tihon literally got down on his knees, as Agnete recalls, confessed that he loved her more than he did his own mother,[27] and begged her to marry him.

On April 20, 1942, the two wed in a widely publicized ceremony at the Alexander Nevsky Church. Outside, throngs of spectators, curious to see the elder son of the daughter of Alexander III and Empress Marie, had to be held back by police.

Newsreel cameras captured a wistful Olga, dressed in a

flowered hat and simple cloth coat, waving to the newly married couple as they climbed into a car that drove them back to Knudsminde. Since Tihon had to report to army headquarters the next morning, the honeymoon consisted of an intimate dinner celebration, attended by both Tihon's and Agnete's family members. Danish papers revelled in playing up the seeming mismatch of Tihon, the grandson of a tsar, and Agnete, the daughter of a shopkeeper. Little could they have known of Tihon's youthful dreams of becoming nothing more than a shopkeeper himself.

Against the backdrop of the Second World War, petty bickering arose between Agnete and Olga over insignificant problems. Olga decried Agnete's method of stacking dishes after a meal, so that the bottoms got dirty, and remonstrated with her for eating strawberries from the garden instead of picking them for dinner. As a victim of numerous Russian famines, Nicolai berated Agnete for not eating the skins of her baked potatoes.

Agnete and Ruth also clashed. According to Agnete, when Olga gave Agnete a diamond brooch as a wedding present, Ruth snatched it, and holding it under a bright light, loudly declared it a fake.[28] Agnete found Ruth's sloppiness appalling, as well as her dependence on Mimka to clean up her room, including emptying her chamber pot.

While still living at Knudsminde, Ruth and Guri had two children—a girl named after Olga's sister, Xenia, and a boy named Leonid. Olga had hoped that Xenia would be born on her birthday, June 1. Ruth gave birth to Xenia on June 19, 1941 and felt guilty disappointing her mother-in-law. Olga instantly adored the little girl, who became the subject of dozens of her paintings.

In 1943, Tihon, dressed in civilian clothes, was arrested by the Germans and charged with being a spy, after he was apprehended on the street taking photographs of German-occupied buildings. He spent one month in jail and, when he was released, returned home.

At home his mother's open-door policy regarding visitors was beginning to cause severe embarrassment to the Danish royal family.

Many Russian émigrés had joined the German army in a bid to drive the Communists out of Russia. Some of these émigrés arrived in Denmark alongside the German occupiers. Once these émigrés knew Olga was in Denmark, they began to knock on her door to pay homage. There is no evidence that Olga tried to discourage these visits, though her daughter-in-law Agnete denies their frequency. "A group of Russians dressed in German uniforms came to the house one Sunday afternoon and my mother-in-law gave them tea, but that was it. Somehow the rumours got started from there."29

If it is true that Olga rose above her dislike of Germans by feeding, sheltering and giving moral support to White Russians in German uniforms, she undoubtedly did so out of her natural open-heartedness and genuine love for Russian peasants loyal to the Romanov family, rather than any passionate attachment to Nazi propaganda. Always her own woman, it probably never occurred to her, or she dismissed as preposterous, any criticism from outsiders, including the Danish royal family, that her actions could be interpreted as complicity.

Even if the Germans had succeeded in conquering Russia and were interested in restoring to it some form of monarchy, it is doubtful that the happily independent Olga would have been among those triumphant family members anxious to return to business as usual. She had long ago escaped the imperial yoke and had no desire to return.

The same might not be said for other members of the family. Grand Duke Cyril, the Romanov Nicholas stripped of his title for marrying a commoner, had settled in the Riviera after the Revolution and considered himself the legitimate successor to the Russian throne, working to bring salvation to his country. After his death in 1938, his son, Grand Duke Vladimir, believed by certain factions of the family to be the new rightful heir to the Romanov throne, was reputed to be in active negotiations with Hitler over the restoration of the monarchy in Russia.

In an extraordinary letter kept at present at the Foreign Policy Archive of the Russian Federation, a secret source stated, "In early September this year [1941] an agreement was concluded between Germany and Russian Grand Duke Vladimir whereby Germany gave its consent to the restoration of the monarchy of the Romanovs. That state should establish a national-socialist or fascist regime. The non-Russian countries of the Soviet Union would be associated into a new Russia within a single union. The Grand Duke would renounce all claims over Poland. In execution of this agreement, the Grand Duke issued guidance to the White émigrés to collaborate with countries that are at war with the USSR."[30]

The ultimate failure of the German army to defeat Russia placed in danger not only Olga but the Russian émigrés who had initially supported the German cause, but defected when they sensed the war was lost. Suddenly, Stalin's Communist troops, which had overtaken Berlin, were a hair's breadth away from the Danish border and not of a mind to look benevolently on Olga's continuing habit, even after the war, of taking these Russian émigrés into her home.

A disgusted Olga accused the Germans of being less concerned with implementing an effective government in Russia than in slaughtering thousands of innocent men, women and children. "They blundered so badly when they broke into Russia," she said. "Hitler kept saying that he meant to free my countrymen from the Reds. The Germans should have formed units of local government composed wholly of Russian members and set up a national administration. Instead, they rushed into pillage and to murder, sparing neither women nor children and they lost on all counts."[31]

Christian X lived long enough to see Denmark liberated on May 5, 1945. He died two years later, whereupon his son Frederik IX and his wife, Ingrid, assumed the throne.

With the war over, Russian émigrés in Denmark who had defected from the German army had nowhere to turn. If they returned to Russia, they faced execution in Stalin's death camps; if they stayed, the Danes would simply return them to Russia. According to Olga's son Tihon, Olga approached Prince Axel, the grandson of King Christian X, to ask him to intercede on behalf of those Russians who were now surrounded by enemies, but her request was turned down.

Tihon believed that a Danish policeman, who was an acquaintance of Olga's, for a time agreed to pick up these inhabitants of a political no-man's land and smuggle them onto ships heading for South America in an effort to prevent them from being repatriated to Russia.

In spite of Tihon's beliefs, both daughters-in-law deny that Olga took Russian émigrés who were also German army defectors into Knudsminde, either before or after the war. "I lived there, I should know,"[32] says Agnete. But amid the festive atmosphere of the farmhouse where people came and went at all hours of the day and night, it is possible that a few escaped both Agnete's and Ruth's notice. Once the war was over, Ruth was in an even less advantageous position to be aware of the presence of émigrés, since between 1946 and 1948, she and Guri, now a lieutenant in the Danish Royal Army, had moved closer to his army garrison in the town of Holbaek, with their young children, Xenia and Leonid.

In retaliation for Olga's apparent efforts to protect the émigrés, the Soviet Government sent Denmark an official note accusing Olga and the Roman Catholic Archbishop of Denmark (a distant acquaintance) of being the two main co-conspirators in helping what the Soviets called "the enemies of the people" to run away from a "well-deserved" revenge.[33]

Shortly after the note was sent, highly placed Communist operatives descended on the State Archive of the Russian Federation in Moscow to rifle through personal documents and letters of Olga's that had been confiscated after the Revolution, possibly in an effort to uncover some incriminating evidence of some prior collusion with German officials through her marriage to Oldenburg.

Olga and her family members in Denmark eventually began receiving threatening phone calls. On his trips out to Olga's house, the butcher's son noticed strangers congregated on neighbours' doorsteps asking inhabitants if they had noticed any suspicious activity on Olga's part. The Kremlin would in all likelihood have eventually pressed for the extradition of Olga and her family to Russia to face justice. It is possible that the Soviets might even have kidnapped the family.

Finally, in 1948, the King bluntly informed Olga that Denmark could no longer guarantee her safety. As a result, at the age of sixty-six, Olga once again faced exile.

Queen Elizabeth and King George VI asked Sir Edward Peacock to find out if the family might be welcome in Canada, a British colony. Peacock quickly wrote to A.H. Creighton, the head of the Canadian Pacific Railway, to see if some red tape could be cut to facilitate the family's departure.

Canada had a desperate need for skilled farmers. In the late 1940s, Creighton was in charge of importing what were called "agricultural immigrants," mostly European farmers, into Canada to work the vast stretches of uncultivated land. Nicolai's farming skills fit the bill, and an offer to emigrate was made.

The British and Canadian governments were very concerned about the safety of their high-profile immigrants. J.S.P. Armstrong, who was the agent general of the province of Ontario in England, was contacted urgently in April of 1948 by Scotland Yard to confirm whether Canadian authorities would give Olga and her family adequate protection.[34]

As soon as Olga was asked to leave the country, Ruth and Guri also chose to go. "I was expecting my third child," said Ruth. "It was hard, very hard to say good-bye to my parents and friends here at home. A few days before we left, Queen Ingrid came out to Knudsminde to say good-bye. The queen was alone and drove the car herself. As a goodbye gift, she gave Mama [Olga] a Danish flag."[35] The smallness of the gesture gave it all the earmarks of an insult.

Knudsminde was sold on April 4, 1948, to a man named Henry Peterson, along with most of the furnishings and paintings from Hvidøre.

Edith Dyregaard Jensen, a family friend, recalls that "there were many tears" on the day the family left Denmark for good. "Olga said she always hoped she would be buried at the Kierkegaard Cemetery in Ballerup, but now knew she wouldn't be."[36] Tatiana Gromova, then in her mid-eighties, decided to remain in Denmark, so the only servant who journeyed with the family was eighty-three-year-old Mimka.

On May 5, the family took one last stroll through the grounds of Knudsminde, posing in their Sunday best for pictures for a Danish magazine photographer. A positive spin was put on the family's decision to leave. They were said to be seeking new challenges in a new land, as yet unidentified. Most readers, however, knew or guessed the truth, that if Olga hadn't left of her own accord, she would have been forced out.

CHAPTER NINE

DISPLACED PERSON

THE FAMILY'S FIRST STOP WAS in London to visit the Grand Duchess Xenia. The couple stayed at Wilderness House, Hampton Court Palace, which George VI had placed at Xenia's disposal, while the rest of the family, including Mimka, stayed in London at an old castle that had been turned into a hotel. Agnete, who often visited Wilderness House, recalls Xenia as "a small, doll-like thing," whose grandsons "bicycled through the flower beds,"[1] earning a stern rebuke from an exasperated King George.

If the aging Xenia still resembled a doll, then the twenty-two-room Wilderness House was a doll's house, complete with cobwebs and uninvited guests of the eight-legged variety. The glory of old Russia was again on display at tea time one afternoon as servants laid out on hand-painted Russian porcelain an assortment of cheeses for the guests to sample. The spell was broken only when Agnete noticed small white worms crawling out from under one of the slices.

Guri and Ruth's daughter, Xenia, recalls British food as "the worst [we] had experienced. It was 1948, everything was rationed. We survived on mutton. The English don't know very much about boiling and roasting mutton. It was like eating woolen socks."[2]

While at Hampton Court, Olga was visited by J.S.P. Armstrong, who provided her with information about the Canadian way of life, including details about the cost of living, and of housing.[3] A servant ushered him into a small ground-floor dining room, where Olga soon joined him, looking pale and tired. A damp chill permeated the dwelling, despite the summer season. Olga's most urgent concern was finding a "safe haven" for her children and grandchildren.[4]

Distracted by agonizing back pain, Nicolai accepted unenthusiastically but without argument Olga's decision to move the family to Canada. Tihon and Guri, on the other hand, were ecstatic, viewing Canada as a place where they might be able to establish identities of their own, separate from their mother's.

Agnete's reaction, however, was by far the most negative. She continued to insist that any notion of Stalinist threats was a fabrication and blamed her brother-in-law Guri for the family's exodus from Denmark, which she saw as pointless. "Guri was doing badly in the army and thought there might be more money and opportunity in the United States or Canada," she says. "All those rumours about the family being threatened by Stalin's communists is nonsense. He couldn't have cared less about us. Guri and Ruth should have gone to Canada by themselves, so the rest of us could have stayed where we were."[5]

On May 29, less than a week before the voyage, a desperately homesick Olga wrote notes to her friends in "my little beloved Ballerup."[6] "We are missing Ballerup and all the kind faces and all our friends. We never get vegetables. They are much more expensive than home. We've got plenty of milk, and the white bread is also good. Last weekend I went to the countryside with old friends, and it was lovely. England is beautiful. On Wednesday we will depart. Think about us—in the sea."[7]

Two or three days before the family left for Liverpool, several large containers and trunks arrived from Denmark filled with clothes, furniture and paintings. Among those items Olga arranged to ship to Canada were a favourite love seat and royal porcelain. There were also various-sized semi-precious stone Fabergé sculptures of animals such as fish, monkeys, rabbits, lions and even a squirrel; and most precious to her, a small round Fabergé table inlaid with pebbles collected off a beach by her father.

Other valuables included pastel-coloured Fabergé picture frames; Empress Marie's travelling case, containing a sterling-silver pitcher, wash basin, brush and comb; Alexander III's jade letter opener, with a circlet of diamonds on its handle; and numerous icons imbedded with semi-precious stones, including the one alleged to have been retrieved by Alexander Sokolov from the body of Grand Duchess Elizabeth (wife of Grand Duke Serge, the man responsible for the Khodinka Field catastrophe), who was thrown alive into a mine shaft in Alapaevsk the day after the murder of Nicholas and his family.

Despite her haste, Olga also managed to retain the jewels that Mimka had smuggled out of the Sergievskaya Street house. Among these items was a bow-shaped diamond hair comb once belonging to Catherine the Great, a ruby and diamond Red Cross brooch, several small Fabergé eggs of various sizes, and a gold medallion containing a black cross, a portrait and a lock of Empress Marie's hair.

If Denmark's political seas seemed rough, Olga faced even rougher seas during her transatlantic voyage to Canada on board the *Empress of Canada*. Chief Steward R. Bartlett noted in his ship's report that the "exceptionally rough weather for the first few days caused a great deal of seasickness amongst the passengers."[8]

On that first night, as Ruth tucked her two children into their bunks, and Guri, Tihon and Agnete prowled the ship's well-stocked first-class cocktail lounge, Olga, warmed by Nicolai's reassuring embrace, stood astern the vessel wistfully watching the twinkling lights of Liverpool recede into the distance. Undoubtedly she knew that June 4, 1948 marked the last time she would see Europe.

The voyage took five days. On-board entertainments in first-class included orchestral music and movies. Little excitement occurred beyond the apprehension on June 4 in the crew recreation room of two stowaways who turned out to be deserters from the 14/20 K Hussars. Three days later, a first-class passenger was caught in the wind while walking from the port to starboard side of the sun deck and was "blown into a ventilator catching his left knee."[9]

For Agnete, who seemed immune to seasickness, an already self-described "fun" voyage improved even more when a male passenger fell "madly in love" with her.[10] Olga and Mimka meanwhile were content to lie on deck chairs, feeling the salt-flecked wind rustle their hair. As the vessel slowly approached its destination of Montreal, Xenia and Leonid ran up on deck and took turns peering through binoculars.

The ship docked in Montreal at 6:30 a.m. on Thursday, June 10. As soon as they disembarked, the family members had to shake the hands of dozens of well-wishers among the Russian émigrés who had gathered on the narrow dock.

After lunching with a German count, the group boarded a train for the last leg of their journey, a five-hour trip to Union Station in Toronto.

As the train slowly rounded the bend toward track eleven, a crowd of newspaper reporters and photographers on the platform began jostling each other to get the best vantage point from which to interview "the great lady and her party of nine."[11]

"Sister of Last of the Czars Arrives in Ontario to Farm," announced *The Evening Telegram*, beneath a photograph of Olga, Ruth, Xenia, Leonid and Mimka, sitting in a row on a wooden bench in the station. It was ungenerously noted that the former Grand Duchess wore a "crumpled blue tweed suit, flat tan-colored oxfords and dowdy hat," but that otherwise "her every gesture implied vigorous good health." Seven-year-old Xenia, bewildered by the mass of flashbulbs, defensively clutched a doll to her chest.[12]

Despite the cynicism associated with their jobs, the reporters were nonetheless impressed by Olga's still-regal bearing as they trailed her out of the station and across the street to the Royal York Hotel. "Quite impervious to the stir she was creating, the Grand Duchess strode through the station, clutching a massive bouquet of yellow and red roses in one hand and a heavy brown satchel in another," they wrote. "Offers of assistance were smilingly declined."[13]

The family lugged their belongings up the staircase rising to the magnificent lobby of the hotel decorated with Persian rugs and Bavarian crystal chandeliers. The strains of Chopin's "Prelude" filtered out from a bar adjoining the lobby.

Mimka enthusiastically approved of the magnificence of Olga's new home, pointing out that "the place being more or less the size of a palace, it was fitting that her mistress should stay there,"[14] until Olga took her aside and quietly informed her that the party would inhabit only one suite rather than the entire building. Meanwhile a phobic Nicolai, accustomed to only low-rise buildings in Denmark, balked at boarding the elevator that carried the family to the twentieth floor.

At last the family entered the enormous suite reserved for them by the American consul Malcolm Doherty, a family friend. Someone had placed a dish of bread and salt on a side table. Leonid immediately raced around the room, pulling the chains that turned lamps on and off. As Olga helped Mimka remove her coat, reporters questioned Tihon and Nicolai about their future plans.

Unlike Olga, the two men seemed concerned with preserving a certain regal image, despite the fact that Olga was the only member of royalty in the room. A proud Tihon, credited by the newspapers with having served with "the underground forces during the Second World War," told reporters that he thought "the Russian people would welcome a return to the Tsarist regime." Asked whether he had received word recently about conditions in Russia, he replied with a wide grin, "No, Uncle Joe doesn't write me too often."[15]

Nicolai, of the "leonine head and gruff" manner, attempted to eject reporters from the suite. "My wife is very tired," he said, removing his coat, "she has had a hard day." He did not correct reporters when they referred to him as Colonel as opposed to the more correct Lieutenant-Colonel and disclosed that the family was on its way to starting "a small dairy farm" just outside Toronto. "We could not bring much money out of Denmark, we cannot buy a big farm," he admitted.[16]

Soon after, he complained that he too was tired and wanted nothing more than to go to bed. By now, he was pale, and the dampness of the sea voyage had greatly aggravated his spinal condition.

When reporters questioned the reasons for the family's rapid departure from Denmark, Olga diplomatically attributed it to her fear that communism might spread throughout some of the northern countries of Europe.[17] The complete truth would have been harder to explain.

After two days, Olga, who felt conspicuous in her new opulent surroundings, accepted an invitation to stay at the home of Russian émigrés. Once there, members of Canada's most influential families flocked to her side, including Lieutenant-Governor of Ontario John Keiller-Mackay, and his wife, Katherine; the Gladstone Murrays; and Babs Messervey, a wealthy resident from the posh neighbourhood of Rosedale. "Babs bought a lot of jewellery from my grandmother," remembers Xenia, "My grandparents loved her and so did I. Tihon hated her, he was jealous of her, her money, and her rich friends."[18]

Katherine Keiller-Mackay recalls that, to preserve Olga's dignity, Babs Messervey acted as a go-between in the sale of Olga's jewellery. "She would come to our houses and unfurl a roll of jewellery," she says. "There were small pieces, not usually costing more than a few hundred or a few thousand dollars. A lot of the women from Rosedale came to select certain trinkets. I bought a bow-shaped hair comb"[19] (the one that had belonged to Catherine the Great is now in the possession of Nancy Jackman, the sister of Hal Jackman, another former Lieutenant-Governor of Ontario). Later, Babs would discreetly forward the proceeds to Olga.

It is strange that a cash-strapped Olga preferred to give her most extravagant jewellery to her daughters-in-laws and friends, while offering for sale only "trinkets." One contemporary antique dealer believes that if Olga had sold even a fraction of the Fabergé items her mother had smuggled out of Russia, she could have been "set for life."[20] A possible explanation could be that she didn't want to sell those items that might have provided income for her sons after her death. Certainly, she helped them out financially during her lifetime, providing capital not only for down payments on their two homes, but toward the investment in two apartment buildings on Lake Shore Boulevard.

Tenacious reporters again caught up with Olga in July 1948 as she was partying at the home of the Gladstone Murrays. In an *Evening Telegram* article entitled "They Are Safe," Olga chalked up her rapid departure from Denmark to intuition. "We were too close," she said, referring to the proximity of their Danish home to the Russian border.

When asked about living conditions in Denmark under the German occupation, Olga tersely described them as uneasy. With a romantic flourish, it was clear that the press had decided to wrap a protective arm around their country's politically "embattled" new arrival. The article concluded, "The Communists could have and might have demanded return of the Grand Duchess and her family to Russia. The Canadians will not."[21]

As eager as Canadians were to help, Olga, with typical stubbornness, chose to find the family's first home through the classified-ad sections of Toronto's newspapers. In July, she settled on leasing for $300 a month a smallish house on fashionable Delisle Street near the corner of Yonge Street and St. Clair Avenue. Behind its white wooden shutters and lattice work, the gingerbread-coloured house was a far cry from the splendour of Gatchina Palace, and in such confined surroundings family fights inevitably erupted.

Tihon and Guri were already sending their résumés to prospective employers, but few jobs were available for two home-tutored military men. Nor were the young men keen to help their parents "farm" their soon-to-be-purchased property outside of town, since each son had decided to find a separate home for himself and his family.

A.H. Creighton, who was alternately referred to by Olga as a "nurse" and "guardian angel," had the improbably long title of District Superintendent, Department of Immigration and Agricultural Development, Canadian Pacific Railway. Because of this position, Queen Mary and, through her, Edward Peacock entrusted him with the job of finding the perfect rural home for Olga, Nicolai and Mimka at a "reasonable price." The department Creighton worked for was created in 1880 when twenty-five million acres of wilderness were sold by the Dominion of Canada to the Canadian Pacific Railway. Under the agreement, the railway was required to push through a railroad and open up the west. People were sought to occupy and develop the adjacent land.

Immigration agents were sent to the British Isles and other areas of Europe to attract settlers to "colonize" the west. After this successful colonization, the department then continued to settle people on other than its own property and to see that they were successfully relocated. After World War II, European farmers became a hot commodity.

Creighton, who was in charge of immigration for the province of Ontario, found many returning European soldiers—farmers whose land had been ravaged by wartime violence—and even some former members of the nobility eager to escape the ghosts of the past and establish themselves in a country with a short history and even shorter memory.

By mid-summer of 1948, Creighton had found a permanent home for the beleaguered Kulikovskys in a township named Nassagaweya, an Indian word literally meaning "a high place from which the water is separating," in Campbellville, Ontario. Because he didn't identity the buyers, the ten-room red-brick three-storey home situated atop a hill amid one hundred acres of prime farmland covered with tall grass was purchased at the then relatively low price of $14,000.

Once the sale was finalized, Creighton forwarded the trunks and containers from Denmark to the home. As soon as they arrived, the first pieces of furniture removed were the beds, the love seat and Nicolai's favourite armchair. "There is no room for all the garbage,"[22] Olga complained, referring to the priceless antiques she laboriously unwrapped. By midsummer, to escape the heat, they slept side by side near an ice-box located on the floor of an open veranda attached to the house.

Even the fussy Mimka approved of the house. To spare her from having to climb the steep staircase, Olga placed her in a room on the ground floor just beside the kitchen. "Happily, my old maid 'Mimka' is quite happy here and even likes the food I cook, so that is a great comfort. She has a good character—also good humour and enjoys life and loves us all too,"[23] she wrote to Queen Mary.

With Mimka virtually infirm, Olga, who was battling arthritis and a failing memory, had to learn quickly how to manoeuvre her way around a kitchen. "I have become a bungler," she complained to friends. "I forget everything, run around the kitchen looking for something, and it is either in my hand or on the shelf right in front of me. . . . [My] electric stove frightened me at first, but the results are encouraging. I am reading a book on electric stoves and learning."[24] In time, Olga would master her two favourite dishes: lemon cake and pot roast.

Tihon, Guri, their wives and the grandchildren had moved in temporarily until the men could find jobs. The sheer relief at escaping the scrutiny of the media in Toronto had unleashed the family's playful side, and soon, improbable as it seemed, Nicolai "started to dance and sing—a sign of pleasure,"[25] noted Olga. In her spare time, Olga also constructed for her adored granddaughter Xenia intricately detailed doll's houses using egg cartons, swatches of fabric, buttons, and any other bits and pieces she found lying around the house.

By September, Sir Edward Peacock was sent by Queen Mary to check on Olga's health and how she was settling in. He arrived with Creighton for tea one afternoon, dressed in an oversized straw hat and three-piece suit. Ironically, despite or perhaps because of his attire, the relentless pounding of the sun soon flushed his face so badly that Olga grew concerned for *his* health.

Once the initial rush of excitement subsided, Nicolai had to turn his attention to hiring staff to work the property. An old farmhand named Arijs was summoned from Knudsminde and a married couple was brought over from England. The husband rotated the crops every year, while the wife, who resembled "a small skinny monkey"[26] in Olga's words, cooked meals, finally allowing Olga time to pursue her painting.

Every few weeks, Olga sent her watercolours to Henry Petersen in Denmark, who sold them to a growing audience of buyers. Her favourite subjects were the two-storey barns located on the property. "You will probably think there is nothing beautiful about them," she wrote to a friend. "No, there is something special about them that attracts me. I do not know what exactly it is—but when the evening sun lights up the top, and the sky is pale green with orange clouds—and trees in the background—it is so beautiful!"[27]

Jersey and Holstein cows were bought, along with two black "farm-working" horses. Livestock, including pigs and chickens, were crowded into barns. "Because of the wolves, we had to bring the animals inside [barns] for the night,"[28] remembers Xenia. Each morning, Olga's border collie named Sammi fetched the paper from the box at the end of the farm's long gravel driveway and carried it in his teeth to the family's breakfast table.

Despite the family's apparent bliss, there were a few miscalculations. As a kind of consolation prize for having evicted them from their country, the Danish government sent the Kulikovskys a state-of-the-art thresher that one observer described as being "as big as an apartment."[29] Too complicated to operate, it remained for years in its box, alongside a smaller box filled with spare parts. So many curious neighbours came around to stare at the "monument" that one neighbour suggested Olga should "sell tickets for the show."[30]

For the most part, while in Nassagaweya, Olga tried to erase all traces of her identity. Neighbours referred to the couple simply as the Colonel and Mrs. Kulikovsky. One of the few journalists permitted to interview Olga for a Canadian magazine intermittently called her Your Majesty and Your Reverence until a visibly irritated Olga said, "My name is Mrs. Kulikovsky, and if you don't want to call me that, it's 'Her Imperial Highness.'"[31]

Every Sunday Nicolai and Olga drove fifty miles to Christ the Saviour Church in Toronto. Olga wrote in a letter that most of the Russian émigré parishioners made her "feel at home," without paying "any particular attention to rank."[32] However, occasionally an admirer did approach her. "Her appearance was quite shockingly shabby, there were loose threads hanging from her sweater and most of her nails were broken," says one, who met Olga after a service and said to her, "I have always admired you and your family so much, and it is such an honour to have you attend our church."

Considering herself more commoner now than royal, Olga gazed at the woman with mirthful eyes that looked right into the soul, eyes so reminiscent of her brother Nicholas's, and replied simply "Why?"[33]

Once a year, as a favour to Tihon, a less than regally attired Olga did agree to attend the annual White Russian Army ball held in various auditoriums throughout Toronto in honour of her father's Akhtyrsky Regiment. As the former honorary colonel of the regiment, she attracted substantial press attention by her attendance at these fundraising events in support of the émigrés.

USING IN PART MONEY THEIR mother gave them, the two sons placed down payments on homes of their own on Haig Street in Port Credit, just west of Toronto. Each took odd jobs, then lost them. Guri sold insurance by day and worked in a brickyard by night. Highly ambitious, he eventually obtained his Bachelor of Arts degree from the University of Toronto, where he also secured a job teaching Russian Literature.

After several false starts, Tihon, through a family friend, finally landed a job selling artwork at Eaton's, Canada's largest department store chain. Later he found work as a draftsman for the Department of Highways.

Exposed as children to the luxuries of Hvidøre and to visits by various crown heads of Europe, and pampered by an adoring Olga, who had waited so long to have children with the man she loved, both sons found it difficult to adapt to the rhythm and mores of ordinary working folk. After all, even their father, as an ex-military man, was forced through circumstances to live off the money his wife brought to the relationship.

Tihon's poor written English contributed further to his inability to achieve a career status similar that of his brother. In at least one newspaper interview, he fudged his true line of work. Waylaid by reporters shortly after returning from a trip to the United States in the early fifties, he did not correct a reporter's description of him as an architect, rather than an art salesman.

On the whole, of the two adult brothers, Tihon was the more sweet natured and better liked. Friends recall him as a man who enjoyed good jokes, good wine, and knew how to party.[34] He and Agnete, regarded by one friend as "a little bit of a flirt,"[35] hosted cocktail parties, which Olga attended. "She would sit on the couch and receive guests with a big smile on her face,"[36] Agnete says.

The serenity of Ruth and Guri's life was, however, superficial. Shortly after they moved into their new home, Ruth gave birth to their third child, Alexander, but by this time Guri's gaze had already begun to stray in the direction of other women. "As soon as he came to Canada, he went crazy for girls,"[37] Ruth recalls.

Eventually, Guri worked for Philips, an electronics manufacturer, where a co-worker remembers him as "highly meticulous and detail-oriented."[38] He was a self-absorbed parent, however, and given to flashes of temper and fits of frustration.

Of all Guri's children, Xenia, despite her ability to grasp English, had the hardest time adapting to life in a new country. "When we went to school, they shouted D.P.s after us. It is an insult and means displaced persons. But we weren't. We were immigrants. It is disgusting to be called something like that. In those days I was a little annoyed with my grandparents. We were in the papers, because *they* were somebody."[39]

*I*N 1951, THE PUBLICATION OF Sir Frederick Ponsonby's memoirs sent shock waves throughout the family. Ponsonby stated that in 1929 Empress Marie's jewels had been appraised at and subsequently sold for £350,000 and that "The King had this large sum put in trust for the Grand Duchesses."[40] Olga had never received any more than the £40,000 from her share of the £100,000 advance offered by Mr. Hardy of Hennell and Sons jewellers in London, so Ponsonby's extraordinary statement now left her wondering where the additional £250,000 had disappeared to.

Suspicion immediately fell on Queen Mary, who had purchased the bulk of the gems. One theory speculated that the Queen might have covertly retained the balance of £250,000 to compensate for the monetary support her husband gave to Empress Marie and her family during their first early days of exile in Denmark.

The most popular theory was that Mary, so renowned for seeking out bargains, took advantage of the 1929 stock-market crash and paid far below the appraised market value for the sisters' gems, resulting in Olga and Xenia's receiving less than a third of what the gems were really worth.

Despite the pleas of her sons, Olga chose not to demean her dignity by investigating the matter. "Why create unnecessary bitterness?"[41] she argued.

When asked in later years, Sir Edward Peacock could shed no light on the matter, except to hypothesize that Ponsonby's memory must have been incorrect.

It would take forty years to resolve the mystery of where the so-called "missing" £250,000 went. Tragically, by then, Nicolai, Olga, Guri and Tihon would all be dead.

ANY EMBARRASSMENT OLGA might have suffered over her rightful inheritance did not prevent her from remaining characteristically creative. In October 1951, *The Globe and Mail* announced a showing of "Paintings and Water Colours by Olga Kulikovsky, former Grand Duchess of Russia" at Eaton's art gallery, where Tihon worked. The ad stated that "The watercolours are delicately executed still life and landscape subjects of great charm and personal warmth," including as a postscript, "These paintings are for sale at modest prices." Olga was under no delusion that the paintings' greatest value lay anywhere but in their signatures.

Wealthy society matrons such as Mrs. Creighton and Mrs. Messervey attended the show. Wearing a now-ubiquitous beret, Olga held court in the second-floor gallery where her paintings were displayed. Most cost between $200 and $250. Twelve were scooped up quickly before the evening was through, a significant feat since Olga admitted that people increasingly preferred buying prints over paintings because they were cheaper.

Reviewers of the show extolled the artist's cheerful optimism rather than analyzing the technical merits or often brooding subtexts of the works. Pearl McCarthy, columnist for *The Globe and Mail,* noted the work possessed "the one old-fashioned trait which keeps art always new and young—a search and respect for what is delightful."[42]

Olga's lifelong chameleon-like talent for adapting to any environment also drew praise. *Globe and Mail* columnist Lotta Dempsey stated, "Her misty snow scenes have so strong a feeling of the Ontario countryside that one wonders how, indeed, this woman of so many cataclysmic experiences since her birth in a Royal Russian palace has so quickly absorbed the peace and quiet of an early winter evening in the Canadian country."[43]

AT THE SAME TIME THAT Olga was attempting to distance herself from her past, more Romanov family claimants attempted to draw her back in. One woman in Toronto repeatedly bombarded Olga with letters. Without explicitly identifying herself as Anastasia, the woman implied that she was a close relative who insisted on the right to meet with Olga.[44]

Olga sent a note refusing to see the woman, which failed to stop the woman from writing. Finally, her letters became so "piteous," in Olga's words, that the kind-hearted Olga relented and agreed to meet with the woman in Campbellville. However, as soon as the woman arrived at the train station in the nearby town of Moffat, Nicolai ambushed her on the platform and said something so intimidating that the woman left immediately, silenced for good.[45]

Japan produced yet another Anastasia, who became so

vociferous that the Russian bishop in Tokyo, a friend of Olga's, wrote to her to say that the woman was "creating quite a stir, even in Asia. You must do something to stop it."[46]

"What was there that I could do?" Olga responded. "All my relations and myself received conclusive proofs of the massacre. It was pure cruelty on the part of those adventurers to assume those identities—always with the hope of material gains. But there was nothing for me to do. I could not stoop to expose those shameful tricks. I could only ignore them. But all of it tortured me."[47]

Olga's reference to receiving conclusive proofs of the massacre may have been a slip of the tongue. At the time she made the comment, the 1950s, no bones of the imperial family had been officially discovered and identified through DNA analysis. The statement therefore provides further evidence that she may have indeed opened the box of remains sent to her in Denmark in 1920 by Alexander Sokolov, the White Army investigator, and despite her family's objections, accepted the contents as part of the remains of her brother and his family.

*B*Y THE END OF 1951, THE strain of trying to manage a farm through yet another frigid winter took its toll on Nicolai's already fragile health. For days on end he could not even rise into a sitting position, his fused discs shooting burning pains down each leg. Slippery driving conditions prevented Olga from shopping in Campbellville. Finally, with the assistance of A.H. Creighton, the couple reluctantly put the house on the market.

"[They] are selling the farm, which is a pity, but are unable to cope with it any longer—too tiring—and costs too much,"[48] wrote Xenia to Queen Mary.

The Campbellville farm was sold in November to Wolfgang von Richthofen, a distant relative of the World War I flying ace, the Red Baron. Wolfgang agreed to assume the $6,000 mortgage, and offered $12,000 for the house.

Gisela von Richthofen and her husband remember keenly the first time they met "Mrs. Kulikovsky." On the drive out to the farm the agent had simply described the owners as an old Russian couple. After the trio toured the property, which Wolfgang noted was in "terrible shape," they approached the side door of the house and knocked. "A tall and bony woman appeared," recalls Gisela. "She had grey hair tucked back and wore slippers, just as you would imagine a Russian farmer's wife."

The friendly woman, whom they were soon introduced to as Mrs. Kulikovsky, welcomed them into the living room and went back into the kitchen to make them some tea. Along with the agent, the von Richthofens settled themselves into the spacious living room, and chatted. Soon, the woman reappeared bearing a tray of tea and cookies. After a half-hour or so of conversation, Gisela asked if she might use the washroom, which was located just off a corridor at the top of the staircase, and there she received a shock.

"In the upper corridor, a huge photo was hanging on the wall showing wounded soldiers in bed, Mrs. Kulikovsky in a nurse's attire, and Nicolas II beside her," remembers Gisela. "I said to myself, 'That must be the one that sits down there.'"

As she re-entered the living room, Gisela could not

disguise the look of surprise on her face from Wolfgang and quietly whispered in his ear her suspicions about the identity of the woman currently chatting with the agent. Less shy than his wife, Wolfgang promptly asked Olga who she was, and received confirmation that she was indeed none other than Grand Duchess Olga Alexandrovna, sister of Tsar Nicholas II.

"We never got over it," says Gisela. "She was the last thing on earth we thought we would find in a Canadian farm house."

Fortunately, just as the deal was finalized, Creighton found another home for Olga and Nicolai in Cooksville, Ontario, "not far from my boys," said Olga. Construction on the house would not be completed until April, meaning that Olga and Nicolai were temporarily homeless. The von Richthofens quickly came to the rescue, and invited the couple to remain in the Campbellville house until the other house was completed.

The two families kept as separate as possible, but the von Richthofens occasionally got a glimpse of Olga's selective squeamishness. One day Wolfgang noticed one of Nicolai's fine horses lying down on the cold winter ground in great distress from colic. Nevertheless, Nicolai and Olga delayed calling in a vet. "No one seemed to care," Wolfgang recalls.

A few days later the von Richthofens found a dead mouse in the kitchen, a sight that reduced Olga to tears. "She got hysterical. 'Oh, the poor little dead mouse. Oh, my little mouse,'" says Wolfgang. "That's very typical of Russians. They are very emotional about certain things; other things, no."

In January 1952, the Kulikovskys held a livestock sale, overseen by Tihon and Guri, but as a result of disorganization and poor planning, the sale went badly. The von Richthofens blamed the sons, whom they found "very strange. The boys were supposed to handle the paper work . . . but it was a hopeless task. They couldn't figure out which paper belonged to which cow. It was terrible!"[49]

At last the April morning arrived when Olga once again said goodbye to a home she had hoped would be her last. A rented truck was filled with the same canisters and trunks she had brought from Denmark. The elderly couple huddled close together in the cab of the truck as it pulled away, Mimka behind them in a car driven by Tihon.

CHAPTER TEN

COOKSVILLE

FTER TIHON AND GURI's fumbling of the auction of the Campbellville farm, Olga and Nicolai wound up with a fraction of the windfall they expected to receive from the sale of their machinery and livestock. Tired and somewhat dispirited, they moved into a five-room, one-and-a-half-storey home at 2130 Camilla Road in Cooksville, Ontario, less than half a mile from the Queen Elizabeth Highway, named after the daughter-in-law of the infamously frugal Queen Mary.

Generously described by Olga as "quite a little palace," the home was a glorified doll's house surrounded by two acres of uncultivated land. The claustrophobia of the living room was alleviated by a large bay window, along whose panes Olga placed Fabergé bottles, jars and figurines, many of which, with Olga's bemused indulgence, ended up being chipped and broken by neighbourhood children who used them as toys.

One object Olga did attempt to protect was a velvet-lined wooden box containing the silver chain, small scent bottle and other trinkets given to her by her niece Anastasia.

A bedroom and kitchen completed the rooms on the ground floor. Upstairs were two bedrooms, inhabited at various times throughout the 1950s by, among others, her sons Guri and Tihon, after their marriages collapsed, granddaughter Xenia, and Olga's faithful maid, Mimka.

By 1952, Nicolai, six feet two inches in his prime, had shrunk more than four inches due to the arthritic degeneration of his spinal discs. Rather than take prescription medications, which he distrusted, he began to toy with homeopathic remedies.

A.H. Creighton's son, Robert, who was in medical school at the time, recalls Nicolai asking about the merits of royal bee jelly, which was alleged to have healing properties. Both father and son felt Nicolai nurtured his pain in order to gain sympathy from his long-suffering wife. "My father rather considered him to be a malingerer," says Robert. "He was always very stern and never took part in festive occasions, preferring to sit in a corner and brood."[1]

Bolstering Robert Creighton's claim are photos of Nicolai at parties, wearing festive hats and a scowl. Decorative cards sent to the Creightons, hand-painted by Olga, expressed the Kulikovsky family's best wishes, but were always signed simply, "Olga."

Mary Turner, a childhood friend of Olga's granddaughter Xenia, recalls Lieutenant-Colonel Kulikovsky as a "forbidding character, almost scary."[2] One occasion, however, provided levity. The Lieutenant-Colonel habitually hung his leather coin pouch from the arm of his favourite rocking chair. One day, while he dozed, the two girls noticed that the pouch had a hole in it which grew bigger the more their fingers worked at it. Eventually, they succeeded in releasing several coins to the floor. Scooping them up, they hurried to the local sweet shop.

Within two months of moving to Cooksville, Mimka suffered a stroke, which left her blind and almost completely paralyzed. Despite the arthritis already attacking her joints, Olga threw herself into nursing her great friend and kindred spirit of over fifty years. Drawing on her strengths as a former nurse, Olga administered nightly sponge baths, murmured softly in Russian, and stroked the old woman's head. On the morning of January 24, 1954, eighty-seven-year-old Mimka died peacefully in her mistress's arms.

Mimka's death marked the first in a series of tragedies that marred the last half-decade of Olga's life. There were few people to whom Olga showed more physical tenderness than this selfless servant who, risking starvation and death, smuggled Olga's jewels out of the Sergievskaya Street house, thereby providing Olga with some of the money necessary to feed, clothe and care for not only herself but her family.

Mimka, who never married, remained in the shadows. Even Olga's first daughters-in-law recall very little of her, except that she always ironed shirts on time, made the family's beds, changed the grandchildren's diapers, and sewed torn hems.

To this day, Olga's granddaughter Xenia tears up when recalling the quiet self-sacrifices of Mimka, who provided not just the financial means by which the family survived, but her loving care. When Xenia was laid up in bed sick, it was Mimka who brought her medicine and laid cool cloths on her feverish forehead. In many ways, Mimka became Xenia's Nana Franklin.

Approaching a bookshelf in her home in Denmark, Xenia removes a jewellery box from a shelf, and withdraws from it a pretzel-shaped sapphire-and-diamond pin Mimka left her in a small white envelope on a bedside table just before she died. It was almost the old woman's only bequest, since she was too poor even to draft a will.

She was buried at York Cemetery on what felt like "the coldest day of the year,"[3] recalls Ruth, who was among the small group of mourners gathered at the grave. Today, virtually obscured by the deep shadows of a giant maple, lies Mimka's flat gravestone, a Russian cross and her date of death chiselled on its face. In death, as in life, she remains mere yards from her mistress's side.

Part of Olga's spirit died after the loss of Mimka. Her excursions into the outside world became less frequent, though certainly more bizarre. Emancipated from the strictures of wealth and its strict code of conduct, Olga indulged her natural eccentricity. When she and Nicolai dined out, her habit of requesting doggy bags for leftovers caused friction between the couple. "She didn't stop merely at doggy bags for her own food," says Xenia. "She would glance at other tables people had left and take that food too. My grandfather would practically deny he knew her."[4]

Nicolai's pain was particularly acute because his wife always remained for him that slightly unattainable silk-gowned figure, locking eyes with him at the military parade at Pavlovsk Palace, where they first fell in love. Her fall in status caused him to withdraw into himself. Whenever he picked up a paper, it contained some article, usually factually inaccurate, describing Olga as merely a "pig farmer," or "fallen Romanov princess."

Olga compensated for her losses by getting even with all the society matrons of questionable artistic sensibilities who paid enormous sums of money to acquire a former Grand Duchess's signature affixed to the bottom of what Olga made sure was second-rate art. "I'm off to paint some cabbage roses,"[5] she'd tell Xenia, as she slapped paint onto canvas in an indiscriminate manner.

Without Mimka, Olga settled into a daily routine. Before the first bird sang, she rose from bed, threw on an old housedress, and yanked on a pair of gumboots. In the kitchen she brewed tea you could stand on in the priceless silver samovar smuggled out of Russia among her mother's possessions. Breakfast was day-old toast, smothered in butter.

When she was finished, she assisted Nicolai out of bed and seated him beside his radio. How far away, yet inescapable, the past must have seemed in the quiet of her tiny home as she dusted furniture, including a sideboard that once belonged to her aunt, Queen Alexandra, and a portrait of Alexander III, sliced from its frame in the Alexander Palace by Felix Yusupov, one of the murders of Rasputin. If she ever grieved over what she had lost, she never showed it.

Cleaning was a job she approached with little enthusiasm and less skill. The hands that once bore diamonds and eyeball-sized rubies, developed calluses. Arthritis gnarled her knuckles. Feet that had once slipped effortlessly into satin shoes now swelled so badly she was forced to soak them every night in buckets of cool water. She gave up trying to wear nylons after a series of mishaps involving the garters sent them cascading to her knees. Efforts to tie the tops of the nylons in knots around her thighs cut off the circulation in her legs and whenever she tried to sit, witnesses would hear the most godawful pop.

While it was still dark, accompanied by her border collies, Tannhauser and Laddie, she toured Newland nursery, just across the gravel road from her home. Strolling alone along its winding paths, bordered on each side by a profusion of wisteria and white marguerites, she must have noted how strongly its lush greenery resembled that around some of the finest palaces of Europe, her former playgrounds.

In that brief interval of time before the curtain of night rose into day, Olga strolled with ghosts. In addition to her mother, father and two brothers, there were Sandro, George V, Grand Duke Ernst of Hesse-Darmstadst and Princess Beatrice (Baby Bee). Even Misha's son George was dead, killed in an automobile accident in 1931.

On February 6, 1952, Queen Mary's son King George VI was added to that list. Olga sent Mary a short letter of condolence, "With all my heart & soul I sympathize with you in this great sorrow—you have so much to bear, I know and I feel so with you. One can't find words at such times—but I love you and—well, that is all. God bless you dear, your beloved Olga."[6]

In spite of her pain, Olga was still capable of deriving devilish amusement from being around people who didn't have the slightest notion of who she was. In December 1952, she and Tihon, who was driving her into Toronto, stopped at the Cooksville post office to pick up a registered package from Queen Mary, containing a Christmas gift of a calendar filled with private family portraits of the British royal family.

When they emerged from the building, they noticed a

group of women shivering in the cold, waiting for a bus into the city. Olga invited three ("couldn't alas! take them all,"[7] she said) to ride into town with her and Tihon. Two of the women turned out to be British, and squealed with delight when Olga handed them a beautiful calendar, explaining that she had just received it from "a dear friend in England."[8]

Olga and Tihon smiled at each other when they heard oohs and aahs emanating from the women in the back seat who excitedly flipped through the calendar. Later Olga wrote to Queen Mary describing the encounter, "They love you all and were excited and pleased to see all your pictures. They didn't know *you* had sent them—but said, 'how lucky you are to have such a lovely calendar from England.'"[9]

Though Olga spent a lifetime trying to sublimate her imperial bearing, the monarch slumbering beneath the mask of humility could unexpectedly be roused. When a friend once interpreted the Bible as saying that at the end of time, kings and queens would be viewed on the same level as commoners, Olga slammed her hand against the dining-room table, and stomped out of the room. Moments later, she recovered her composure and conceded that the Bible was probably right.[10]

On another occasion, when a neighbourhood child ran up and asked, "Are you really and truly a princess?" Olga replied with only the faintest bit of haughtiness, "I am most certainly not a princess, I am a Russian Grand Duchess."[11]

On March 24, 1953, eighty-five-year-old Queen Mary died in the comfort of Marlborough House, with several servants and family members by her side. Olga did not waste time indulging in bitterness, regret or recriminations. Nevertheless, one can only imagine how galling it must have been in the coming years to see photographs showing her mother's finest gems fastened around the hands and necks or propped atop the heads of Mary's relations, including Queen Elizabeth II, Princess Margaret and Princess Marina of Kent.

As THE FIFTIES SLIPPED BY, the Kulikovskys lived very quietly on Camilla Road. Sunny days found Olga digging vigorously with bare fingers through the soil of her garden. Children waved at her as they rode by on their bikes, unaware of her illustrious past.

Now and then she invited children in to eat cookies she'd baked. At this time, baking was an anomaly for her. More typically she and her husband were reduced to eating fruits and vegetables out of cans.

Crumbs were not wasted, but scattered across the front lawn of the property, along with saucers of milk. "My uncle, a veterinarian, sent me out to speak to her about all the cats those saucers of milk attracted," says William Pinkney, a teenager at the time he met the Grand Duchess. "She met me at the door categorically refusing to stop feeding the cats, saying 'there's always room for one more.'"[12]

Eventually Pinkney began to visit Olga on a regular basis. His impression of her remains vivid: "She had an awesome demeanour, which was instantly intimidating; she once told me that she wished she'd come to Canada earlier because it was so much like Russia."[13] Pinkney believes she had a soft spot for the dispossessed because she had been driven from so many homes.

The bargain basement cafeteria in Eaton's department

store played host to Olga whenever she craved bacon and eggs. Shoppers did not even glance at the plainly dressed former Grand Duchess as she perched on a swivel seat before a U-shaped counter.

Once or twice a week, she carried a fishnet bag to a small market on Lake Shore Boulevard, where she patiently waited in line at the meat counter as her butcher, Mr. Shaw, wrapped her selection. Joining her on these trips might be any one of a number of local admirers whose fan letters intermingled in her letter box with those from Buckingham Palace and from other members of the extended royal families of Europe. "She answered every letter she received, even from strangers," remembers Xenia. "Some of the greedy ones couldn't believe that she didn't have money."[14]

One of these fans was Ed Ewing, who was a twenty-one-year-old amateur genealogist living in Hamilton when he summoned the courage to telephone Olga. Shortly afterwards, he found himself at her front door, holding a hand that had a "terrific grip" for an old woman. Her kitchen was in a state of "benevolent chaos."[15] Making no distinction between Ewing and royalty, she gave him a tour of the house, pointing out in particular the precious round occasional table, consisting of inlaid granite pebbles personally collected from a beach by her father, Alexander III.

Ewing was startled during his first visit when he was invited to share tea with Olga's family members and friends, including Captain Konstantin Martemianoff, the Russian émigré and member of her father's Horse Guard. Martemianoff had introduced himself to Olga in church, and with his family thereafter devoted their lives to her service.

At least twice a month, Olga visited the Martemianoffs'

home for hearty Russian dinners, where she happily peeled potatoes beside the kitchen sink, chattering in Russian to Konstantin's wife, Sinaida, as the latter stirred simmering pots of stew.

In 1954, the residents of Camilla Road experienced a flurry of excitement when Princess Marina of Kent, the widow of the Duke of Kent, visited her cousin Olga. "Our parents told us to buy new dresses,"[16] Mary Turner says of her playmates in the neighbourhood.

The gravel road that led north from the Queen Elizabeth Highway to Olga's home was paved especially for the occasion—but just as far north as Olga's home, where it again petered out into gravel. Murmuring excitedly, the neighbours watched the black limousine slowly pull up in front of the plain brick house. They applauded softly as the elegant woman wearing a black and white polka-dot dress, with a red cashmere sweater draped across her shoulders, stepped out of the car.

A reception line greeted Princess Marina on the front lawn: Olga and Nicolai and their two sons, accompanied by their wives, all meticulously dressed. The two daughters-in-law were particularly concerned with one-upping each other in the clothing department, with Agnete claiming victory. "If you look at Ruth's face, you'll see how miserable she was that I looked so much better than she did,"[17] she says today.

Marina and Olga embraced warmly and kissed each other's cheeks. Afterwards, with her high heels sinking into the soft earth of the front lawn, Marina walked arm in arm with Olga into the house, where they drank tea, ate store-bought cookies and spoke for more than half an hour.

Princess Marina, who was staying at the Royal York

Hotel, complained of sleep deprivation due to the loud rumble of trains close by at Union Station. Later the two women strolled down to the banks of the creek behind Olga's house and stood talking a while longer, while six bodyguards hovered nearby, trying to look inconspicuous.

Out of respect for Olga, the neighbours hung back and made as little noise as possible. As Princess Marina returned to her limousine at the conclusion of the visit, a neighbour's daughter ran up and presented her with a basket of freshly picked peaches. A news photographer's camera flashed just as the Princess leaned down to accept the basket, exposing more royal assets then she had intended.

Olga continued to attract an eclectic assortment of friends. One of the best known and by far the most unorthodox was James Rattray, a wily millionaire mining prospector, who owned an enormous estate named Barrymede on the outskirts of Mississauga. On the surface, Rattray was an upper-class bohemian, but his roots were buried deep in conservative Scots Presbyterian soil.

Rattray had a passion for creative people of all types, including artists and writers who visited his mansion to ride horses from his small stable, or play on the property's miniature golf course. Dozens of neighbourhood children were invited each year to participate in elaborate Easter-egg hunts. Each summer, Rattray hosted a horse-jumping competition, where Olga was given the honour of bestowing ribbons and silver dollars to the winners.

Olga, who preferred travelling the ten miles to Rattray's house on foot, painted nature scenes from her favourite location—a vinyl car seat that had been dumped amid the tall grass in one of the estate's fields. "She always wore very cheap clothes, usually housedresses and open-toed sandals," says Marjorie Wooten, Rattray's niece. "Her face was extremely weather-beaten, but she had a beautiful smile."[18] Rattray was a great fan of Olga's work, and hung dozens of her watercolours on the bedroom walls of his home.

Pat Moore, a neighbour of Rattray's, was impressed by Olga's friendly manner and "incredibly kind" eyes, which she describes as being filled with "humour and vivaciousness." She recalls, "My son was outside playing and I called him inside to introduce him to Olga. I could have died when I noticed he had sand caked all over his hands. Olga took both his hands in hers, leaned forward, and said, 'Oh, I have little boys who have dirty hands too.'"[19]

Now an attractive young woman, Olga's granddaughter Xenia was invited each summer to Deepwater, Rattray's summer camp situated on the Lake of Bays in northern Ontario, where she swam and rode horses. Barely into her teens, Xenia was already considered a beauty, possessing her father's high colour and her mother's dark hair and eyes.

At the same time that Olga visited the estate, the newly released movie *Anastasia,* starring Ingrid Bergman, was playing in theatres. Curious guests couldn't help but ask Olga what she thought of the film, and of the woman in Germany who still claimed in newspaper articles to be Anastasia.

Olga's reply was adamant, "I think [the film] was well done and quite exciting, but the whole thing is so foolish . . . [It] is the ghost of the unhappy Anastasia that is still around. I have said once and for all that it is a scam. I don't know who is behind that unfortunate person, but she is not Anastasia. The real one was killed together with the others, about that there is no doubt."[20]

Olga was also unsparingly tough about Herluf Zahle's participation in the controversy. She said, "I do think that the Danish minister, the chamberlain Zahle in Berlin, unwittingly became the cause of all the fuss. He believed her and championed her cause, which he should never have done. But with this wind in her sails, she took off, the poor woman.

"I had to go to Berlin myself, of course, and that only seven years after the real Anastasia had been killed; I have never doubted that it was a scam . . . Anastasia will continue to haunt, as long as this unhappy person in Germany is alive; I cannot do any more than I have done to dispel all these fantastic notions."[21]

These were bold words, but somewhat disingenuous on their face. For one thing, Olga did not "have" to go to Berlin to identify the claimant; rather she chose to go, over the strenuous objections of her family. Second, her assertion of "never doubting" that the claimant was not Anastasia can at least be questioned in light of the abundance of gifts she bestowed on the patient shortly after visiting with her in the German hospital.

And there was a third question mark in the air. Marjorie Wooten, James Rattray's niece, recalls questioning Olga in private about the true identity of Mrs. Tschaikovsky. Seated in the screened veranda, beneath the fading light of a summer's evening, Olga admitted to Wooten that she had indeed recognized Mrs. Tschaikovsky as Anastasia, because Tschaikovsky knew the pet name for her dog. "Why did you change your story?" Wooton asked her.

With this, Olga shook her head, sighed, and replied almost inaudibly, "Family pressure."[22]

If Olga's recognition of Mrs. Tschaikovsky's identity was contradictory, her prediction that Anastasia would "continue to haunt as long as this unhappy person in Germany is alive" proved correct. Mere months after her assertions that there was nothing more she could do to dispel all the "fantastic" notions surrounding the true identity of Mrs. Tschaikovsky, Olga was called upon to give a deposition in Toronto concerning the true identity of Mrs. Tschaikovsky. Her appearance was precipitated by a lawsuit in Germany concerning the rights to the inheritance of what Mrs. Tschaikovsky described as "a vast Romanov fortune" in the Bank of England.

*I*N 1933, OLGA, XENIA, Michael's wife Natasha, the Grand Duke of Hesse and Empress Alexandra's sisters Irene and Victoria asked the Central District Court in Berlin to rule that all of Nicholas II's children were dead, and that they be recognized as the collateral heirs to any possible Romanov money in German banks.

In 1938, the Berlin Court issued a Certificate of Inheritance to all the named parties. Soon after, the Mendelssohn Bank in Berlin paid out three hundred thousand marks (about six thousand Canadian dollars, the balance of the Romanov money) to the named beneficiaries.

As soon as they had paid out the balance of the account, authorities within the Mendelssohn Bank, for unknown reasons, took it upon themselves to inform Mrs. Tschaikovsky, whom they referred to as "Imperial Highness" of the withdrawal of the money, and to advise her "to protect herself by demanding the withdrawal of the Certificate of Inheritance." It was the beginning of a colossal legal battle that would span several decades.[23]

In August of 1938, Mrs. Tschaikovsky lodged in Berlin a Petition for the Revocation of the Certificate of Inheritance. Though that initial petition was ultimately denied, Tschaikovsky filed numerous appeals.

Disbelieving Sandro's contention that "Beginning with the summer of 1915, there was not a farthing left in the Tsar's name in the Bank of England, nor any other bank outside Russia,"[24] Tschaikovsky insisted that relatives of the Tsar's daughter, particularly Grand Duchesses Olga and Xenia, had wrongfully denied her identity and prevented her from acquiring the money her father, Nicholas, had deposited for her in foreign banks, especially in England.

Numerous investigations into the holdings in the Bank of England failed to yield any evidence of assets belonging to Nicholas. Several witnesses present during Nicholas's reign agreed that during the First World War, he liquidated most of his personal funds in England to subsidize the purchase of munitions for the Russian army. This was also Olga's and her sister Xenia's understanding.

Sir Edward Peacock also tried to put out the fire started by the rumour of tsarist money existing in the Bank of England. "I am pretty sure that there was never any money of the Imperial Family of Russia in the Bank of England, nor in any other bank in England," he told biographer Ian Vorres for Vorres's book, *The Last Grand Duchess*, adding, "Of course it is difficult to say 'never,' but I am positive at least there was never any money after World War I and during my long years as director of the Bank."[25]

By 1958, most of the recipients of the three hundred thousand marks released to the Romanov beneficiaries in 1938 were dead, including Michael's wife, Natasha, Grand Duke Ernst of Hesse and Princess Irene, Alexandra's sister. Olga's sister, Xenia, had not even bothered to pick up her share of the money, nullifying any question of wanton greed on her part.

Nevertheless, Mrs. Tschaikovsky, having failed repeatedly in the German courts to achieve recognition as Anastasia, remained determined to obtain her share of the bank's payment to the beneficiaries, this time with interest. In order to do so, Tschaikovsky accused a relative of the Tsar's daughter of "wrongfully denying her identity and spending her money."[26] The target of the accusation was Barbara of Prussia, or Duchess Christian Louis of Mecklenburg, the granddaughter of the deceased Princess Irene. Duchess Barbara had received through her grandmother a portion of the money paid out by the Mendelssohn Bank.

Another recipient of some money, the late Grand Duke Ernst of Hesse's son, Prince Louis of Hesse, soon became Duchess Barbara's co-defendant. The only reason Olga and Xenia were not included as co-defendants at this late date was that they lived outside the jurisdiction of the Hamburg Court, where the case was heard, and where Tschaikovsky was a citizen. This did not, however, prevent them from being questioned as witnesses.

Gunther von Berenberg Gossler, the attorney for Barbara of Prussia, believes Tschaikovsky, rather than being what he called a "common swindler," suffered from a psychopathological condition known as auto-suggestion, in which an individual, confronted with clues to her identity from outsiders, represses facts about her own past in favour of experiences she has heard from other sources. In a conversation with Michael Thornton, a journalist who held power of attorney for Tschaikovsky in England, Gossler admitted, "Tschaikovsky will win you over because she has astonishing suggestive power."[27]

Eventually the German court's tendrils reached Olga, the only person, aside from Herluf Zahle, alleged to have heard from Mrs. Tschaikovsky's own lips the unproved story of a vast fortune existing in either the Bank of England or a bank in England.

Mrs. Tschaikovsky was adamant that she had only mentioned "the subject of the Tsar's money" with Olga at the Mommsen clinic in 1925 because she thought she had only hours to live. Later she suspected that Olga and Xenia used the information against her in an effort to do everything possible to block her chances of gaining recognition as Anastasia.

Gleb Botkin, the son of the imperial physician Evgeny Botkin, who became an ally of Mrs. Tschaikovsky, went so far as to refer to Olga and Xenia as the "two greedy aunts" who attempted to "attain the Tsar's fortune for themselves."[28]

Despite decades-long protestations to the contrary, one fact became certain, that there was simply no money to be had. Olga effectively argued, "Would my mother have accepted a pension from King George V if we had any money in England? It does not make sense."[29]

The question then remained of where the money had gone. Tschaikovsky's attorney, Edward Fallows, finally concluded that any Romanov money left in British banks was probably used to subsidize the capitalization of the

Anglo-International Bank, the Bank of England's largest subsidiary, of which Peter Bark was the President." Fallows further concluded that the Romanov family had been "duped," by Bark, "just as surely as Anastasia had."[30]

Despite the obstacles in her way, Mrs. Tschaikovsky never stopped trying to establish her identity as Anastasia. To the credit of her loyal allies, who sacrificed their health, fortunes and reputations to defend her, the quest ultimately became more one of principle than of money.

In March of 1959, the German court hearing Mrs. Tschaikovsky's claims for recognition would summon Olga to a judge's chambers in Toronto to give a formal deposition describing exactly what had occurred in that German hospital room so many years before, and to provide her official opinion concerning the true identity of Mrs. Tschaikovsky. With great reluctance, the aged and ailing Olga finally appeared.

For someone who had spent two-thirds of her life trying to escape the past, it was about to catch up with her with a vengeance, making her sometimes contradictory behaviour toward Tschaikovsky a matter of public record. Her testimony would be one of the last official acts of her life, and the stress implicit in it would almost kill her.

CHAPTER ELEVEN

BROKEN THREADS

OLGA HAD TWICE ESCAPED assassination, first by a nurse at the army hospital in Kiev, then by the Yalta Soviets at Ay-Todor. As the sister of a vanquished monarch, she had been forced into a nomadic existence, never to return to her beloved Russia. At seventy-two years of age, she was still stirred awake by the ghostly hands of her murdered siblings, Nicholas and Michael, and especially by her favourite niece Anastasia, whose imposters continued to show up on her doorstep, or write letters demanding money from their "aunt." In the end, though, her most devastating sadness arose from the marital woes and financial worries of her two sons, Tihon and Guri.

Of all the Kulikovskys, Olga worked hardest to keep the family together. Her efforts would be sorely tested by two events that occurred in the mid-1950s: Tihon's and Guri's divorces from their respective wives, Agnete and Ruth.

In the early fifties, Princess Xenia, the granddaughter of

Olga's sister, Xenia, travelled from England to Canada to visit following the breakup of her marriage. She lived for a time at Olga's house. For Tihon, bored with the routine of married life with a working-class girl, Agnete, Xenia represented his return to aristocratic respectability. A courtship soon commenced.

When Xenia moved to California, Tihon followed. Upon his return from one of these trips, the man who had wept when Agnete initially refused his marriage proposal thirteen years before, and who had professed to love her "more than he did his own mother," coldly informed her that he had fallen in love with another woman. "We would never have divorced if [Xenia] hadn't met Tihon. We had a good life,"[1] Agnete says in retrospect.

After Tihon broke the news, the depression that had gripped so many previous members of her family began to drag Agnete down. She yearned for Denmark and took a trip there and then to Brazil in 1954. While she was away, Tihon moved out of the home the couple had shared on Haig Boulevard and into his parents' home.

While in Brazil, Agnete fell in love with a man named Wilfred Diestal who accompanied her back to Canada and took up residence in the Haig Boulevard house. It was there on August 27, 1956 that she was served with divorce papers, accusing her of adultery, despite the fact that it had been Tihon who had fallen in love first.

Without her husband's income, Agnete was forced to look for work. With virtually no skills or education, she took a part-time job selling shoes at Simpson's department store. A short stint as a model for Creeds furriers ended abruptly when she encountered romantic problems with a member of the management team. When the relationship with Diestal failed, she sold the house and, with Tihon's permission, kept the profits.

This time she had to relocate alone. Thirty-seven and childless, she moved into an apartment in the west end of Toronto, finding work as a waitress in an all-night restaurant. It was hot, demanding work, brutal on the feet, and despite the fact she appreciated being able to come and go according to her own hours, she lapsed into near-suicidal depressions.

When the marriage ended, so did her relationship with Olga. "She cut me off just like that," she says. "She adored Tihon, though, and went along with almost any decision he chose to make."[2]

Today Agnete lives in a Danish retirement home near Guelph, Ontario, with her second husband, Egon, and still laments the past: "I married into one of the wealthiest most influential families in the world, and look where I am now,"[3] she says, gesturing toward the trailer homes that dot the property.

In addition to the profits from the sale of the house, she took with her from the marriage items of jewellery her mother-in-law had given her. One of those items was a slightly damaged Fabergé pearl-and-diamond-studded umbrella handle which she tried to sell to Dr. Morton Shulman, a wealthy Canadian author, television personality and Romanov-phile. Shulman, she says, promised to pay her $2,000 for the piece sight unseen over the phone, but after viewing it, halved the price. "He had broken my dream,"[4] she says. Shulman denies the accusation. "I made a bid of seven-hundred dollars for the handle, sight unseen, through my New York agent, but did not buy it," he says, insisting that it "subsequently sold to someone else for $10,000."[5]

Tihon's fortunes didn't fare much better than his ex-wife's after the end of their marriage. Shortly after he had moved out of the couple's home in 1954, he proposed to Princess Xenia. Olga, preoccupied with the declining health of her husband, saw the impending marriage as a hopeful sign for the future. She was stunned, therefore, when Xenia rejected Tihon two days before the scheduled nuptials. The reason could not have been more pedestrian. Xenia, it seems, did not wish to move from California to Toronto, while Tihon did not want to move from Toronto to California.

A barometer of Olga's frustrations at what she viewed as superficial North American mores are contained in a letter she wrote around that time to a friend in Denmark. "Imagine, my son didn't get married," she wrote. "He flew to the USA California in November for his wedding. Everything had been said and [he] was very happy. So the day before she said No. And now he is here again. [It] was such a shock for the three of us. Now, thank God, he is happy again. The women are strange. Most of them don't know what they want themselves. This one said that Tihon was too good for her (that is true too)."[6]

Devastated, Tihon was forced to sell a house he had already bought for his prospective bride and to remain in one of the upstairs bedrooms of the cramped Camilla Road home. Across the hall was the bedroom of his niece, Xenia. She had moved there once her father and mother began experiencing problems of their own. Once again, Olga had become the family's rock. Like his father, Tihon retreated into himself. He went to work, came home, cut the lawn, did odd chores for his parents, but otherwise withdrew into deep despondency. "He used to sit on his bed by the hour, with those miniature soldiers of his,"[7] says Xenia, referring to the three-quarter-of-an-inch-high lead soldiers painted by Tihon in the exact likeness of great figures from history, including his own uncle, Nicholas II, on horseback.

The collapse of Tihon's marriage to Agnete was followed almost simultaneously by the dissolution of Guri's marriage to Ruth, the shy former shopgirl. Once the picture of happy domestic bliss, the couple broke up when Guri fell in love with an attractive redhead named Asa Lefebvre, who, by an unfortunate happenstance, was Ruth's hairdresser.

In April 1956, Ruth visited Denmark. During her absence, Guri wrote to tell her that he did not wish her to come back, as he might "do without [her]."[8] The day after Ruth returned home, Guri packed his bags and said he was leaving her to live at an undisclosed location with Asa. Asa, a married woman, left her husband at the same time.

The divorce settlement filed by Ruth entitled her to the proceeds from the sale of her and Guri's home, also on Haig Boulevard, plus a portion of the profits from the sale of two apartment buildings on Lake Shore Boulevard in Toronto that Guri co-owned with his mother and brother.

Guri agreed to pay for the Danish boarding-school education of the two boys, which he was not able to sustain for more than two months since he was temporarily unemployed. Ruth was also allowed to keep all the jewellery given to her by her mother-in-law, a not inconsiderable amount.

In the end, Ruth was granted custody of the three children and returned to Denmark with Leonid and Alexander.

Xenia, now sixteen, asked if she could stay and finish school in Canada. It was decided that she would live permanently with her grandmother Olga in the home on Camilla Road.

As the divorce dragged on, the court assigned investigators from the Children's Aid Society to assess the suitability of the former Grand Duchess and her husband as surrogate parents. It seems incredible that the child Olga had given birth to just prior to her perilous escape from Russia returned the favour by expecting his elderly mother to care for a daughter he abandoned just when she needed him most. Court records indicate that Guri visited Xenia only twice in the period of a year.

In its final report the court described Xenia as a "healthy, most attractive and impatient young woman who has given her future plans considerable thought."[9] At the time her parents separated, she was an honour student and a first-rate basketball player. Under the guidance of her grandmother, she drew "excellent figures." Thanks to both her grandparents, the atmosphere of the Camilla Road house was described as one of "great warmth and love."[10] Perfunctorily dismissing the rather extraordinary revelation that Olga was "the daughter of Alexander III, the Tsar of Russia," the Children's Aid Society chose to concentrate on Olga's "strengths" as a "most active and vivacious person, keenly interested in art." Nicolai was described as merely a "retired farmer." The report concluded that despite their advanced years, the couple possessed "a great deal of stamina and foresight."[11] They would need it for the road ahead.

*above: Olga painting
nature scenes with her
canine friend in
Denmark (1930s).*
(Photo: Ballerup
Engmuseum)

*right: Mrs. Tschaikovsky
a.k.a. "Miss Unknown"
later known as
Anna Anderson.*

At Knudsminde, saying farewell to Denmark, May 1948.
(Photo: Agnete (Kulikovsky) Petersen)

left: Olga, wearing ten-pound diamond necklace, circa 1906

below: Living in relative poverty in Cooksville, circa 1954.
(Photo: Galina Martenianoff)

above: Campbellville farmhouse, Canada. (author photo)

below: Cooksville house, Canada. Olga's last home. (author photo)

Princess Marina of Kent assists Olga down the steps of the Cooksville house, Tihon and Agnete in background (1954).

above: An ailing Nicolai is visited by his doctor in the Cooksville house, as a wistful Olga looks on. (Photo: Galina Martemianoff)

below: James Rattray watches Olga paint perched atop a discarded car seat (Canada). (Photo: Mary Lou Burton)

above: (top left) The Martemianoffs' Gerrard Street apartment, where Olga died. (author photo)

below: A long journey from Gatchina Palace—the room where Olga died, 1960. Note Fabergé dog and photo of Nicolai on table. (Photo: Galina Martemianoff)

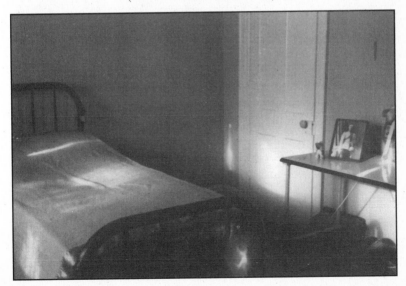

The three angels of Olga's last days: (above left) Captain Konstantin Martemianoff, (above right) Sinaida Martemianoff, (below) Galina Martemianoff. (Photos: Galina Martemianoff)

UPON RETURNING TO DENMARK, Ruth opened a wine and tobacco shop, and like her former sister-in-law Agnete, supplemented her living by selling some of the pieces of jewellery given to her by her former mother-in-law. A boyfriend who jilted her made off with some pieces, including a ruby necklace worth several thousands of dollars. Because Ruth's business acumen was unsophisticated, the remaining pieces sold for a song.

Once Guri and Ruth's divorce was declared final, Olga grew depressed at the estrangement from her grandchildren, whom she adored. "It is a sad story that my son Guri has suddenly left his family. We are very distraught and grieving about it. Now we never see them anymore,"[12] she wrote.

Indeed, Olga would never see grandson Alexander (Ruth and Guri's youngest son) again, though she and Leonid (the couple's second son) continued to write letters to each other and he returned to live with her in 1958.

Olga lamented to a friend that for a year or two, the only way she got news about her grandsons was through magazine articles about Ruth and the children published in Denmark. "So, you saw the big Leonid with his mother and little brother in the magazine. . . . [N]obody has thought of sending me pictures from the magazine, and I want so much to see them."[13]

By the late 1950s, Xenia had blossomed into a stunningly beautiful Ava Gardner lookalike, much sought after by members of the opposite sex. In the evenings she and her grandmother listened to radio shows, played cards, or read Frank Slaughter and A. J. Cronin novels. "Our temperaments were very alike,"[14] says Xenia, who admits that her grandparents discussed sexual matters with her in a frank and forthright manner. Nicolai, who had waited so long to marry the unattainable Olga, even advised Xenia to emulate her grandmother by considering herself "like a Cadillac—hard to get."

Although she tried to conform to the sedate pace of her grandmother's house, Xenia was overwhelmed by adolescent restlessness. Her unhappiness was most certainly exacerbated by what she perceived as abandonment by her parents. Her father, then working as a translator five hundred miles away at Carleton University in Ottawa, continued to ignore her. After completing high school, she enrolled in the furniture and interior design program at Ryerson Institute of Technology, but quit when she discovered she had no talent for woodworking. Eventually, she quit school altogether, and when not modelling her spectacular figure in Philips stereo ads, demonstrated kitchen appliances at Eaton's. Friends recall her as beautiful, if a little egotistical, and passionate about small sports cars. "I was a menace behind the wheel,"[15] she laughs.

Leonid moved back to Canada in 1958, and he and Xenia terrorized their grandparents as only teenagers can: Leonid zooming around on a motorcycle; Xenia staying out late with boys. By this time, Olga's arthritis pained her so severely that she could barely lift her arms above her head to fix her hair. Medications she took did little to reduce swelling. Meanwhile Nicolai's infirmity worsened almost daily.

Olga's publicly sunny disposition differed markedly from the one she revealed in letters to friends. "Pussi [Xenia's nickname] and Leonid are absolutely no help," she complained in one. "They are both so preoccupied by their own lives that they think I can manage on my own without help from them. That's what young people are like here."[16]

In a letter from Hampton Court, Xenia commiserated with her sister's plight, "Pussi's unbelievable selfishness is really too much . . . [a] good spanking is what she needs, she used to be so nice to you and you enjoyed having her—you said she helped keeping the rooms clean and with the washing up, etc. . . . a great mistake as well that the children are left to have their own way and their betters elders are reduced to silence." In a reference to what must have been Pussi's racy reading material of the time, Xenia wrote in the same letter, "those beastly sex magazines ought to be forbidden by law, why doesn't the church protest?"[17]

By 1958, NICOLAI'S SPINAL problems had drastically worsened. Pictures from this period show Olga trying to avert her eyes from the emaciated figure of her husband slumped hollow-eyed in his easy chair. During the last weeks of his life, he slept fitfully on the living-room sofa, not wishing to wake his wife by tossing and turning.

On August 11, 1958, out of instinct, Olga rose in the middle of the night to see if her husband needed anything. "I found him awake and he smiled at me. When I got up in the morning, I found him gone. In a way it was such a relief to have him spared all further suffering."[18]

Despite being raised in one of the most aristocratic

families in Russia, the man who captivated the ladies as a charismatic blue-eyed "God Apollo" on horseback owned pathetically few possessions upon his death. Under the General Description of Property section of his will is listed $6,633 (money secured by mortgage); $3,850 cash in the bank; a $1,495 Ford automobile; $120 in household goods and furniture; and $25.47 in clothing and jewellery—a total estate worth $12,123.47.

Olga and Nicolai's love story survived a revolution, two world wars and exile. They were married more than four decades, traversed three continents, raised two children, and ultimately lived only for each other.

With Nicolai's death, Olga lost her most compelling reason for living. "When my father-in-law died suddenly, Mama [Olga] all at once lost some of her sparkling charm and her indomitable spirits," says Ruth. "But [Nicolai] was still close to her. 'I feel as if he is with me here in my living room still,' she wrote to me in a letter before she grew so weak and feeble that she could no longer write."[19]

Tihon attempted to compensate for his father's absence. After work, he mowed the lawn and each Sunday faithfully drove Olga to church. Eventually he rebounded from his former bride-to-be's rejection of him by falling in love with a Hungarian woman named Livia Sebesteyn, whom he met at a "When in Rome, do as the Romans do" toga theme party he threw at his Mississauga home in the spring of 1958. The couple seemed perfectly matched, each of them having lost family members and property to the Communists who swept through Eastern Europe.

Neighbours recall that Olga spent increasingly less time outside the house and when she did, she was "hobbled with a big third leg," as she called the cane she leaned on because of her worsening arthritis.

O N MARCH 23, 1959, a reluctant and ailing Olga was summoned to the German consulate in downtown Toronto to give the deposition she had so long been dreading in the false Anastasia case, which had already become the longest running case in the history of the German courts. Every possible effort was made to make Olga comfortable. Her testimony was heard *in camera* in a judge's chambers.

Two attorneys took turns asking Olga to recount her experiences with Mrs. Tschaikovsky, beginning in 1925. A visibly irritated Olga initially refused, whereupon the atmosphere in the room became as chilly as the air outside. When she finally relented, Olga proved herself to be a less than malleable witness. She described Tschaikovsky as not a "crazy" woman, but one "affected by an obsession" and blamed Ambassador Zahle for attempting to unfairly influence Olga to look favourably upon the claimant. "When I met with the envoy [Zahle] in Berlin I found out that the latter had already been dealing with the clearing up of the identity of the plaintiff for some time and that he took great interest in this matter,"[20] she said.

Olga claimed that she knew Tschaikovsky was not Anastasia immediately upon entering the hospital room with Ambassador Zahle, unwittingly lending credence to Zahle's suspicions that she might have made up her mind to dismiss the claimant even before seeing her. Olga cited the shape of Tschaikovsky's nose, the broadness of her forehead, the position of her eyebrows, her large mouth compared with Anastasia's small one and the tone of the claimant's voice as reasons for denying her authenticity. Olga also pointed out that Anastasia was capable of running her tongue into her nostrils,[21] though it will remain a mystery whether she ever asked the claimant to demonstrate this unusual feat.

When Olga showed Tschaikovsky a photograph of the real Anastasia's massage therapist (Anastasia suffered back damage in her teens which required two years of treatment), the claimant failed to recognize her, providing Olga with even more ammunition in her testimony to the court. Tschaikovsky also failed to recognize Nicolai, of whom Olga claimed the real Anastasia had been, she said, "especially fond."[22]

According to Olga, immediately after her first visit, she informed Zahle that she categorically dismissed the claimant's authenticity and wished to return home to Denmark, whereupon Zahle pressed her to stay, arguing that several visits would be necessary in order for her to render a fair judgement. Olga's statements regarding Zahle's tenacity on behalf of Tschaikovsky are consistent with Zahle's own words in a letter he wrote shortly before Olga's visit, in which stated unequivocally, "I shall do everything possible to see that the Grand Duchess' visit lasts until she in my opinion has been able to form a true picture."[23]

Though years later Olga would condemn Zahle's strong-arm tactics, her negative feelings about him were not evident in an October 31, 1925 letter she wrote to him in which she not only expressed her and her husband's "warmest thanks" for Zahle's hospitality, but added that "there are still many strange and inexplicable facts not cleared up."[24] This simple phrasing would haunt Olga for the rest of her life. Under questioning by the Hamburg court in 1959, she attempted to deny being the author of the letter at all, referring to it as one that "I was *supposed* to have written to Ambassador Zahle." Later, she tried to justify her seemingly inconsistent statements by stating testily, "*If* I wrote this letter, then I can say no more today why I used these words, as it was in my opinion certain that the person I had visited [was] not Anastasia."[25]

The most blatant inconsistencies, however, lay in the highly personal letters and gifts that Olga sent to the claimant months after her visit. Instead of admitting that she continued to be conflicted about the claimant's identity, Olga blamed Zahle for initiating the letter-writing campaign, explaining, "I remained in *loose* contact with the patient for a short period of time because I considered her a sick person and I wanted to act friendly towards her."[26]

Most importantly, in her 1959 testimony Olga implied that she was highly insulted by the insinuation that she discussed financial matters with the claimant, including any conversations about any Romanov fortune existing in the Bank of England. She also dismissed any suggestion that at the conclusion of her visit, Tschaikovsky rose up and kissed her hand, explaining that "it was not the custom at the court of the tsar that the daughters of the tsar kissed their aunt's hands; not even that of their grandmother."[27]

As the afternoon dragged on, Olga's responses to questions became increasingly "curt and evasive."[28] When one of the attorneys asked her if she had ever discussed Mrs. Tschaikovsky's case with her mother, Empress Marie, Olga snapped tensely, "In our family, it was not customary to discuss things all that much."[29]

Without counsel to protect her, Olga eventually grew alarmed that she was being trapped into answering questions she did not properly understand.[30] Wolfgang von Richthofen recalls finding out that near the end of her testimony, in which she repeatedly denied ever recognizing Tschaikovsky as her niece, Olga suddenly became so completely hysterical that a doctor had to be summoned to the premises.[31]

Rising painfully to her feet, Olga refused to answer any more questions and, despite the pleas of the German Consul, stormed out of the room where she had the even more unhappy experience of running straight into a woman from Illinois also claiming to be Grand Duchess Anastasia. "Aunt Olga! Dear Aunt Olga. . . . At last . . . "[32] the woman cried out upon seeing her "dear aunt." Without even glancing at the woman, Olga fled the building and climbed into a taxi, which carried her back to her small sanctuary on Camilla Road.

Several Canadian newspapers took note of Olga's visit to the consulate. One headline screamed: "Czar's Kin 'Joke' Woman Here Says." Unaware that the case involving the recognition of Tschaikovsky as Anastasia would drag on in the court of public opinion until definitive DNA tests could be completed in 1994, reporters optimistically concluded in 1959 that, "It is Mrs. Kulikovsky's testimony that should close the bizarre mystery."[33]

The average beat reporter could not have been expected to understand the labyrinthine twists and turns the Tschaikovsky case had already taken, due in part to Olga's contradictory actions and statements over the years, including the one Harriet Rathlef-Keilmann said Olga made in 1925, in which she said that prior to her visit to the German asylum, she had received a telegram from her sister, Xenia, forbidding her to recognize Tschaikovsky as Anastasia.

Around the same time that Olga gave her deposition in Canada, a British writer visited Grand Duchess Xenia in England to ask about her feelings concerning the Tschaikovsky affair and to investigate Rathlef-Keilmann's claim that Olga said Xenia had sent a telegram.

According to Michael Thornton, the writer who met with Xenia, despite her "extreme frailty, Xenia had a sharp and clear memory"[34] of events preceding Olga's visits to Tschaikovsky and emphatically denied ever sending a telegram to Olga concerning Tschaikovsky. Instead, she told Thornton she blamed Gleb Botkin (the son of the imperial physician who died with the imperial family):

> Botkin said the most terrible lies about my sister and me. According to Botkin, I was supposed to have sent Olga a telegram saying, 'On no account recognize Anastasia.' That was a fantasy. I never sent any telegrams, or gave my sister any advice about her visit to Berlin. We were all apprehensive about the wisdom of her going, but only because we feared it would be used for propaganda purposes by the claimant's supporters. To suggest that either Olga or I would refuse to recognise a much-loved niece because of money— money that did not even exist—was cruel and wicked.[35]

In defence of her sister, Xenia added, "My sister Olga felt sorry for that poor woman. She was kind to her, and because of her kindness of heart, her opinions and motives have been misrepresented."[36]

Whether to improve her image, portray Rathlef-Keilmann as a liar, or because it didn't exist, in her sworn testimony before the Hamburg court, Olga vehemently denied the existence of the telegram in question, stating, "I can swear to God that I did not receive before or during my visit to Berlin, either a telegram or a letter from my sister Xenia advising that I should not acknowledge the stranger."[37] Bolstering her claim is the fact that the telegram has never surfaced among the many papers associated with the "false Anastasia case."

The truth about whether or not Olga ever received a telegram from Xenia may never be known, but one thing resulting from the sisters' apparent disagreement became clear: the only thing consistent about the Anastasia case was its inconsistencies. In the end it would be a stretch of the imagination to believe that Olga visited Tschaikovsky as a result of duress exerted upon her by Ambassador Zahle. More likely her interest in the claimant was piqued by the unique experience of gazing upon someone like herself: an eternal outsider, her nose pressed firmly against the glass.

IN JUNE 1959 QUEEN ELIZABETH and her husband, Prince Philip, sailed into Toronto harbour aboard the royal yacht, *Britannia*. A few days after her arrival the Queen gave a lavish luncheon on board ship to which Olga was invited. Katherine Keiller-Mackay recalls that the event was filled "with some degree of uneasiness."[38]

Neighbours in Cooksville prevailed upon Olga to buy a new dress for the occasion. As usual, Olga picked the simplest frock available and this time she wore on her head "the most hideous straw hat I ever saw,"[39] recalls Xenia.

Olga climbed unsteadily up to the top of the gangplank to the ship's deck, where a young officer unexpectedly barred her path.

"What is your business here, Madam?" he asked, looking askance at her open-toed sandals and cheap vinyl purse.

"I have come to lunch with Her Majesty," Olga responded, withdrawing from her purse her engraved invitation. As soon as he heard the refined cadence of her speech, the officer recognized Olga as a woman of considerable breeding. Without bothering to check the invitation he simply, and with considerable embarrassment, permitted her to pass.

The Queen had been told where Olga would be standing in a semi-circular receiving line in the ship's dining room. A hush fell over those assembled as Olga walked into the room clad in her simple dress and fur wrap. "She looked nervous," Mrs. Keiller-Mackay recalls. "We were all afraid the Queen might overlook her and she might be hurt."[40]

Keiller-Mackay's fears were unfounded. As soon as the Queen entered the banquet room, she walked briskly toward Olga and, to an almost audible sigh of relief on the part of the guests, gently placed an arm around Olga's shoulders and guided her toward the head table.

Olga's visit on board the *Britannia* marked the last

time she would visit with any member of European royalty.

⤬

*T*OWARD THE FALL OF 1959, Olga's health drastically deteriorated. In September she managed, through much pain, to make it to Tihon's wedding to Livia, which took place at Christ the Saviour Church in Toronto. She wore a belted knee-length striped dress and a flowered hat. After the ceremony, she was driven to Tihon's house, where she presented bread and salt to the newlyweds. Olga was relieved that Tihon had found a partner to care for him for the rest of his life. "I now have time to tell you our news," she wrote to a friend shortly after the wedding. "My dear Tihon has become happily married. This time it is an attractive and sweet woman, just the one for him. They are so fond of each other, understand each other. I love her. She is so good and kind to me, so I am happy for both of them."[41]

Guri, meanwhile, married Asa Lefebvre, the woman accused of breaking up his marriage to Ruth. The couple eventually settled in Ottawa with Asa's two children from her first marriage.

Unlike Tihon, Guri was rarely present during Olga's final illness. He visited the Cooksville house infrequently, in spite of the fact that both his daughter Xenia and son Leonid lived there.

The pace of Olga's illness quickened as virtually overnight she developed new and more frightening symp- toms. She became highly anemic and light-headed and lost more weight than she could afford, considering how thin she was to begin with. "I don't seem to feel I shall ever be well again,"[42] she wrote to Ed Ewing in late 1959. Ruth concluded that, more than anything else, Olga was suffering from a "broken heart."

Like her father, Olga harboured a deep suspiciousness toward doctors, which made her susceptible to the advice of laymen, including those of the royal variety. Queen Louise of Sweden suggested the secret to her recovery lay in drinking fresh lemonade every morning, a remedy Olga tried until its novelty wore off. A doctor suggested a shot of vodka would do her good. "I never put it to the test," said Olga. "The man had a very red nose."[43]

Queen Louise of Sweden offered to send over one of her maids to help Olga turn the chaos of her home into some kind of order, but Olga demurred. Neighbours dropped in regularly to wash up dirty dishes, dust, and launder clothes, but it was clear to them that Olga was beginning to slip away.

Ed Ewing visited Olga in December of 1959 and was, he said, "astonished" and "weakened" by what he saw. She was so weak that she could not go to her door to greet him, but merely waved at him from her seat on her divan by the large front window. She seemed "a far distant thing from the vibrant, living Olga of a few weeks back,"[44] he recalls.

In her last letter to Ewing, Olga wrote, "I won't write and don't write to me, as it is so difficult for me to write— perhaps in Summer if I am any better—and not just a crippled skeleton."[45]

In September 1959, Olga's good friend James Rattray died of cancer. He left ten thousand dollars to Olga in his will, and two thousand dollars to Olga's granddaughter

Xenia, with strict instructions that "this sum must not be paid to her father under any circumstances."[46] Rattray's suspicions about the integrity of Guri's character would be borne out months later when Olga herself lay dying.

Ed Ewing last visited with Olga near Easter of 1960. She was sitting in her kitchen, "wrapped in a shawl, looking very old, and much more weakened than before,"[47] he observed. He never visited the house again.

The next time Olga's name appeared in the paper it was under an article in the *Toronto Telegram* entitled: "Grand Duchess Olga III, Unaware Her Sister Dead." Indeed, on April 20, 1960, the day that eighty-five-year-old Xenia was felled by a heart attack, Olga was in Toronto General Hospital fighting for her own life.

In spite of their marital estrangement and her widowhood of many years, Xenia was laid to rest beside Sandro in a small cemetery in Menton, France. Attending the service were Xenia's daughter, Irina, and her husband, Felix Yusupov, as well as Princess Marina of Kent. Xenia left behind an estate worth over £117,000 (close to a million dollars in Canadian funds in 1960), considerably more than her sister Olga's, reactivating rumours that she had indeed received a larger cut of money from the sale of Empress Marie's jewels.

Back in Toronto, a decision had to be reached concerning where Olga would go once she was released from hospital. She was now clearly too weak and intermittently disoriented to fend for herself. The doctors at Toronto General Hospital quickly concluded that nothing further could be done for Olga. The diagnosis, though never publicly confirmed, was believed to be cancer. Appalled by the indifferent treatment she received in the hospital, where no one was aware of her former rank and prestige, Captain Martemianoff told his family, "The Last Grand Duchess will not die in a cold hospital between people she doesn't know."[48]

Arrangements were hastily made for Olga to be taken to a tiny room on the second floor of the Martemianoffs' home on Gerrard Street in the east end of Toronto. Pitifully few possessions were brought with her, just her favourite orange china cup and saucer, a small Fabergé dog and a framed picture of Nicolai in his uniform of the Blue Cuirassiers.

Critics have made much of the fact that Olga did not choose either of her two sons to care for her as she lay dying, but Galina Martemianoff insists that Olga specifically did not want to burden her two sons, especially the newly married Tihon. Instead, she chose to stay at the Martemianoffs' home, where she could receive round-the-clock nursing and love.

"The Martemianoffs were marvellous people," says Tanya Wyches, a good friend of Tihon's. "It was a blessing from heaven, what happened."[49]

"It was a wonderful solution," agrees Michel Wyches, Tanya's husband. "If Olga stayed in Cooksville, she would have required nursing all the time. Nobody could afford that."[50]

"By the time she arrived, she was drifting in and out of consciousness," remembers Galina, who operated a hair salon on the ground floor of the house. "Out of the blue, she sat up and asked, 'Where is my husband?' We could tell her mind was drifting back to the past."[51]

Years later when questioned about why he did not insist on taking care of the mother who so adored him, Tihon buried his head in his hands and with his voice breaking, replied, "I can't talk about it."[52]

Ruth is less than forgiving of Tihon's actions during Olga's last illness, and accuses him of holding a dying Olga "under siege" in the Cooksville house prior to her trip to the hospital. According to Ruth, when Babs Messervey tried to visit Olga to tell her something that would affect her will, Tihon inexplicably turned her away. "We'll never know what it was she wanted to say,"[53] she notes, ruefully.

Soon after he heard about the desperate state of Olga's health, Sir Edward Peacock made arrangements to visit the Martemianoffs. "His representative kept phoning in advance to say 'Don't forget that he is coming.' I said, 'what do you expect, that I put down a red carpet?'"[54] Galina says.

Peacock's arrival at the Martemianoffs' home started on an inauspicious note when, thinking Galina was a maid, he handed her his umbrella and hat. "Grand Duchess Olga didn't want to look at him,"[55] Galina recalls of the brief visit.

Indeed, over the final days and weeks of Olga's tumultuous life, the only person who could comfort her was, as usual, a child—Galina's eight-year-old-son Nikita. "You want maybe some ice-cream?" he would ask, to which Olga would always nod yes. "She would eat out of love for him because she was refusing food from everyone else,"[56] says Galina.

As he sat on a small stool beside Olga's bed, Nikita tenderly spoon-fed her the ice-cream. Feeling the soothingly cool liquid slide down her throat must have reawakened in the deepest recesses of Olga's memory the hours she had spent at her dying father's side, also feeding him ice-cream.

While Olga lay near death in Toronto, a young and frightened Xenia, who had already been traumatized by the death of her grandfather, was hiding out in the Cooksville house so no one would discover that she had become pregnant. Since Leonid had moved back to Denmark, the only other person Xenia had to rely on was Tihon, who brought her money now and then to help her buy groceries.

Before long, Tihon and Guri began turning up at the Cooksville house for the sole purpose of removing Olga's valuables. At first they were "discreet," says Xenia, "because they knew I was living there alone."[57] When Xenia moved to Ottawa to await the birth of her baby, however, Guri rented a truck and virtually ransacked the dwelling, removing "almost all, even the Persian carpets, including my personal one which was never returned. Also my paintings," says Xenia. Several other valuables, including Anastasia's box, were inexplicably swept into the trash by Tihon. In retrospect Xenia is blisteringly blunt about the actions of both her father, Guri, and her uncle, Tihon. "Oh yes, I have a lot to love my family for. Gold-diggers, greedy, you name it!"[58] she says.

Unquestionably, for whatever reason, as their mother lay dying at the Martemianoffs' home, Guri and Tihon chose to make a priority out of securing possession of their mother's Russian imperial treasures, though both already knew that Olga had bequeathed everything to them in the will she signed on December 15, 1958, three months after Nicolai's death.

Xenia, who saw her grandmother's original will, is adamant that Tihon and Guri forced Olga to draft a new one three months after Nicolai's death, in order to disinherit the grandchildren. "Originally my grandfather and grandmother had identical wills. They left a portion of their estates to the grandchildren. After my grandfather died, Guri and Tihon got my grandmother to change her will, cutting us out altogether, so they could get everything."[59]

Nicolai's will, filed on August 10, 1956, divided all his personal property into six equal shares, to be divided among Tihon, Guri, Ruth, Xenia, Leonid and Alexander. Olga's will, filed two years later, following not only the death of Nicolai, but Ruth's divorce from Guri, makes no similar provision for the grandchildren. Despite Xenia's suspicions, it is impossible to prove that Olga was persuaded to sign a new will leaving everything to her two sons, to the exclusion of the grandchildren. Nevertheless, the bitterness resulting from the will continues to this day.

By all accounts the last moments of Olga's life were terrible. The young Russian doctor attending her was distracted that night by the imminent birth of his first child. As the hours ticked by, he sped back and forth between the maternity ward and Olga's bedside, where Tihon and the Martemianoff family murmured prayers above the rumble of streetcars outside the window. "When Olga became very bad, the doctor decided to get morphine," says Galina. "While he was gone, Olga died. . . . It was a blessing for him because he would think he gave her morphine and she died."[60]

On November 30, 1960, more than five hundred mourners filled the oppressively hot Christ the Saviour Cathedral in Toronto, where Olga lay in state. Hundreds of mourners from among the Russian émigré classes spilled out onto the sidewalks, crying copiously. Wreaths arrived from members of royalty all over the world. Queen Elizabeth was one of the first to send a telegram of condolence to Tihon and Guri, as did Lady Astor, as well as members of the royal houses of Norway and Denmark.

There were some political holdouts. The Greek Consul explained that he could not attend as "an official representative," since his country "had recognized the Communist regime." The Estonians felt it would be tasteless to attend since they "used to oppose Tsarism as much as they opposed Communism."[61] The Americans, on the other hand, developed selective amnesia about Olga's identity.

The Russian imperial standard and the Union Jack hung from the four corners of the catafalque where Olga's coffin was placed. Four giant incense candles burned continuously. At one point an eerie cloud of smoke seemed to hover momentarily above Olga's head.

Standing guard at each end of the coffin were members of both Nicolai's Cuirassier Regiment and Olga's Akhtyrsky Regiment. One officer's presence was particularly moving. He was the same officer who had attempted to stop Olga from boarding the *Britannia* during the Queen's visit one year before. His attendance was a belated act of contrition.

A.H. Creighton served as a pallbearer, alongside Tihon, Guri and members of the Akhtyrsky Regiment. John and Katherine Keiller-Mackay, who had been in the Yukon Territory, flew back in time for the Sunday requiem mass.

After a three-hour service, the procession drove to York Cemetery under a slate grey sky to lay Olga's body beside her beloved Nicolai, and yards away from her faithful servant Mimka. "Life is not the same without her; the house is so empty now,"[62] Mrs. Martemianoff wept to Ian Vorres, who was covering the event.

As a final loving gesture, Father Diachina of Christ the Saviour Church sprinkled a handful of Russian soil over the coffin as it was slowly lowered into the earth.

CHAPTER TWELVE

AFTERMATH

AFTER SEEING HER FAMILY'S palaces ransacked and priceless possessions destroyed by the Bolsheviks, Olga admitted she had come to view material possessions as ephemeral, and the riches of nature, eternal. In her later years, she lived in an ultimate state of grace, eschewing ornamentation and empty rituals. Except by relative standards, however, she was not poor.

Upon her death, she left an estate worth more than $200,000 (comparable to more than a million Canadian dollars by today's standards). Most of it was tied up in stock and bond holdings. This estimate was calculated before adding the combined value of all the material assets Olga smuggled out of Russia which, before Guri appropriated them, were stored in trunks in the basement of the Cooksville house. One contemporary appraiser who has seen a portion of these possessions places their current worth at a "conservative" one and a quarter million Canadian dollars.[1]

In compiling the inventory of the estate, Tihon and Guri estimated the value of her clothing and jewellery assets at a mere $50, while the household goods and furniture were clocked in at $300. These figures are most certainly vastly below independent estimates. For instance, the sideboard belonging to Queen Alexandra alone would have been appraised at several thousand dollars.

As is already known, just weeks before Olga's death, Guri and Tihon took possession of those assets in the Cooksville house that might for sentimental reasons be sought out by disgruntled family members. Guri removed several dozen of Olga's paintings, her paint set, photograph albums, many sets of hand-embroidered linen, furniture, numerous pieces of jewellery, jewel-encrusted icons, property originally belonging to Alexander III and several original letters dating back to Olga's years in the Crimea.

By all accounts, Tihon fared less well, but still managed to retrieve a number of valuable icons, pieces of crystal, silver flatware, Royal Copenhagen porcelain (some hand-painted by Olga), Fabergé frames and, most importantly, the Fabergé round table with inlaid stones. There were also ruby and diamond pendants, gold medallions, bracelets and necklaces.

Michel and Tanya Wyches agree that "the parting was not fair between the two brothers," and that Guri "had a much bigger part than Tihon. Guri didn't act the way he should, he took a little bit of an advantage, [he] was not a gentleman,"[2] Michel Wyches says.

Persistent rumours circulate today amongst antique dealers about the whereabouts of two important items still believed to be missing from Olga's estate: Alexander III's silver samovar and the single strand of perfect pearls Olga wore around her neck all her life and many believed she had been buried wearing. "We thought they were fake," says Galina Martemianoff, who can't remember whether Olga wore them in her casket or not.

In a 1964 interview with a Danish magazine, Olga's former daughter-in-law Ruth vehemently insisted that "The chain of genuine pearls, which she [Olga] always wore around her neck, she took with her into her grave."[3] This statement is probably wrong. As a convert to Russian Orthodoxy, it is surprising that Ruth did not remember that the Orthodox church forbids the deceased to be buried wearing any jewellery. As a result, rumours surrounding the possible theft of the pearls continue.

Within weeks of Olga's death, Xenia, along with her new baby named Paul, tried to return to the Cooksville house, but according to Ruth, found herself locked out by Guri. "I didn't know he [Guri] was going to be so awful,"[4] Ruth says.

When Paul was two months old, Xenia decided to move back to Denmark to live with Ruth. Soon after she arrived, she found work in the post office, where she remains today, married for the third time, and the mother of four children, still moved to tears by traumatic memories of her lonely last few months in Canada.

Six years after Olga's death, Guri finally decided to find out what had happened to the "missing" £250,000 mentioned in Sir Frederick Ponsonby's 1951 memoirs. His first line of inquiry was Hennell and Sons jewellers in London whom he asked for an inventory of the number of jewels sold and to whom. Since Hennells had new owners, the appropriate records could not immediately be found. As soon as it received a down payment for the search, Hennells promised to produce a detailed list of the seventy-six jewels sold, how much was realized on the sales, and which pieces were returned to Olga and Xenia. According to Suzy Menkes, author of the 1985 book *The Royal Jewels*, after receiving the list from Hennells, Guri forwarded it for examination to Buckingham Palace and the Lord Chamberlain's office. The matter was then placed in the hands of the Queen's solicitors. Menkes explained:

> They examined the papers—which have now been sent to Windsor—and discovered the truth: Queen Mary had held on to the jewels until 1933; she had then claimed that the Depression and the collapse of the pearl market had reduced their value; she paid only 60,000 pounds. In 1968, forty years after the Empress Marie's jewels had cascaded from their box, Queen Mary's granddaughter, the Queen, settled the debt.[5]

It is virtually certain that in 1968 Tihon did not know about Guri's attempts to search for answers regarding the "missing" £250,000. After their mother's death, the brothers rarely corresponded. As a result, Menkes's 1986 claims regarding Guri's settlement from Queen Elizabeth served as a shocking revelation to Tihon and galvanized him into action.

As soon as he read Menkes's book, Tihon wrote a letter to Buckingham Palace attempting to confirm whether Guri had indeed received compensation in 1968. Sir Robert Fellowes, the Queen's secretary, categorically denied that any payment had been made by the Queen to the Kulikovsky family in 1968.

To this day, Menkes believes that Buckingham Palace "fudged" the truth by stating that no settlement had been made in 1968, cleverly sidestepping the possibility that money might have been paid to Guri in some other year after Olga's death.

As to where she found out about the possibility of a settlement being made in 1968, Menkes says, "I was told about the saga of Queen Mary and the Empress Marie's jewels first by the Marchioness of Cambridge (since deceased). The idea that the Queen had settled with Guri Kulikovsky was told to me as a possibility by the then Crown jeweler, but he was very circumspect. I was then told categorically that a settlement had been made and that the papers were at Windsor by Marcus Bishop, then at the Lord Chamberlain's office in London."[6]

There is currently no way to confirm whether Guri actually received a settlement from Queen Elizabeth. However, friends and acquaintances of the family still question how Guri could afford to buy an enormous home and property in the Ottawa Valley. "How is it that Guri had an estate in Ottawa?" the Wyches ask. "He had a poor job in the beginning. How did he afford the house?"[7]

After receiving his response from Buckingham Palace, Tihon felt he was being duped. He shared Menkes's suspicions that Mr. Fellowes's denial of payments being made in 1968 was a cute technicality masking the possibility that payments had been made in some other year besides 1968. Feeling stonewalled, he wondered whether his loyalty toward the British royal family had simply reduced him to play the role of patsy, while Guri was rewarded with a pay-off because he had made himself a pest.[8]

Conversely, Tihon labelled as scandalous the possibility that Buckingham Palace was telling the truth in denying any settlement was made in any year. Whether there was a payment or not, Tihon felt the only honourable thing for the royal family to do was to compensate him accordingly.[9]

Regrettably, due to a change in ownership, Hennells was never able to locate and forward to Tihon the inventory of the seventy-six items sold back in late 1929 and 1930. Tihon died of a heart attack on April 14, 1993, never discovering the fate of his grandmother's jewels.

Guri died in 1984, but Tihon didn't attend the funeral. Even more sadly, it wasn't until 1997 that Guri's children found out when their father had died, how, and where he was buried. More than thirteen years after his death, they made tentative inquiries into whether they might be entitled to any assets of his estate, only to discover that he had never filed a will.

With the assistance of the current managing director of Hennells, one year after Tihon's death, William Clarke, author of the book *The Lost Fortune of the Tsars,* finally located the "long lost" inventory of jewels (see p. 261). Any question of Queen Mary defrauding the two sisters was finally, and belatedly, put to rest, when the list revealed that, despite the Depression, she had bought most items of jewellery at or above their appraised market value. Clarke writes:

> Thus the idea that Queen Mary used her privi-
> leged position to acquire at knock-down prices
> the Romanoff jewels her daughters-in-law,

granddaughters and other royals are still seen wearing is not justified by the evidence of the original master list kept by Hennells. Nor is the suggestion, first raised by Sir Frederick Ponsonby, that up to 350,000 pounds had been realised from the sale of Empress Marie's jewels, anywhere near the truth. The missing 350,000 can now be safely ignored. The 136,624 finally realized from the sale is not significantly higher than the figure of 'about 100,000 pounds', Sir Edward Peacock mentioned as receiving as trustee in 1929. Sir Edward was right: Ponsonby's memory had clearly failed him.[10]

What remains shocking to Clarke is that the British royal family itself did not attempt to clarify the discrepancy, but chose instead to allow the Kulikovsky family to twist in the wind with uncertainty. Therefore, the answer to the question of where Guri obtained enough money to buy expensive property may simply lie in his sale of those items he managed to retrieve from the Cooksville house.

By contrast, just as he had done when the brothers gambled at card games in Denmark so many years before, Tihon hung onto his share of most of the items formerly in his mother's possession.

*T*HIRTY-FOUR YEARS AFTER Olga's death, the solution to the mystery concerning the true identity of Mrs.

Tschaikovsky, later known as Anna Anderson, was finally confirmed through DNA analysis. She was identified conclusively as Franziska Schanzkowska, a Polish factory worker. It would be too easy to dismiss Schanzkowska as merely one of the best in a long line of "confidence tricksters." By all accounts, her words and actions had no performative quality to them. Her resemblance to the real Anastasia was beyond eerie, especially the malformation of the foot, the scar on her shoulder and the malformed middle fingers of her hands.

There is little doubt that her passionate speech, bearing and carriage were impressive enough to plunge "Aunt" Olga into decades-long uncertainty and guilt. Nevertheless, the woman caught up for so many years in a netherworld of mental illness and depression was an imposter.

Calling her physical resemblance to the real Anastasia "incredibly lucky," Michael Thornton, who held Tschaikovsky's power of attorney in England, said of Tschaikovsky:

> She could be as charming as she was sometime querulous and she was never less than a deeply fascinating and enigmatic personality. But from my earliest meeting with her . . . I formed the immediate impression that this was not someone who had spoken English from childhood, as Anastasia certainly had. It was someone who had learned English later in life . . . The Polish identity, therefore, was to me always a possibility, and it is a curious streak of inverted snobbery in human nature that suggests that a Polish peasant cannot transform herself into a princess. Why ever

not? Great actresses, often of the most humble origins imaginable, do it on a daily basis.
Madame du Barry began life as a Paris street
walker. Franziska Schanzkowska had 64
years—longer than Queen Victoria's reign—
to perfect her role, and sometimes played it
to perfection, if a trifle too grandly.[11]

On February 17, 1970, fifty years to the day since she
was rescued from the Landwehr Canal in Germany, and
twenty-four years before DNA analysis confirmed her lineage, the German court ruled that Tschaikovsky's identity had
been "neither established nor refuted." The case was effectively over.

The existence of any Romanov money held in British
banks had long since been confirmed as nonexistent. On the
day of the verdict, even Tschaikovsky/Anderson seemed
tired of the decades-long battle. Her husband, Jack Manahan, whom she had met when she emigrated to the United
States in 1968, spoke for her when he said, "I feel this is a
case to go before the bar of history."[12]

He was wrong. After countless appeals, counter-appeals,
allegations and counter-allegations, little could he have predicted how dramatically a thin slice of his wife's flesh could
silence the majority of conspiracy buffs.

*T*ODAY PAUL KULIKOVSKY LARSEN, the son Xenia gave
birth to in Canada in 1960, keeps his great-grandmother
Grand Duchess Olga's memory alive in a small museum he

and his friend Jorgen Bjeergaard run just outside the little town of Ballerup, Denmark. Funded in part by the Ballerup Historical Society, the museum attracts hundreds of visitors from all over the world each year, who peer through glass cases at Olga's christening gown, paintings, letters, porcelain and intimate family photographs.

BACK IN 1991, WHEN THE imperial family's bones were first found, Olga's son Tihon was asked to provide a blood sample for DNA analysis against what was believed to be the femur of his uncle, Tsar Nicholas. Despite the impassioned pleas of Britain's Dr. Peter Gill and Russia's Dr. Pavel Ivanov, the DNA experts conducting the analysis of the bones, Tihon and his wife Olga informed them that they would not cooperate with any testing of the bones unless it was conducted under the auspices of both the Russian Government and the Orthodox Church.

In addition, Tihon told Ivanov that he thought "the whole business was a hoax," and remonstrated with him for working in conjunction with a British scientist in light of how cruel England had been to the Tsar and "to the Russian monarchy."[13]

Ivanov decided there was no use arguing with Tihon and instead approached Grand Duchess Xenia's great-granddaughter Xenia Sfiris for a blood sample, as well as Queen Alexandra's (Dowager Empress Marie's sister) great-grandson James George Alexander Banerman Carnegie, the third Duke of Fife.

Unlike Tihon, both descendants gave blood samples

without a fight. As the world now knows, the DNA extracted from the descendants proved virtually conclusively that one set of bones found in Russia belonged to Tsar Nicholas II. Afterwards it was easy to test the remainder of the bones and confirm that they belonged to the other members of the imperial family and their retinue. Only the whereabouts of the bones of Anastasia or Maria and Alexei remain a mystery.

Meanwhile, back in Toronto, hopeful that the Russian Government and the Orthodox Church would eventually work in tandem, Tihon had a change of heart and decided to donate a blood sample for examination to Dr. Evgeny I. Rogaev, a Russian molecular geneticist working out of the University of Toronto. Dr. Rogaev, in association with the Centre of Forensic Sciences, conducted an independent study through the University of Toronto. Not surprisingly, the comparison of Tihon's DNA to that of the Tsar showed virtually identical matches in sequences, although Rogaev felt additional independent tests on the Tsar's bones were needed before definitive results could be obtained.

Five years after Tihon's death, his widow, Olga, remains unconvinced that the bones found near Ekaterinburg belong to Nicholas and his family. As a result, she refused to attend Russia's official burial of the bones, which occurred at the St. Peter and St. Paul Fortress in St. Petersburg at noon on July 17, 1998, the eightieth anniversary of the imperial family's murder. Romanov family descendants who attended the ceremony wept when they realized that each family member's incomplete set of bones had been stacked inside a child-sized coffin.

The horror of the violent deaths of Nicholas and his family remained a taboo subject in Olga's life. Although she appeared outwardly sunny, experience had taught her that whatever happiness she found could and would be taken away from her. There were times, even in bucolic Canada, when reawakened anxieties and fears for her safety forced her to place a loaded pistol under her pillow at night. Luckily, these times were few. For the most part, she looked toward the future rather than dwelled on the past. She understood, even accepted, with a kind of bittersweet fatalism, her ultimate reversal of fortune and the brutalities of revenge.

List of Jewels in Sale

1. Eight diamond flowers on white silk collar
   Returned to H.I.H. Grand Duchess Xenia at Windsor, by registered post

2. Eight diamond ornaments on black silk
   Sale of these ornaments suspended on H.I.H. Grand Duchess Xenia's instructions, July 18, 1929

3. Small diamond bow hair ornament
   Sale of these ornaments suspended on H.I.H. Grand Duchess Xenia's instructions, July 18, 1929

4. Diamond stiff band bracelet
   Bracelet mount returned Buckingham Palace. Loose diamonds returned as above [No. 1] following withdrawal from sale

5. Ruby and diamond stiff band bracelet
   Returned to H.I.H. Gand Duchess Xenia at Frogmore Cottage, by registered post

6. Necklace of 144 pearls (small) with large pearl drop
   Sold to Lord Lascelles

7. Pearl and diamond collar with sapphire and diamond clasp
   Bought by Queen Mary; returned to her at Windsor by A.W. Hardy

8. Pearl and diamond row
   Returned to H.I.H. Grand Duchess Xenia at Frogmore Cottage, by registered post

9. 275 pearls =
   1. 45 pearls with 2 diamond tulips;
   2. 49 pearls with 2 diamond tulips;
   3. 55 pearls with 2 diamond tulips;

4. 60 pearls with 2 diamond tulips;
5. 66 pearls with 2 diamond tulips
   All sold (including No. 44)

10. 33 pearls diamond cluster snap and tulips
10a. 32 pearls with two diamond tulips
   Sold. Further cheque sent

11. Diamond Star Order of St. Andrews (sic)
   Sold

12. Small pearl and diamond collar on black velvet
   *Returned to H.I.H. Grand Duchess Xenia at Frogmore Cottage, by
   registered post*

13. Yellow diamond hair pin
   Sold

14. White diamond hair pin
   Sold

15. Three single stone diamond hat-pins
   Sold

16. Diamond feather hat-pin
   Sold

17. Diamond and pearl drop hair pin
   Sold (including No. 76)

18. Four tortoiseshell and rose diamond hair pins
   Valued and left at Windsor

19. Ten jewelled hat-pins
   Valued and left at Windsor

20. Spinel, diamond and gold cross
   Sold

21. Ruby, diamond and gold cross (16 small rubies)
   Valued and left at Windsor

22. Diamond and sapphire cross
   Valued and left at Windsor

23. Diamond cross with head of Saviour inset
   Valued and left at Windsor

24. Diamond, pearl and black enamel cross
    Sold

25. Ruby, pearl, diamond and enamel cross
    Returned to H.I.H. Grand Duchess Xenia at Frogmore Cottage, by registered post

26. Round garnet and diamond pendant
    Left at Windsor

27. Garnet, sapphire and diamond pendant on platinum chain
    Sold to H.R.H. Princess Royal

28. Diamond eagle set in silver on gold pendant on gold chain
    Left at Windsor

29. Diamond flexible bracelet set pearl, ruby and sapphire
    Left at Windsor

30. Diamond bracelet with cabochon sapphire centre
    Sold

31. Gold chain bracelet set 1 turquoise and 1 diamond
    Returned to H.I.H. Grand Duchess Xenia by registered post

32. Gold chain set rubies and diamonds with gemset easter egg
    Left at Windsor

33. Moonstone and cabochon sapphire chain
    Left at Windsor

34. Turquoise and diamond chain
    Left at Windsor

35. Black chain with 9 drop pearls and rondelles
    Left at Windsor

36. Small sapphire chain
    Left at Windsor

37. Pearl and diamond pendant with miniature and three pearl drops
    5 miniatures returned to Buckingham Palace by hand, June 10, 1929

38. Diamond heart-shaped brooch with crown and ribbon and two miniatures
    Sold

39. Diamond and ruby brooch with two miniatures
Sold

40. Diamond brooch with two bouton pearls and one pearl drop
Returned to H.I.H. Grand Duchess Xenia at Frogmore Cottage, by registered post

41. Turquoise and diamond pendant
Returned to H.I.H. Grand Duchess Xenia at Frogmore Cottage, by registered post

42. Oval cabochon sapphire and diamond oval cluster brooch and pearl drop
Sent by hand to H.M. Queen Mary, Buckingham Palace. Sold to H.M. Queen Mary

43. Sapphire and diamond crown-shaped brooch
Sold

44. Large sapphire and diamond oval cluster brooch
Sold (amount included in cheque for no. 9)

45. Large cabochon sapphire and 4 diamonds brooch
Left at Windsor. Brought in later to Hennells by H.I.H. Grand Duchess Xenia. Sold

46. Cabochon sapphire and diamond brooch
Left at Windsor. Brought in later

47. Pearl and diamond twist brooch
Sold to Queen Mary and taken by A.W. Hardy to Windsor

48. Large pearl and diamond 2 stone brooch with smaller diamonds
Sold

49. Pearl and diamond cluster brooch
Sold

50. Diamond circle brooch with pearl and diamond in centre
Left at Windsor

51. Diamond bow with pearl drop
Returned to H.I.H. Grand Duchess Xenia at Windsor, by registered post

52. Diamond sword brooch with 3 pearls
Sold

53. Baroque pearl and diamond trefoil
Returned to H.I.H. Grand Duchess Xenia at Hennells

54. Cabochon emerald, ruby and diamond brooch
Sold

55. Cabochon emerald, ruby and diamond brooch
Sold

56. Diamond circle brooch with 2 rubies and 1 diamond in centre
Returned to H.I.H. Grand Duchess Xenia at Hennells

57. Star ruby, catseye and diamond double circle brooch
Left at Windsor

58. Diamond scroll brooch with ruby and diamond centre
Left at Windsor

59. Two smaller brooches similar to No. 58
Left at Windsor

60. Cabochon ruby and diamond bar brooch
Left at Windsor

61. Diamond heart brooch with 1 small ruby
Returned to H.I.H. Grand Duchess Xenia at Hennells

62. Ruby and diamond trefoil pendant
Returned o H.I.H. Grand Duchess Xenia at Hennells

63. Bouton pearl pin
Sold

64. Ruby and diamond bow brooch
Left at Windsor

65. Diamond brooch with 2 ruby and sapphire flowers
Left at Windsor

66. Ruby cross with rose diamond border
Left at Windsor

67. Ruby cross with diamond border (smaller)
Left at Windsor

68. Cabochon sapphire and diamond quatrefoil brooch
    Returned to H.I.H. Grand Duchess Xenia at Hennells

69. Diamond trefoil brooch
    Left at Windsor

70. Sapphire and diamond trefoil brooch
    Left at Windsor

71. Pearl and enamel tassel
    Left at Windsor

72. Cabochon sapphire and rose diamond long brooch
    Sold to H.M. Queen Mary

73. Turquoise and diamond heart brooch
    Sold

74. Diamond and ruby arrow brooch
    Returned to H.I.H. Grand Duchess Xenia at Hennells

75. Diamond and black onyx bow brooch
    Left at Windsor

76. Diamond amitie brooch
    Sold (amount included in cheque No. 17)

Notes

Chapter One ⌘ Childhood

1 Charles Lowe, *Alexander of Russia* (New York: MacMillan and Co., 1895), p. 26.

2 Grand Duke Alexander, *Once a Grand Duke* (London: Cassel, 1932), p. 61.

3 Lowe, *Alexander of Russia*, p. 20.

4 Diary entry of Tsarevich Alexander Alexandrovich, dated June 25/July 7, 1865, State Archive of the Russian Federation (hereafter referred to as GARF).

5 Undated letter from Elizabeth Franklin to Empress Marie Feodorovna, GARF 642/2946 3.

6 Ibid., 642/2946 3-4.

7 Ibid.

8 Ibid.

9 June 23, 1984 letter from Elizabeth Franklin to Empress Marie Feodorovna, GARF 642/2946 1.

10 Ian Vorres, *The Last Grand Duchess* (Athens: Finedawn Publishers, Psaropoulos, 1985) p. 24.

11 Vorres, *Last Grand Duchess,* p. 23.

12 Vorres, *Last Grand Duchess,* p. 40.

13 June 18, 1893 letter from Grand Duchess Olga Alexandrovna to Empress Marie Feodorovna, GARF 642/2414 6.

14 Undated letter from Grand Duchess Olga Alexandrovna to Empress Marie Feodorovna, GARF, 642/2414 5-6.

15 Undated letter from Grand Duchess Olga Alexandrovna to Empress Marie Feodorovna, GARF, 642/2414 83.

16 Undated letter from Grand Duchess Olga Alexandrovna to Empress Marie Feodorovna, GARF, 642/2414 5-6.

17 March 10, 1898 letter from Grand Duchess Olga Alexandrovna to Empress Marie Feodorovna, GARF, 642/2414 81.

18 Ibid.

19 Vorres, *Last Grand Duchess*, p. 27.

20 Ibid., p. 28.

21 Ibid., p. 48.

22 Ibid., p. 48.

23 March 10 1898 letter from Grand Duchess Olga Alexandrovna to Grand Duke Nicholas Alexandrovich, GARF, 642/2414 81.

24 Vorres, *Last Grand Duchess*, p. 33.

25 September 3, 1892 letter from Grand Duchess Olga Alexandrovna to Empress Marie Feodorovna, GARF, pp. 2-3.

26 Grand Duchess Olga Alexandrovna, "Hjemmet I Gatchina," *Berlingske Tidende* (Copenhagen, 1941).

27 Vorres, *Last Grand Duchess*, p. 35.

28 Lowe, *Alexander of Russia*, p. 254.

29 Vorres, *Last Grand Duchess*, p. 34.

30 Ibid., p. 34.

31 Ibid., p. 34.

32 Ibid., p. 43.

33 Ibid., p. 43.

34 Christmas 1897 letter from Olga Alexandrovna to His Royal Highness George V, Royal Archives, Windsor RA GEOV AA43/81.

35 Vorres, *Last Grand Duchess*, p. 43.

36 November 6, 1888 letter from Empress Marie Feodorovna to Kaiser Wilhelm II of Germany, cited in Inger Liste Klausen, *Dagmar. Zarina Fra Danmark (Copenhagen: Lindhardt og Ringhoff, 1997),* p. 190.

37 Vorres, *Last Grand Duchess*, p. 29.

38 November 6, 1888 letter from Empress Marie Feodorovna to Kaiser Wilhelm II of Germany, cited in Inger Liste Klausen, *Dagmar* p. 190.

39 Lowe, *Alexander of Russia,* p. 258.

40 Ibid., p. 260.

41 Vorres, *Last Grand Duchess*, p. 30.

42 Ibid., p. 32.

43 Lowe, *Alexander of Russia,* p. 259.

CHAPTER TWO ∞ TURNING THE PAGE

1 Charles Lowe, *Alexander of Russia* (New York: MacMillan and Co., 1895), p. 201.

2 June 7, 1894 letter from Olga Alexandrovna to Empress Marie Feodorovna, GARF, 642/2414 13-14.

3 Ian Vorres, *The Last Grand Duchess* (Athens: Finedawn Publishers, Psarapoulos, 1985), p. 53.

4 Ibid., p. 52.

5 Golos minuvshego (voice of the past), 1917, No. 5-6, p. 100, cited in Maria Feodorovna, Empress of Russia, An exhibition about the Danish princess who became Empress of Russia (Copenhagen: Christianborg Palace, 1997) p. 250.

6 Vorres, *Last Grand Duchess,* p. 59.

7 Grand Duke Alexander of Russia, *Once a Grand Duke* (London: Cassel, 1932), p. 120.

8 June 7 1894 letter from Olga Alexandrovna to Empress Marie Feodorovna, GARF, 642/2414 13-14.

9 Alexander, *Once a Grand Duke,* p. 132.

10 Ibid.

11 Ibid. p. 133.

12 Lowe, *Alexander of Russia,* p. 286.

13 Grand Duke Konstantin Konstantinovich, cited in Andrei Maylunas and Sergei Mironenko, *A Lifelong Passion* (London: Weidenfeld & Nicholson, 1996) p. 117.

14 October 18/30 letter from Empress Marie Feodorovna to Queen Louise of Denmark, GARF, Cat no. 137.

15 Ibid.

16 Ibid.

17 Alexander, *Once a Grand Duke*, pp. 168-169.

18 Ibid., p. 135.

19 Ibid., p. 169.

20 November 19, 1894 letter from Nicholas II to Grand Duke George Alexandrovich, cited in Maylunas and Mironenko, *Lifelong Passion*, p. 124.

21 November 16, 1894 letter from Empress Alexandra of Russia to Queen Victoria, cited in Maylunas and Mironenko, *Lifelong Passion*, p. 112.

22 Vorres, *Last Grand Duchess*, p. 49.

23 Alexander, *Once a Grand Duke*, p. 139.

24 April 27, 1896 letter from Nicholas II to Empress Marie Feodorovna, cited in Maylunas and Mironenko, *Lifelong Passion*, p. 141.

25 May 12, 1896 diary entry of Grand Duchess Olga Alexandrovna, GARF 643 4-5.

26 Ibid.

27 May 13, 1896 diary entry of Grand Duchess Olga Alexandrovna, GARF, 643 4-5.

28 May 14, 1896 diary entry of Grand Duchess Olga Alexandrovna, GARF 643 4-5.

29 Ibid.

30 Ibid.

31 Ibid.

32 May 16, 1896 letter from Empress Marie Feodorovna to Queen Louise of Denmark, GARF, Cat. No. 137.

33 Francis W. Grenfell, John A. Logan and Kate Koon Bovey, *Coronation of Czar Nicholas II* (Toronto: Pavlovsk Press, 1997), p. 14.

34 Alexander, *Once a Grand Duke*, p. 171.

35 Grenfell, Logan and Bovey, *Coronation of Czar Nicholas II*, p. 14.

36 Ibid.

37 May 18, 1896 diary entry of Grand Duchess Olga Alexandrovna, GARF, 643 7-8.

38 Ibid.

39 Alexander, *Once a Grand Duke*, p. 172.

40 May 18, 1896 diary entry of Grand Duchess Olga Alexandrovna, GARF, 643 7-8.

Chapter Three ∞ A Wedding

1 Undated 1900 diary entry of Grand Duchess Olga Alexandrovna, GARF, 643 4-5.

2 Ian Vorres, *The Last Grand Duchess* (Athens: Finedawn Publishers, Psaropoulos, 1985), p.80.

3 Ibid.

4 Undated 1900 diary entry of Grand Duchess Olga Alexandrovna, GARF, 643 7-8.

5 Vorres, *Last Grand Duchess*, p. 82.

6 Ibid., p. 85.

7 Ibid.

8 Edward J. Bing, *The Letters of Tsar Nicholas and Empress Marie* (London: Ivor Nicholson and Watson Ltd., 1937), p. 148.

9 Ibid.

10 Prenuptial document relating to marriage of Grand Duchess Olga Alexandrovna, Russian State Historical Archives, St. Petersburg, 486 48 139 9.

11 Ibid.

12 July 3, 1901 letter from Empress Marie Feodorovna to King Christian IX of Denmark, GARF 642 86.

13 Alexander Bokhanov, *Nicholas II* (Moscow: Russian Printhouse, 1997), p. 100.

14 July 4, 1916 letter from Grand Duchess Olga Alexandrovna to Tsar Nicholas II of Russia, GARF, 601 1316.

15 Vorres, *Last Grand Duchess*, p. 87.

16 Ibid., p. 88.

17 Prenuptial document relating to marriage of Grand Duchess Olga Alexandrovna, Russian State Historical Archives, St. Petersburg, 486 48 139 9.

18 Vorres, *Last Grand Duchess*, p. 92.

19   Ibid.

20   Ibid., p. 98.

21   January 3, 1903 letter from Empress Marie Feodorovna to King Christian IX of Denmark, GARF 642.

22   Vorres, *Last Grand Duchess,* p. 89.

23   Ibid., p. 90.

24   May 6, 1902 letter from Prince Peter of Oldenburg to Grand Duchess Olga Alexandrovna, GARF, 643 30.

25   Ibid.

26   Ibid.

27   May 5, 1902 letter from Prince Peter of Oldenburg to Empress Marie Feodorovna, GARF, 642 2440.

28   May 7, 1902 letter from Prince Peter of Oldenburg to Empress Marie Feodorovna, GARF, 642 2440.

29   Vorres, *Last Grand Duchess,* p. 89.

30   September 14, 1902 letter from Prince Peter of Oldenburg to Empress Marie Feodorovna, GARF, 642 2440.

31   Vorres, *Last Grand Duchess,* p. 94.

32   Alexander, *Once a Grand Duke,* p. 211.

33   Vorres, *Last Grand Duchess,* p. 105.

34   Ibid.

CHAPTER FOUR ⌇
WAR, MARITAL WOES AND A MAD MONK

1   Richard Pipes, *A Concise History of the Russian Revolution* (New York: Vintage Books, 1995), p. 36.

2   Ibid., p. 35.

3   Ibid., p. 36.

4   January 1, 1904 letter from Grand Duchess Xenia Alexandrovna to Tsar Nicholas II, cited in Andrei Maylunas and Sergei Mironenko, *A Lifelong Passion* (London: Weidenfeld & Nicholson, 1996), p. 238.

5   Grand Duke Alexander of Russia, *Once a Grand Duke* (London: Cassel, 1932), p. 213.

6 S. Witte, *Memoirs* (New York: Doubleday, Page, 1921), p 49.

7 Alexander, *Once a Grand Duke*, p. 214.

8 Pipes, *Concise History*, p. 36.

9 January 25, 1894 letter from Grand Duchess Xenia Alexandrovna cited Maylunas, Mironenko, p. 239.

10 Ian Vorres, *The Last Grand Duchess* (Athens: Finedawn Publishing, Psaropoulos, 1985), p. 119.

11 Edward J. Bing, *The Letters of Tsar Nicholas and Empress Marie* (London: Ivor Nicholson and Watson Ltd., 1937), p. 184.

12 December 4, 1904 diary entry of Grand Duke Konstantin Konstantinovich, cited in Maylunas and Mironenko, *A Lifelong Passion*, p. 251.

13 Vorres, *Last Grand Duchess*, p. 120.

14 Ibid.

15 Ibid.

16 Ibid.

17 January 9, 1905 diary entry of Tsar Nicholas II, cited in Maylunas and Mironenko, *A Lifelong Passion*, p. 256.

18 May 10, 1905 diary entry of Tsar Nicholas II, cited in Maylunas and Mironenko, *A Lifelong Passion*, p. 274.

19 Alexander, *Once a Grand Duke*, p, 225.

20 July 22, 1906 letter from Nicolai Kulikovsky to Grand Duchess Olga Alexandrovna, GARF, 662 1.

21 V. Trubetskoy, "A Cuirassier's Memoirs" *Nashe nasledie*, Moscow 2-4 1991, p. 60.

22 Ibid., p. 61.

23 Ibid.

24 Vorres, *Last Grand Duchess*, p. 105.

25 Trubetskoy, "A Cuirassier's Memoirs," p. 61.

26 Ibid.

27 October 16, 1906 letter from Tsar Nicholas II to Prime Minister Styolypin, cited in Maylunas and Mironenko, *A Lifelong Passion*, p. 296.

28 Vorres, *Last Grand Duchess*, p. 143.

29 Joseph T. Fuhrmann, *Rasputin, A Life* (New York: Praeger Publishers, 1990), p. 26.

30 Vorres, *Last Grand Duchess*, p. 143.

31 Fuhrmann, *Rasputin*, p. 25.

32 Vorres, *Last Grand Duchess*, pp. 138-139.

33 Ibid., p. 142.

34 Ibid., p. 138.

35 Ibid., p. 139

36 Ibid.

37 Ibid.

38 Undated 1907 letter from Grand Duchess Olga Alexandrovna to Empress Marie Feodorovna, GARF 643-1242.

39 Ibid.

40 Vorres, *Last Grand Duchess*, p. 139.

41 Ibid.

42 Ibid.

43 Ibid., p. 140.

44 Rosemary and Donald Crawford., *Michael & Natasha* (Vancouver/Toronto: Douglas & McIntyre, 1997), p. 218.

45 Fuhrmann, *Rasputin*, p. 49.

46 Letter from Empress Marie Feodorovna, cited in V.N. Kokovtsov, *"Iz moyego proshlogo." Vospominaiya: 1903-1903,* vol. 2, Paris, 1933, p. 35.

47 Maurice Paleologue, *An Ambassador's Memoirs* (New York: Doran, 1925), p. 331.

48 Lukhomskii, Memoirs of the Russian Revolution. (London: Unwin, 1922), p. 27, cited in Fuhrmann, *Rasputin*, p. 65.

49 Vorres, *Last Grand Duchess*, p. 142.

50 Letter of Empress Alexandra citied in Fuhrmann, *Rasputin*, p. 90.

51 Fuhrmann, *Rasputin*, p. 49.

52 Ibid., p. 102.

53 Anna Vyrubova, *Memoirs of the Russian Court* (London: MacMillan, 1923), p. 159.

54 Protopresviter Georgi Shavelsky, *Memoirs of The Last Protopresviter of The Russian Army and Navy, "Krutiskoe Patriarsheye Podvorie"* (Moscow: Publishing House of The Russian Church, 1996), p. 104.

Chapter Five ∽ Love on the Battlefield

1 Edward J. Bing, *The Letters of Tsar Nicholas and Empress Marie* (London: Ivor Nicholson and Watson Ltd., 1937), pp. 283-284.

2 Rosemary and Donald Crawford, *Michael & Natasha* (Vancouver/ Toronto: Douglas & McIntyre, 1997), p. 50.

3 Ibid., p. 50.

4 November 21, 1912 letter from Tsar Nicholas II to Empress Marie Feodorovna, cited in Andrei Maylunas and Sergei Mironenko, *A Lifelong Passion* (London: Weidenfeld & Nicolson, 1996), p. 363.

5 Richard Pipes, *A Concise History of the Russian Revolution* (New York: Vintage Books, 1995), p. 56.

6 Ian Vorres, *The Last Grand Duchess* (Athens: Finedawn Publishers, Psaropoulos, 1985), p 129.

7 Ibid.

8 Ibid., p. 130.

9 Undated letter from Grand Duchess Olga Alexandrovna to Grand Duchess Xenia Alexandrovna, GARF, 643 2414.

10 Olga Alexandrovna, "Mit Hojeste Onske," *Berlingske Tidende* (Copenhagen: 1941).

11 July 4, 1916 letter from Grand Duchess Olga Alexandrovna to Tsar Nicholas II, GARF, 601 1316.

12 April 7, 1915 letter from Grand Duchess Olga Alexandrovna to Nicolai Kulikovsky, GARF, 643 28.

13 July 4, 1916 letter from Grand Duchess Olga Alexandrovna to Tsar Nicholas II, GARF, 601 1316.

14 November 1914 letter from Grand Duchess Olga Alexandrovna to her four nieces, Olga, Tatiana, Maria, Anastasia, GARF, 643 28.

15 Ibid.

16 April 4, 1915 letter from Grand Duchess Olga Alexandrovna to Nicolai Kulikovsky, GARF, 643 28.

17 March 26, 1916 letter from Empress Alexandra to Tsar Nicholas II, cited in Maylunas and Mironenko, *A Lifelong Passion*, p. 462.

18 May 16, 1916 letter from Grand Duchess Olga Alexandrovna to Tsar Nicholas II, GARF, 643 28.

19 Vorres, *Last Grand Duchess*, p. 149.

20 June 18, 1916 letter from Grand Duchess Olga Alexandrovna to Tsar Nicholas II, GARF, 601 1316.

21 Ibid.

22 Ibid.

23 December 25-26, 1914 letter from Grand Duchess Olga Alexandrovna to Nicolai Kulikovsky, GARF, 643 28.

24 Ibid.

25 July 4, 1916 letter from Grand Duchess Olga Alexandrovna to Tsar Nicholas II, GARF, 601 1316.

26 July 18, 1916 letter from Grand Duchess Olga Alexandrovna to Tsar Nicholas II, GARF, 601 1316.

27 September 9, 1916 letter from Tsar Nicholas II to Empress Alexandra, cited in Joseph T. Fuhrmann, Rasputin, A Life (New York: Praeger, 1990), p. 180.

28 Lili Dehn, The Real Tsaritsa (New York: Little Brown and Company, 1922), p. 141.

29 April 16, 1915 letter from Grand Duchess Olga Alexandrovna to Nicolai Kulikovsky, GARF, 643 1316.

30 May 22, 1916 letter from Empress Marie Feodorovna to Tsar Nicholas II, cited in Bing, Letters of Tsar Nicholas, p. 297.

31 Vorres, Last Grand Duchess, p. 150.

32 September 19, 1916 letter from Tsar Nicholas II to Grand Duchess Olga Alexandrovna (courtesy of Paul Byington).

33 November 19, 1916 letter from Grand Duchess Olga Alexandrovna to Tsar Nicholas II, GARF, 601 1316.

34 Ibid.

35 Ibid.

36 Alexander, Once a Grand Duke, p. 273.

37 November 10, 1916 letter from Grand Duchess Olga Alexandrovna to Tsar Nicholas II, GARF, 601 1316.

38 Ibid.

39 Ibid.

40 Ibid.

41 Olga Alexandrovna, "Hjem Til Danmark," Berlingske Tidende (Copenhagen: 1941).

42 Marie Rasputin, *My Father* (New Hyde Park, New York: University Books, 1970), p. 31.

43 Undated 1916 letter from Grigory Elfimovich Rasputin to Tsar Nicholas II, cited in Fuhrmann, *Rasputin*, p. 194.

44 Vorres, *Last Grand Duchess*, p. 145.

CHAPTER SIX ∞ ESCAPE

1 March 4, 1917 telegram from the former Tsar Nicholas II to Grand Duke Michael, cited in Rosemary and Donald Crawford, *Michael & Natasha* (Vancouver/Toronto: Douglas & McIntyre, 1997), p. 308.

2 March 13, 1917 letter from Grand Duchess Olga to Grand Duchess Xenia, GARF, 662 212.

3 Grand Duke Alexander, *Once a Grand Duke* (London: Cassel, 1932) p. 287.

4 Ibid., p. 288.

5 Rosemary and Donald Crawford, *Michael & Natasha*, p. 295.

6 Ibid., p. 314.

7 March 3, 1917 diary entry of former Tsar Nicholas II, cited in Andrei Maylunas and Sergei Mironenko, *A Lifelong Passion* (London: Weidenfeld & Nicolson, 1996), p. 551.

8 March 13, 1917 letter from Grand Duchess Olga to Grand Duchess Xenia, GARF, 662 212.

9 Ibid., GARF 662 221.

10 Ibid.

11 Ibid., GARF 662 221 5.

12 Ibid., GARF 662 221 6.

13 Ibid., GARF 662 221.

14 Ibid.

15 Ian Vorres, *The Last Grand Duchess* (Athens: Finedawn Publishers, Psaropoulos, 1985), p. 154.

16 Olga Alexandrovna, " Flugten Til Krim," *Berlingske Tidende* (Copenhagen), 1941.

17 Vorres, *Last Grand Duchess*, p, 157.

18 Ibid.

19 Rosemary and Donald Crawford, *Michael & Natasha,* p. 324.

20 Ibid., p. 326.

21 Ibid.

22 May 4, 1917 letter from Empress Marie Feodorovna to Prince Valde-mar of Denmark, GARF, Cat No. 138.

23 Undated letter from Prince Peter of Oldenburg to Empress Marie Feodorovna, GARF, 642 2440.

24 November 21, 1917 letter from Empress Marie Feodorovna to for-mer Tsar Nicholas II, cited in Edward J. Bing, *The Letters of Tsar Nicholas and Empress Marie* (London: Ivor Nicholson and Watson Ltd., 1937) p. 301.

25 Vorres, *Last Grand Duchess,* p. 159.

26 Alexander, *Once a Grand Duke,* p. 308.

27 Olga Alexandrovna, "De Holdes Mandtal," *Berlingske Tidende* (Copen-hagen), 1941.

28 Vorres, *Last Grand Duchess,* p. 160.

29 Alexander, *Once a Grand Duke,* p. 313.

30 October 13, 1917 letter from Grand Duchess Olga Alexandrovna to former Tsar Nicholas II, GARF, 643 28.

31 Ibid.

32 Olga Alexandrovna, "En Bitter Afsked," *Berlingske Tidende* (Copen-hagen), 1941.

33 Olga Alexandrovna, "Hos Kuban-Kosakkeine," *Berlingske Tidende* (Copenhagen), 1941.

34 Olga Alexandrovna, "Hjem Til Danmark," *Berlingske Tidende* (Copen-hagen), 1941.

CHAPTER SEVEN ∞
EXILE AND A WOMAN NAMED "MISS UNKNOWN"

1 January 20, 1922 letter from Grand Duchess Olga to unknown recipient, GARF, 642 1212.

2 *Hvidøre—an historical treasure trove* (Copenhagen: Novo Nordisk A/S, 1993).

3 Grand Duke Alexander, *Always a Grand Duke* (New York: Farrar & Rinehart Inc., 1933), p. 108.

4 Ernst Bodenhof, undated personal essay entitled *"Grand Duchess Olga."*

5 Ian Vorres, *The Last Grand Duchess* (Athens: Firedawn Publishers, Psaropoulos, 1985), p. 169.

6 Alexander, *Always a Grand Duke*, p. 113.

7 May 15, 1926 letter from Grand Duchess Xenia Romanov to King George V, Royal Archives, Windsor RA GEOV AA43/238.

8 John F. O'Connor, *The Sokolov Investigation of The Alleged Murder of The Russian Imperial Family* (New York: Robert Speller & Sons, Publishers, Inc., 1971), pp. 176-189.

9 Statement made by William Pinkney to author, April 10, 1997.

10 July 24, 1916 letter from Grand Duchess Olga Romanov to Grand Duchess Maria Romanov, GARF, 643 28.

11 November 24, 1914 letter from Grand Duchess Olga Alexandrovna to her nieces, Grand Duchesses Olga, Maria, Tatiana and Anastasia Nicholaevna, GARF, 643 28.

12 Vorres, *Last Grand Duchess*, p. 110.

13 Ibid.

14 Ibid., p. 109.

15 Letter of Nurse Chemnitz, a member of the Dalldorf Asylum nursing staff, cited in Peter Kurth, *Anastasia: The Life of Anna Anderson,* Fontana Collins, 1983, p. 36.

16 Letter from Grand Duchess Olga Alexandrovna to Shura, cited in *I am Anastasia, The Autobiography of The Grand-Duchess of Russia* (New York: Harcourt, Brace and Company, 1958), p. 141.

17 Statement of Harriet Rathlef-Keilmann, cited in Kurth, *Anastasia,* p. 149.

18 Statement of Pierre Gilliard, cited in Kurth, *Anastasia,* p. 149.

19 Kurth, *Anastasia,* p. 145.

20 Statement of "Miss Unknown," cited in Kurth, *Anastasia,* p. 151.

21 October 27, 1925 letter from Danish Ambassador Herluf Zahle to Count Moltke (courtesy of Dick Schweitzer and Marina Botkin Schweitzer).

22 Ibid.

23 Harriet Rathlef-Keilmann, *Anastasia,* (New York: Payson and Clarke Ltd., 1929), p. 99.

24 Ibid.

25 Ibid.

26 Zahle, letter of October 27, 1925.

27 Rathlef-Keilmann, *Anastasia,* p. 100.

28 Ibid., p. 100.

29 Ibid., p. 101.

30 *I Am Anastasia,* pp. 154-155.

31 Zahle, letter of October 27, 1925.

32 Rathlef-Keilmann, *Anastasia,* p. 106.

33 Affidavit of Rathlef-Keilmann found in Edward Fallows papers, cited in Kurth, *Anastasia,* p. 154. (Interestingly, these statements attributed to Olga do not appear in Rathlef-Keilmann's 1929 book, *Anastasia.*) In Ian Vorres's 1964 book, *Once a Grand Duchess,* Olga denied ever receiving a telegram from her sister regarding the matter of "Miss Unknown."

34 Affidavit of Rathlef-Keilmann, cited in Kurth, *Anastasia,* p. 156.

35 Rathlef-Keilmann, *Anastasia,* p. 106.

36 Alexander, *Always a Grand Duke,* p. 212.

37 Undated letter from Grand Duchess Olga to "Miss Unknown," cited in Gleb Botkin, *The Woman Who Rose Again.* (New York: Fleming H. Revell Company, 1937), p. 97.

38 October 22, 1925 letter from Grand Duchess Olga to "Miss Unknown," cited in Gleb Botkin, *The Woman Who Rose Again,* p. 97.

39 Ibid., October 18, 1925 letter from Grand Duchess Olga, to "Miss Unknown."

40 Interview with Marjorie Wooten, the niece of Canadian mining executive James Rattray, July 1997.

41 Letter from Grand Duchess Olga to Col. Anatoly Mordvinov, former aide-de-camp to Nicholas II, cited in Kurth, *Anastasia,* p. 165.

42 Statement of Grand Duke Andrew, cited in Kurth, *Anastasia,* p. 169.

43 Vorres, *Last Grand Duchess,* p. 179.

44 Ibid., p. 180.

45   Alexander, *Always a Grand Duke,* p. 134.

46   Ibid., p. 213.

47   Vorres, *Last Grand Duchess,* p. 182.

48   Olga Obukhova, "The Romanovs In Denmark." *International Affairs,* Vol. 7, July-August, 1995, p. 101.

49   Ibid.

CHAPTER EIGHT ☜ FIRE SALE

1   Peter Kurth, *Anastasia* (New York: Fontana/Collins, 1983), p. 297.

2   Ibid.

3   Letter from Grand Duke Andrew Romanov to Grand Duchess Olga Alexandrovna, cited in Kurth, *Anastasia,* p. 271.

4   Ian Vorres, *The Last Grand Duchess* (Athens: Finedawn Publishers, Psaropoulos, 1985), p. 183.

5   November 1, 1928 letter from Grand Duchess Xenia Romanov to Grand Duchess Olga Alexandrovna, Windsor Archives, RA GEOV CC 45/729.

6   Ibid.

7   Ibid.

8   Sir Frederick Ponsonby, *Recollections of Three Reigns* (London: Eyre & Spottiswoode, 1951), p. 203.

9   William Clarke, *The Lost Fortune of the Tsars* (London: Orion Books Ltd., 1994), p. 204.

10   Ibid.

11   Ernst Bodenhof (personal unpublished essay).

12   Ponsonby, *Recollections of Three Reigns,* p. 205.

13   Bodenhof.

14   Ibid.

15   Ibid.

16   Vorres, *Last Grand Duchess,* p. 213.

17   Interview with Xenia (Kulikovsky) Nielsen, June 19, 1997.

18   Bodenhof.

19 Interview with Agnete (Kulikovsky) Petersen, July 1997.

20 Statement made by Jorgen Bjeergaard, curator of the Ballerup Engs-museum, Dennmark, June 1997.

21 Interview with Agnete (Kulikovsky) Petersen, July 1997.

22 Bodenhof.

23 Ibid.

24 Interview with Ruth Kulikovsky entitled "The Czar's Daughter," *All For The Ladies* (Denmark), 1967.

25 Ibid.

26 Ibid.

27 Interview with Agnete (Kulikovsky) Petersen, July 1997.

28 Ibid.

29 Ibid.

30 October 28, 1941 letter by unknown source, kept at the Foreign Policy Archive of the Russian Federation, cited in Yuriy Vasilyevich Ivanov, "Archives Shed Light on Candidates for the Russian Throne," *International Affairs,* Vol. 42. January-February 1996.

31 Vorres, *Last Grand Duchess* p. 234.

32 Interview with Agnete (Kulikovsky) Petersen, July 1997.

33 Information contained in documents provided by Olga N. Kuli-kovsky, affirmed by documents contained in British Foreign Office files, FO/371/858/N4230, April 8, 1948.

34 Vorres, *Anastasia,* p. 189.

35 Kulikovsky, "The Czar's Daughter."

36 Interview with Edith Dyregaard Jensen, Denmark, June 1997.

CHAPTER NINE ∞ DISPLACED PERSON

1 Interview with Agnete (Kulikovsky) Petersen, July 1997.

2 Quote of Xenia (Kulikovsky) Nielsen in interview with Erik Bergholt-Svendsen and Jorgen O. Bjeergaard for article entitled "Xenia—Grand Duchess Olga's Grandchild," appearing in pamphlet entitled *Storyfyrstinde Olga,* Byhornet 1/1991, published by the Ballerup Historiske Forening, 1994.

3 Ian Vorres, *The Last Grand Duchess* (Athens: Finedawn Publishers, Psaropoulos, 1985), p. 190.

4 Ibid.

5 Interview with Agnete (Kulikovsky) Petersen, July 1997.

6 August 26, 1948 letter from Grand Duchess Olga Alexandrovna to Rudolf Dyregaard Jensen (courtesy of Edith Dyregaard Jensen).

7 May 29, 1948 letter from Grand Duchess Olga Alexandrovna to Rudolf Dyregaard Jensen (courtesy of Edith Dyregaard Jensen).

8 Excerpt from "Commander's General Voyage Report," S.S. *Empress of Canada*, Canadian Pacific Steamships Limited, June 2, 1948.

9 June 6, 1948 Purser's Report, General Voyage Report, S.S. *Empress of Canada*, Canadian Steamship Limited.

10 Interview with Agnete (Kulikovsky) Petersen, July 1997.

11 "Grand Duchess Takes Her Cake And Salt," *The Evening Telegram*, June 11, 1948.

12 Ibid.

13 Ibid.

14 Vorres, *Last Grand Duchess*, p. 195.

15 "Grand Duchess Takes Her Cake And Salt," *Evening Telegram*, June 11, 1948.

16 Ibid.

17 "They Are Safe," *Evening Telegram*, July 12, 1948.

18 Excerpt from September 28, 1997 letter to author from Xenia (Kulikovsky) Nielsen.

19 Interview with Katherine Keiller-Mackay, July 1997.

20 Interview with Vladimir Purghart, May 1998.

21 "They Are Safe," *Evening Telegram*, July 12, 1948.

22 August 16, 1948 letter from Grand Duchess Olga Alexandrovna to unknown recipient (courtesy of Olga N. Kulikovsky).

23 September 3, 1948 letter from Grand Duchess Olga Alexandrovna to Queen Mary, Windsor Archives, RA GEOV CC 45/1599.

24 August 16, 1948 letter from Grand Duchess Olga to unknown recipient (courtesy of Olga N. Kulikovsky).

25 Ibid.

26 September 3, 1948 letter from Grand Duchess Olga Alexandrovna to unknown recipient (courtesy of Olga N. Kulikovsky).

27 Ibid.

28 Quote of Xenia (Kulikovsky) Nielsen in interview with Erik Bergholt-Svendsen and Jorgen O. Bjeergaard for article entitled "Xenia—Grand Duchess Olga's Grandchild."

29 Interview with Gisela and Wolfgang von Richthofen, June 1997.

30 Ibid.

31 Quote of Xenia (Kulikovsky) Nielsen in interview with Erik Bergholt-Svendsen and Jorgen O. Bjeergaard for article entitled "Xenia—Grand Duchess Olga's Grandchild."

32 August 16, 1948 letter from Grand Duchess Olga Alexandrovna to unknown recipient (courtesy of Olga N. Kulikovsky).

33 Interview with Marie Blagovesmensky, June 1997.

34 Interview with Michel and Tanya Wyches, July 1997.

35 Ibid.

36 Ibid.

37 Interview with Ruth Kulikovsky, June 23, 1997.

38 Interview with Eva Terp, June 1997.

39 Quote of Xenia (Kulikovsky) Nielsen in interview with Erik Bergholt-Svendsen and Jorgen O. Bjeergaard for article entitled "Xenia—Grand Duchess Olga's Grandchild."

40 Sir Frederick Ponsonby, Recollections of Three Reigns (London: Eyre & Spottiswoode, 1951), p. 207.

41 Vorres, Last Grand Duchess, p. 192.

42 Pearl McCarthy, "Season of Autumn Sketching Brings More Than Fine Color," The Globe and Mail, October 6, 1951.

43 Lotta Dempsey, "Person to Person," The Globe and Mail, October 26, 1951.

44 Vorres, Last Grand Duchess, p. 200.

45 Ibid.

46 Ibid., p. 201.

47 Ibid.

48 November 19, 1951 letter from Grand Duchess Xenia Alexandrovna

to Queen Mary, Windsor Archives, RA GEOV CC 45/1748.

49 Interview with Gisela and Wolfgang von Richthofen, June 1997.

CHAPTER TEN ∽ COOKSVILLE

1 Interview with Dr. Robert Creighton, March 1997.

2 Interview with Mary Turner, March 1997.

3 Interview with Ruth Kulikovsky, June 1997.

4 Interview with Xenia Kulikovsky, June 1997.

5 Ibid.

6 February 6, 1952 letter from Grand Duchess Olga Alexandrovna to Queen Mary, Windsor Archives, RA GEOV CC 45/1766.

7 December 5, 1952 letter from Grand Duchess Olga Alexandrovna to Queen Mary, Windsor Archives, RA GEOV CC 45/1818.

8 Ibid.

9 Ibid.

10 Interview with Mary Turner, March 1997.

11 Ian Vorres, *The Last Grand Duchess* (Athens: Finedawn Publishers, Psaropoulos, 1985), pp. 209-210.

12 Interview with William Pinkney, April 1997.

13 Ibid.

14 Interview with Xenia (Kulikovsky) Nielsen, June 1997.

15 Quote from undated essay, "Olga Alexandrovna, Grand Duchess of Imperial Russia, Mrs. Nicolai Kulikovsky," by W. Ed Ewing.

16 Interview with Mary Turner, March 1997.

17 Interview with Agnete (Kulikovsky) Petersen, July 1997.

18 Interview with Marjorie Wooten, June 1997.

19 Interview with Pat Moore, July 1997.

20 Aage Heinberg, article entitled "I Have Found Peace and Harmony," courtesy of Ballerup Engsmuseum.

21 Ibid.

22 Interview with Marjorie Wooten, July 1997.

23 Peter Kurth, *Anastasia* (New York: Fontana/Collins, 1983), p. 368.

24 Grand Duke Alexander, *Always a Grand Duke,* (New York: Farrar and Rinehart Inc., 1933), p. 337.

25 Vorres, *Last Grand Duchess,* p. 246.

26 Kurth, *Anastasia,* p. 375.

27 Quote of Michael Thornton, cited in John Klier and Helen Mingay, *The Quest For Anastasia* (London: Smith Gryphon Limited, 1996), p. 230.

28 Gleb Botkin, *The Real Romanovs* (New York: Fleming H. Revell Company, 1931) p. 91.

29 Vorres, *Last Grand Duchess,* p. 243.

30 Notes from Edward Fallows's papers, cited in Kurth, *Anastasia,* p. 310.

CHAPTER ELEVEN ⌾ BROKEN THREADS

1 Interview with Agnete (Kulikovsky) Petersen, July 1997.

2 Ibid.

3 Ibid.

4 Ibid.

5 Interview with Dr. Morton Shulman, March 1998.

6 March 24, 1957 letter from Grand Duchess Olga Alexandrovna to Vilhelmine Dittman (courtesy of the Ballerup Engsmuseum, Denmark).

7 Interview with Xenia (Kulikovsky) Nielsen, June 1997.

8 Excerpt from September 13, 1956 action for dissolution of marriage between Ruth Kulikovsky and Guri Nikolaevitch Kulikovsky.

9 Ibid.

10 Ibid.

11 Ibid.

12 December 14, 1957 letter from Grand Duchess Olga Alexandrovna to Vihelmine Dittman (courtesy of the Ballerup Engsmuseum).

13 Ibid.

14 Interview with Xenia (Kulikovsky) Nielsen, June 1997.

15 Ibid.

16 September 26, 1959 letter from Grand Duchess Olga Alexandrovna to Vilhelmine Dittman (courtesy of Ballerup Engsmuseum).

17 April 14, 1957 letter from Grand Duchess Xenia Alexandrovna to Grand Duchess Olga Alexandrovna (courtesy of Paul Byington).

18 Ian Vorres, *The Last Grand Duchess* (Athens: Finedawn Publishers, Psaropoulos, 1985), p. 215.

19 Interview with Ruth Kulikovsky entitled "The Czar's Daughter," *All For The Ladies* (Denmark), 1967.

20 Staatsarchiv Hamburg, File 1991 74 O 297/57 Volume 7, pp. 1297-1315.

21 Ibid.

22 Ibid.

23 October 27, 1925 letter from Herluf Zahle to Count Moltke (courtesy of Dick Schweitzer and Marina Botkin Schweitzer).

24 October 31 letter from Grand Duchess Olga to Herluf Zahle (courtesy of Dick Schweitzer and Marina Botkin Schweitzer).

25 Staatsarchiv Hamburg, File 1991 74 O 297/57 Volume 7, pp. 1297-1315.

26 Ibid.

27 Ibid.

28 Peter Kurth, *Anastasia* (New York: Fontana/Collins, 1983), p. 391

29 Ibid.

30 Ibid.

31 Interview with Gisela and Wolfgang von Richthofen, June 1997.

32 Vorres, *Last Grand Duchess*, p. 200.

33 *The Globe and Mail*, March 24, 1959.

34 Excerpt of January 10, 1998 letter from journalist Michael Thornton (former holder of the Power of Attorney for Anna Anderson in England) to author.

35 Ibid.

36 Ibid.

37 Staatsarchiv Hamburg, File 1991 74 O 297/57 Volume 7, pp. 1297-1315.

38 Interview with Katherine Keiller-Mackay, July 1997.

39 Interview with Xenia (Kulikovsky) Nielsen, June 1997.

40 Interview with Katherine Keiller-Mackay, July 1997.

41 September 26, 1959 letter from Grand Duchess Olga to Vilhelmine Dittman (courtesy of the Ballerup Engsmuseum).

42 December 1959 letter from Grand Duchess Olga to W. Ed Ewing (courtesy of Ed Ewing).

43 Vorres, *Last Grand Duchess*, p. 217.

44 Excerpt from undated essay "Olga Alexandrovna, Grand Duchess of Imperial Russia, Mrs. Nicolai Kulikovsky," by W. Ed Ewing.

45 March 22, 1960 letter from Grand Duchess Olga to W. Ed Ewing (courtesy of Ed Ewing).

46 Bequest contained in the June 22, 1959 Last Will and Testament of James Halliday Rattray.

47 Excerpt from "Olga Alexandrovna," by W. Ed Ewing.

48 Interview with Galina Martemianoff, March 1997.

49 Interview with Tanya and Michel Wyches, July 1997.

50 Ibid.

51 Interview with Galina Martemianoff, March 1997.

52 Statement made to author by Olga N. Kulikovsky, June 1997.

53 Interview with Ruth Kulikovsky, June 1997.

54 Interview with Galina Martemianoff, March 1997.

55 Ibid.

56 Ibid.

57 Excerpt from September 28, 1997 letter from Xenia (Kulikovsky) Nielsen to author.

58 Ibid.

59 Interview with Xenia (Kulikovsky) Nielsen, June 1997.

60 Interview with Galina Martemianoff, June 1997.

61 Vorres, *Last Grand Duchess*, p. 224.

62 Vorres, "Handful of Russian Soil on Casket," *The Globe and Mail*, December 1, 1960.

CHAPTER TWELVE ∞ AFTERMATH

1 Paul Byington, Smiths Falls, September 1997.

2 Interview with Michel and Tanya Wyches, July 1997.

3 Interview with Ruth Kulikovsky entitled "The Czar's Daughter," *All For The Ladies* (Denmark), 1967.

4 Interview with Ruth Kulikovsky, June 1997.

5 Suzy Menkes, *The Royal Jewels* (London: Grafton, 1985), p. 52.

6 March 27, 1998 letter from Suzy Menkes to author.

7 Interview with Michel and Tanya Wyches, July 1997.

8 June 16, 1998 letter from Tihon Kulikovsky to Suzy Menkes.

9 Ibid.

10 William Clarke, *The Lost Fortune of the Tsars* (London: Orion, 1994), p. 213.

11 January 10, 1998 letter from Michael Thornton to author.

12 Quote from the *Daily Progress,* cited in Peter Kurth, *Anastasia* (New York: Fontana/Collins, 1983), p 473.

13 Robert Massie, *The Romanovs: The Final Chapter.* (New York: Random House, 1995), p. 93.

SOURCES

ARCHIVES

Archives of Ontario
Ballerup Engsmuseum—The Olga Museum, Ballerup, Denmark
Canadian Pacific Archives
Leeds Russian Archive, University of Leeds
Public Record Office, London
Royal Archives, Windsor Castle
Royal Library, Copenhagen
Russian State Historical Archives, St. Petersburg
School of Slavonic and East European Studies,
    University of London
Senat Der Freien Und Hansestadt, Hamburg Staatsarchiv
State Archive of the Russian Federation

NEWSPAPERS

Berlingske Tidende
Daily Progress
The Evening Telegram
The Globe and Mail
Politiken

MAGAZINES/JOURNALS

All For The Ladies
Chatelaine
Hvidøre—an historical treasure trove,
    Novo Nordisk A/S, Copenhagen, 1993
Maria Feodorovna, Empress of Russia, catalogue of exhibit
    at Christiansborg Palace, Copenhagen, 1997
Saturday Night

WORKS CITED

Alexander (Mikhailovich), Grand Duke. *Always A Grand Duke*. New York: Farrar and Rinehart Inc., 1933.

Alexander (Mikhailovich), Grand Duke. *Once a Grand Duke*. London: Cassel, 1932.

Bing, Edward J. *The Letters of Tsar Nicholas and Empress Marie*. London: Ivor Nicholson and Watson Ltd., 1937.

Bjeergaard, Jorgen O., Jensen, Svend Jorgen. *"Storfyrstinde Olga."* Denmark: Byhornet 1991, Ballerup Historiske Forening, 1991.

Bodenhof, Ernst. *"Grand Duchess Olga"* (unpublished essay, undated).

Bokhanov, Alexander. *Nicholas II*. Moscow: Russian Printhouse, 1997.

Botkin, Gleb. *The Woman Who Rose Again*. New York: Fleming H. Revell Company, 1937.

Botkin, Gleb. *The Real Romanovs*. New York: Fleming H. Revell Company, 1931.

Clarke, William. *The Lost Fortune of the Tsars*. London: Orion, 1994.

Crawford, Rosemary and Donald. *Michael & Natasha*. Vancouver/Toronto: Douglas & McIntyre, 1997.

Dehn, Lili. *The Real Tsaritsa*. New York: Little Brown and Company, 1922.

Ewing, Ed. *"Olga Alexandrovna, Grand Duchess of Imperial Russia, Mrs. Nicolai Kulikovsky"* (unpublished work, undated).

Fuhrmann, Joseph T. *Rasputin, A Life*. New York: Praeger, 1990.

Grenfell, Francis W. Logan, Jr., John A., Bovey, Kate Koon, *Coronation of Czar Nicholas II 100th Anniversary 1896-1996*. Toronto: Pavlovsk Press, 1998.

Hussey, Ruth, and Judith Goulin. *Rattray Marsh, Then And Now*. Toronto: The Rattray Marsh Protection Association, 1990.

I Am Anastasia. New York: Harcourt, Brace and Company, 1958.

Klier, John, and Helen Mingay. *The Quest For Anastasia*. London: Smith Gryphon Limited, 1996.

Kurth, Peter. *Anastasia*. New York: Fontana/Collins, 1983.

Lowe, Charles. *Alexander III of Russia*. London: MacMillan And Co., 1895.

Massie, Robert K. *The Romanovs: The Final Chapter*. New York: Random House Ltd., 1995.

Maylunas, Andrei, and Sergei Mironenko. *A Lifelong Passion*. London: Weidenfeld & Nicolson, 1996.

Menkes, Suzy. *The Royal Jewels*. London: Grafton Books Ltd., 1985.

Paleologue, Maurice. *An Ambassador's Memoirs*. New York: Doran, 1925.

Pipes, Richard. *A Concise History of the Russian Revolution*. New York: Vintage Books, 1995.

Ponsonby, Sir Frederick, *Recollections of Three Reigns*. London: Eyre & Spottiswoode, 1951.

Rasputin, Maria. *My Father*. New Hyde Park, New York: University Books, 1970.

Rathlef-Keilmann, Harriet. *Anastasia*. New York: Payson and Clarke Ltd., 1929.

Shavelsky, Protopresviter Georgi. *Memoirs of The Last Protopresviter of The Russian Army and Navy*, "Krutiskoe Patriarsheye Podvorie." Moscow: Publishing House of The Russian Church, 1996.

Sokolov, Nicholas A., ed. John F. O'Connor. *The Sokolov Investigation*. New York, New York: Robert Speller & Sons, Publishers, Inc., 1971.

Summers, Anthony, and Tom Mangold. *The File on The Tsar*. London: Gollancz, 1976.

Trubetskoy, V. *"Cuirassier's Memoirs."* Moscow: Russian Printhouse, 1991.

Vorres, Ian. *The Last Grand Duchess*. Athens: Finedawn Publishers (Psaropoulos), 1985.

Vyrubova, Anna. *Memoirs of the Russian Court*. London: MacMillan, 1923.

Wheatcroft, Andrew, ed. Lyons, Marvin. *Nicholas II, The Last Tsar*. London: Routledge & Kegan Paul, 1974.

Witte, Sergei. *Memoirs*. Garden City, N.Y: Doubleday, 1921.

$\mathcal{L}$IST OF $\mathcal{O}$BTAINED $\mathcal{P}$ERMISSIONS

The author wishes to thank the following companies and individuals:

Weidenfeld & Nicolson for permission to quote from *A Lifelong Passion*, by Andrei Maylunas and Sergei Mironenko, © 1997; *Michael & Natasha,* by Donald and Rosemary Crawford, © 1997; and *The Lost Fortune of the Tsars,* by William Clarke, © 1994.

Bantam Doubleday Dell for permission to quote from *A Lifelong Passion,* by Andrei Maylunas and Sergei Mironenko, © 1997.

Pavlovsk's Press for permission to quote from *Coronation of Czar Nicholas II,* © 1997.

Xenia Kulikovsky Nielsen, for permission to quote from September 29, 1997 letter to author.

Excerpts from Lotta Dempsey's and Pearl McCarthy's columns reprinted with permission of *The Globe and Mail* newspaper.

Edward Ewing for permission to quote from his personal essay entitled *"Olga Alexandrovna, Grand Duchess of Imperial Russia, Mrs. Nicholai Kulikovsky."*

Letters from Olga to Vilhelmine Dittman, used with the permission of the Ballerup Engsmuseum, publishers of Byhornet/1991, Denmark.

Hamburg court deposition given by Olga in Toronto in 1959 quoted by permission of the Staatsarchiv, Hamburg.

Michael Thornton, for permission to quote from his January 10, 1998 letter to the author.

Ian Vorres, for permission to quote from *The Last Grand Duchess,* Finedawn Publishers (Psaropoulos) © 1985.

Hennell of Bond Street Limited, for permission to reproduce the list of 76 jewels constituting the property of Grand Duchess Olga and Grand Duchess Xenia Alexandrovna.

ACKNOWLEDGEMENTS

FIRST AND FOREMOST I MUST thank Grand Duchess Olga Alexandrovna Romanov, whose extraordinary strength and fearless spirit in the face of almost unimaginable hardships provided ample incentive for me to attempt to document her story.

Three years ago, after reading *The Romanovs: The Final Chapter*, by Robert Massie, I discovered that the last Grand Duchess of Russia had died above a barbershop in Toronto. The apartment, little changed since Olga's death in 1960, is coincidentally located in a run-down neighbourhood less than three miles from where I live. After visiting the location, I realized what a long and harrowing journey it must have been from the marbled hallways of the seven-hundred-room Gatchina Palace, Olga's favourite palace, to here.

There had been one other book written about Grand Duchess Olga's life. In 1959, author Ian Vorres conducted a series of interviews with Olga in her home in Cooksville,

Ontario, which resulted in his excellent biography, *The Last Grand Duchess*. The book contained Olga's often poignant reminiscences about her life, particularly in imperial Russia.

At the time the book was written, neither Vorres nor any other researchers were allowed access into either the State Archive of The Russian Federation, or the Russian State Historical Archive in St. Petersburg, where the Romanov family's letters are stored. Fortunately, today, both archives are open to researchers and they contain dozens of never-before-seen letters to and from Olga, as well as Olga's childhood diaries. Included in her diary entries are detailed descriptions of her brother Nicholas's ornate 1896 coronation and the bloody catastrophe of Khodinka Field, where more than a thousand people were trampled to death attempting to retrieve coronation mugs distributed by the imperial family. There are the affectionate letters of Olga's first husband, Prince Peter of Oldenburg, to a wife he respected yet could not bring himself to love with the intensity and physical expression she so desperately desired. Most poignant of all, however are the passionate love letters a still-married Olga wrote to her lover, Nicolai Kulikovsky, while he fought at the Russian front during World War I, and she worked as an army-hospital nurse. Their romance, carried on amid the destruction of the Russian empire, forms the heart and soul of this book.

Neither archive could have been successfully navigated without the expert help and generosity of several people. Particular thanks to Sergei Mironenko, the director of the State Archive of the Russian Federation; and to Irina Chirkova, Lubov Tuttunick and Irina Biriukova, who made the impossible possible. I am grateful, too, for the guidance of the staff of the Historical Archive of St. Petersburg.

In Canada, I first have to thank Paul Gilbert, who in spite of personal heartbreaks found time to provide me with not only research materials and sources, but honest criticism and unfailing support. He made the trip worthwhile. Others I must thank for their invaluable help include Tanya and Michel Wyches, Sylvia Suchacev, Lorenz Eppinger, Gisela and Wolfgang von Richthofen, the late Katherine Mackay Stewart (formerly Katherine Keiller Mackay), Maria Blavovacheschensky, Mary Turner, Paul Byington, Garry Webster, Ed Ewing, Judith Goulin, Olga N. Kulikovsky, Tom Kneebone, Hugh Brewster, Richard Nahabedian, Olga Cordeiro, Vladimir Purghart, Joel Clark, William Pinkney, Ginevra and Patrick Boal, Agnete and Egon Petersen, Mary Lou Burton, Dr. Robert Creighton, Pat Hat, Rick and Isabelle Solkower, Mike Filey and Michelle and Cathy of the Brampton Court House.

Thanks must also be extended to the Danish, German and Russian translators who were paid less than their patience and skill deserved. They include Eva Terp, Ernst von Bezold and Angela Haberhauer. Special thanks and affection to Yulya Margolin, who with her husband, Misha, sacrificed everything they had ever known and loved to leave Russia for Canada, and instead of looking back, continue to inspire with their ability to stride fearlessly into the future. The obstacles they have overcome on their journey made any obstacles I faced completing this book look insignificant.

In Denmark, I am deeply grateful to Paul Kulikovsky Larsen, Olga's great-grandchild, who despite his busy career, found time to selflessly provide me with much appreciated research and advice. His mother, Xenia (Kulikovsky) Nielsen, though it understandably pained her to do so, bravely shared with me her unique perspective on the upsetting conflicts and controversies surrounding her grandmother Olga's last years in Canada. Despite ill health, Ruth Kulikovsky also provided unflinchingly honest answers to sensitive questions, a testament to the strength of her char-acter. Appreciation too must be extended to Jorgen Bjeergaard, the very capable curator of the Ballerup Engsmuseum, "the Olga museum" based in Ballerup, Denmark; Ole Krog, the curator of the Royal Silver Room at Christiansborg Palace; Louise Illum, the former manager of Hvidøre; Tatiana Meinertz; and Anna Andreasen of the *Politiken* newspaper.

London, England boasts many experts on the subject of the Romanovs. Several invaluable letters contained in the Royal Archives at Windsor Palace would not be available for quotation in this book without the gracious permission of Her Majesty Queen Elizabeth II.

Greatest thanks must also be extended to the late Prince Rostislav Romanov, Michael Thornton, Rosemary and Donald Crawford, William Clarke, Pamela Clark of the Royal Archives at Windsor Palace and Richard Davies, archivist with the Leeds Russian Archive at the University of Leeds.

Those of help from the United States include Dick Schweitzer and Marina Botkin Schweitzer, whose grandfather Evgeny Botkin's courageous decision to serve until death Nicholas II's family has largely been ignored by the history books. Thanks also to Thomas Mansfield for allowing me to bend his ear and sharing with me his expert knowledge of Russian artwork.

Gunther von Berenberg Gossler and Herr Stukenbrock assisted me in retrieving from the Senat Der Freien und Hansestadt Hamburg Staatsarchiv Olga's deposition to the Hamburg court in the Anna Anderson case.

Cynthia Good is a publisher whose incredible energy and enthusiasm inspires those around her, including this author. I owe her deepest thanks for taking a personal interest in seeing this book through to publication. Thanks too for the sound editorial judgement of Jennifer Glossup and the almost miraculous patience and humour of Mary Adachi, who likes her criticisms blunt and her coffee black.

Most importantly of all, my bottomless thanks and everlasting love go to my parents, Leonard and Verna, islands in a raging sea, who listened, laughed, discussed, advised and endured all on this book's journey to publication. I couldn't and wouldn't have wanted to write it without them. Similarly, my brother, John, always displays precisely the kind of acerbic wit that puts nitpicking problems into perspective. And lastly, to Cindy Phenix, I give my heart.

INDEX